Joe Connelly worked for nine years as a medic for St. Clare's Hospital in New York City, where he was born. He lives in New York City and is working on his second novel.

BRINGING OUT THE DEAD

JOE CONNELLY

WARNER BOOKS

A *Warner* Book

First published in the United States in 1998 by Alfred A. Knopf, Inc.

First published in Great Britain by Warner Books in 1998
This edition published by Warner Books in 1999

A CIP catalogue record for this book
is available from the British Library.

ISBN 0 7515 2781 5

Typeset by Hewer Text Limited, Edinburgh
Printed and bound in Great Britain by
Clays Ltd, St Ives plc

Warner Books
A Division of
Little, Brown and Company (UK)
Brettenham House
Lancaster Place
London WC2E 7EN

For those who work in the wells of night

1

I parked the ambulance in front of Hell's Kitchen walk-up number 414 and Larry and I pulled the equipment from the back. It was midnight in April, and the full moon lit the street like a saint's festival, and as I walked toward the blue-covered brownstone, the faces watching from its windows, I thought again of how much I'd needed this night to be quiet, of how I'd walked the seven blocks to work with my shaking hands actually clasped together in the act of praying for a quiet night, and of how, for all that, I'd been dispatched immediately, and without coffee, to this cardiac arrest.

The stoop stairs were littered with revelers drinking and shouting to a radio on the first floor, and when we reached the front gate the singers stopped shouting and then the music was only static. They cleared a lane up the steps, kicking empty cans out of our way, crowding at our sides for the bad news. What apartment? What apartment? Like they were holding lottery tickets no one wanted to win. Oh Jesus it's Mr. Burke, the oldest woman said, and the group gathered behind us to collect the stories of the man from 5A, of his drunken son, his spiteful daughter, his wife the saint, and his bad heart.

The front door opened, a young boy holding it. He was crying, and when we got inside the screams met us on the ground floor and I knew them well, like the patched rotting

1

steps, the gray-yellow paint, and the red steel doors with three locks in every building I've climbed through to get to those screams at the top – they're always at the top. I knew Mr. Burke was dead and what an awful thing to know, and to have learned through time, and to have to climb.

Four flights. We were ushered into a small front room crowded with red velvet chairs and porcelain. Mrs. Burke stood in the center, surrounded by neighbors, and when we entered, their cries became choked voices, and the old woman's eyes had run dry, and she squeezed them tight. Over here, said a man standing in the hallway like a robbed and beaten sentry. He led us past the kitchen and a small bedroom, into a large back room with a king-size bed upon which lay the figure of Mr. Burke. A woman was kneeling over the old man. She looked up briefly as we came in and then turned and pressed her lips against the already colder, flaccid mouth of her father.

"We were just watching television," said the man who led us in, "and Dad yelled out and started punching his chest and before we could do nothing he locked himself in the bathroom. I said we oughta call you guys but he swore us not to. He was crying and I never once heard the old man cry and after a while we couldn't hear anything, so I broke the door in and he was barely breathing. I put him on the bed there and he just stopped."

Larry and I moved the body to the floor. "How long ago did he stop breathing?"

"Maybe ten minutes. The woman on the phone was telling us how to do CPR. Please, you gotta do something. This is gonna kill my mother."

"We'll do all we can," I said, wanting to sound confident, but ten minutes was too long, and CPR on a bed is useless. Even as I pulled out the Ambu-bag I wanted to put it back, to sit with the family and pour a few drinks, toast the life they remembered, for there was nothing to celebrate in the body whose heart I was supposed to start. Patrick Burke's time had come. He probably knew that when he locked the bathroom door.

I opened his mouth and felt a box of cool air pass through my fingers, like the morning breath of heavy snow, the last of his life leaving. I'm sure it was just gas built up in the stomach from CPR, but in the last year I had come to believe in such things as spirits leaving the body and not wanting to be put back, spirits angry at the awkward places death had left them, and though I understood how crazy I was to think this way, I was also convinced that if I looked up at that moment I would see the old man standing at the window, staring out over the tar-paper plots and gray ditches of his birthplace. I didn't have to look; I could feel him there, pressed against the glass, waiting for us to finish.

"Frank, what are you doing?" Larry was hooking up the wires to the electrode patches he'd just placed on Burke's chest. He plugged them into the EKG monitor and turned it on. I opened my eyes. "Come on, Frank, let's move along here."

I put the mask over Burke's face and squeezed the bag, though my heart wasn't in it, hadn't been in a long time, and neither was Mr. Burke's, whose EKG rhythm on the monitor was a flat green line. The spirit was gone. Standing by the window. If we did manage to jump-start his heart, there'd be only blood to fill it.

But my hands took over; they always do: trained on hundreds of cardiac arrests, they're automatic. I pulled out the long steel laryngoscope blade and inserted it into his mouth. Using it like a lever, I lifted the tongue up until I found the white vocal cords, like Roman columns, and I grabbed the thick plastic tube and carefully passed it through those gates, through the dark cartilage of the trachea, into the branched entrance of the lungs. I secured it, hooked the bag up to the tube, and pumped it hard.

I called for a backup. Dispatch said first available, which meant we would be on our own for at least twenty minutes. I didn't want to involve the man's daughter any further, but I needed her hands. She knelt by her father's head and I showed her how and when to squeeze the bag. She tried very hard but was lost looking into his eyes, her head falling back. "Squeeze," I had to keep saying.

Larry was crunching down violently on the man's chest and as I fit into the slim space between the bed and the man's right arm I heard one of the ribs crack, like deep ice in a winter lake. I turned the arm over, found a trace of blue vein, and plunged the needle in. I hooked up the IV and watched the bubbles ride the salt water into his arm.

Epinephrine first, one milligram pure adrenaline, a liquid scream in the vein to make the heart feel it's trapped in a burning shirt factory. Followed by one half milligram of atropine, a more subtle agent that rings an alarm and tells the heart it's not dead, only sleeping. This heart wasn't fooled. I waited a minute and gave him another epi, but the flat line only shivered a moment before flattening again. So I decided to hit him with everything at once, get it over with. I shot in

4

an amp of calcium; gives the heart a Joe Louis punch. I drew up a vial of Isuprel and stuck it into the IV bag and let it run. Isuprel scorches everything in its path. It sets the heart on fire, and the heart can either come back to life to beat the flames out or lie there and burn like dead pine. I added in another epi and atropine and sat back to see what would happen.

The flat line on the monitor ran untouched, seemingly infinite and perfect like the axis of the universe, then suddenly it flexed, then bowed, a minute later exploding into one thousand shaking points. I could see the vibration in the chest under Larry's hands as every muscle in Burke's heart fired wildly in different directions. I charged up the paddles and placed them on his chest, twelve inches apart. "Clear," I yelled. "Clear." The daughter let go and then screamed when the man's frail body left the pinewood floor. The green line continued to dance, so I shocked him again. The man's face reared up to mine like a challenge. His daughter groaned and rubbed the head that had thumped heavily upon her knee.

The shock of defibrillation is like a slap in the face to the hysterical heart. Sometimes the slap alone gets the heart to pull itself together and start beating normally, but often the soft voice and soothing hand of lidocaine is needed. Just relax, the lidocaine says; everything will be all right. I gave him eighty milligrams and prepared to shock again, but the daughter would not let go. "No more," she said, and she was crying. "Please don't." Larry pulled her arms away from her father's face, and I hit him at full power. This time the body hardly moved. There was nothing left. The line on the

5

monitor stopped dancing. It ran straight and smooth and showed no intention of rising. Larry returned to the man's chest, grunting with every compression. I heard another rib snap.

Larry was exhausted. Sweat dripped from his nose onto the man's blue shoulders, and he wheezed with every compression. Larry had trouble mowing his suburban quarter acre without a substantial nap, and a four-flight climb followed by ten minutes of CPR was more than his well-rested body could bear. There were a number of reasons why Larry should have become a plumber or a lawyer – anything except a medic – but chief among them was the way his body moved during CPR. He had a heavy gut, stretched by years of dozing off in his stain-guarded Naugahyde recliner, his head tilted forward just enough for him to swallow his beer without choking. When Larry knelt over the dead, his belly would swing like a bowling ball in a shopping bag. The force of this gyration met the force of gravity somewhere in his lower lumbar and inspired a number of unfortunate reflexes. With each compression, Larry's heels kicked up, his pelvis shot forward, and his head jerked back, giving all present the impression that Larry's work stimulated him far more than most would consider the limits of professional behavior.

"Why don't you let me take over," I said to him, "while you call Dr. Hazmat and ask for an eighty-three." After starting CPR and delivering a regulated set of treatments, medics have to call the on-call physician to receive orders for further treatment, or, as in the case of Mr. Burke, to call a dead man an eighty-three. He had been down over twenty minutes, and by the time Larry woke the doctor and explained the situation it would be thirty. All first-line drugs had been used, with little success. The man was dead. We were tired. It was time to pull out the tubes and catheters, unplug the monitor, put the man back on the bed, cover him, and leave this poor family to their grief. Time to get a cup of coffee and park the ambulance by the river for a few minutes of rest.

I knelt in Larry's place and pressed my hands down on Burke's chest. Under the cracked ribs the heart felt like a flat tire. I apologized to him for both of us and gently built up to a soft, steady rhythm. For the first time I looked around the room, at the dust-covered artifacts of the man's life: unmatched socks under the bed, one gray suit in the closet, pictures scattered on the walls. I thought of all the hours I'd spent in rooms like this, kneeling on the floor, crunching the chests of dead strangers while putting stories together from the pieces they left behind.

Burke's wedding picture sat on the nightstand. He wore a black tuxedo and posed happily with his young bride on the church steps. From the top of the tall dresser in the corner Private Burke stared down, trying to look tough and ready to fight the Communists but succeeding only in looking young. On one side of him was a Purple Heart in a brown velvet case and on the other was a smaller photo, three GIs arm in arm, standing at a muddy crossroads. A signpost listed distances to different cities: NEW YORK, 7,862 MILES; SEOUL, 40 MILES. On the wall above that was a plaque from the *New York Times* to Patrick Burke, forty years of service,

1952–1992. Next to it, a photo of the man in work clothes, hands and feet dark with newsprint, looking small before the blue metal girth of the printer.

Across the bed, above Mrs. Burke's low, wide bureau, was a mirror as big as a bay window. In its glass a dark portrait of Christ stared at me from somewhere behind and above. He was pointing to his chest, to where the red robe opened, the heart wrapped in thorns, crowned by flames.

At the foot of the bed, next to the window that opened on a wall of windows, the Burke family was born and raised. In its center were three collections of bald, smiling babies. Around them the two older sons became boys in baseball uniforms, then high school graduates. One of them, the son who had shown me in, was married near the window and had two smiling boys of his own. The other never made it that far, his life trailing off to the left, a photo of him bundled up and laughing in the snow, two dried-out palm leaves crossed behind the frame.

Both sons' lives appeared foreshortened in some way, shunted aside, as if the boys had been rushed toward adulthood to make room for their sister, the blond-haired freckled-faced favorite, whose life filled more of the wall than the window. I watched her climb out of diapers, start walking, and go to school. She prayed for all of us at her First Communion, loved to paint and play the violin. She won swimming medals and cheer-leading awards, and she always smiled, a smile that grew brighter as her life grew higher, to the top of the wall, queen of the prom, the most beautiful daughter in the world, her place as sacred as the Christ looming behind me.

The girl's life on the wall ended there; no graduation or wedding or babies, nothing superseded that smile, and when I looked at the woman kneeling next to me I understood why. Her face was sharply lined, almost anorexic, still beautiful but harsh and pale as raw quartz. Her blond hair was dyed black and chopped into short, straight bangs. Black makeup ran down her cheeks, and the loose-fitting black tank dress she wore showed the bleached points of her shoulders. It seemed as if she hadn't smiled since that night at the prom, as if she had spent the last ten years fighting her way off that wall, and there, on the floor, as she held her dead father's head between her knees, it seemed she had succeeded miserably.

"Squeeze," I said. I wanted to give some lasting consolation. There was none. "Maybe you should take a break. Your brother could come in for a few minutes and then my partner will be back." "No." She shook her head. "He couldn't handle it." I felt bad for bringing her into this, but she was right: it was a job best done by the already fallen and, in my case, the still falling. I tried to imagine our sitting like that on the Great Lawn in Central Park, a picnic lunch between us on a bright blue and green spring afternoon. I opened the wine and she smiled and stretched her back on a cool breeze. Two young people.

"Do you have any music?" I said.

"What?"

"Music. I think it helps if you play something he liked." I was already using the past tense.

"John," she yelled, "put on the Sinatra."

John came in. He was crying.

"Play the Sinatra," she whispered.

The opening strings of "September of My Years" drifted through the room. Not salsa, I thought, not a good rhythm for CPR, but what music to leave with. Unconsciously I picked up my pace and concentrated on my hands. There was a time when I believed music could make a dead heart beat again, and I once believed my hands were electric and bringing someone back to life was the greatest thing one could do.

I have done CPR in grand ballrooms on Park Avenue and in third-floor dance halls uptown. On Park they stand tall black panels around you to shield the dancers from an unpleasant view, while the band keeps up their spirits with songs like "Put on a Happy Face." Uptown the music never breaks and the dancers' legs whirl around you like a carnival ride. I've worked on the floors of some of the finest East Side restaurants, serenaded by violins while the man at the table next to me cut into his prime rib, and I have worked under the gory fluorescence of basement diners where taxi drivers can order, eat, and be back on the road in ten minutes. I've watched Broadway shows from the front row, kung fu pornography from Times Square balconies. I once brought a bartender back to life on the top of his bar while Irish dance music played. The patrons moved over for us, but no one stopped drinking.

One of my first cardiac arrests was in the Graceland Ballroom. I'd been there the Friday night before, to pick up a young man shot in the head, but this was Sunday afternoon, when families come from all over the city to talk and dance. A salsa band was playing, and the crowd of dancers made a path for us without losing a beat. The man lay dead in the middle of the floor, dead but not lifeless, because nothing could be lifeless in a room so full of laughter and dancing and music that sounded off your heart. We had a backup unit behind us and my partner and I moved perfectly – intubated with an epinephrine on board in twenty seconds. I took over CPR, my hands rising and falling into the rhythm of the music and the dancers' feet stepping nimbly around us to the salsa beat, a pulse of life. On the monitor I watched my compressions become perfect beats, and when I took my hands away the beats continued. "He has a pulse," I shouted, and stuck my thumb up in the air. The man started breathing on his own, and as we pulled the stretcher out the crowd cheered and slapped us on the back and the dancers filled in behind.

Walking from that room I was blessed by life. I had purpose for the first time and it carried me through those early wild years. Only much later did that beat begin to fade, and only recently did it disappear, leaving a cold stone in its place.

Larry had been on the phone ten minutes, and my knees felt as if I'd just spent an hour in a confessional. I had to admit that Burke looked better. The blue was gone from his cheeks, and the broken vessels in his nose had turned a familiar red. He wasn't that old really, barely sixty. I noticed beats on the monitor, too wide to carry a pulse, but they were gathering speed. I pumped on and listened to Sinatra sing of the brown leaves falling down. When I looked up again the beats had tightened. I stopped and found a weak pulse in his neck, which soon became a strong pulse at the wrist. I sat on the bed. His brain was dead; I was pretty sure of that. I checked his pupils; they were fixed in place, but his heart was beating like a young man's. Larry came in.

"It's okay, Frank. We can call it. Eighty-three."

"No we can't," I said. "He's got a pulse."

"No shit."

The daughter looked up. "Is he going to be all right?"

"His heart's beating." I didn't say that he would never wake up and that his heart would beat on as long as machines pumped in food and oxygen – that I was just acting on orders.

The news of Mr. Burke's recovery spread quickly, and soon the living room was full of crying, smiling faces. The backup unit arrived with a longboard and the two EMTs helped us strap the old man in. Larry and I packed up the equipment.

The stairway was tight and it took some time to get down; at each turn we had to tilt the board and pass it hand to hand over the railings, all the time fighting to keep the airway tube in place. The daughter led our procession, glaring at the faces that peered out from every door. When we reached the bottom she waved her arms at the people still sitting on the stoop – "Get out, get out" – pushing the ones on the top until the crowd moved and split, gathering on each side of the front gate to watch us bear Mr. Burke down the last six steps.

At the back doors to the ambulance I felt the rain start. I looked up to where the clouds had moved under the moon, and in the fifth-floor window I saw Mr. Burke standing, watching the proceedings. The light seemed to go through him, his body too thin to stop it, but he felt more real to me than the man strapped to the board, the eyes unblinking in the rain. I held my breath and bent over, waiting for the feeling to pass. When I looked up again, Mrs. Burke had taken his place. She was holding a suit and a pair of shoes; she reached up her arm and the light went off. "Let's go, Frank," Larry said, and together we loaded Burke's body into the back.

There is an old woman named Doris who for years has been wandering the streets of Times Square. She carries all her belongings with her in two tattered canvas bags, and she sleeps in a box next to the playground in Clinton Park. She walks most of the day and night, her bags held just inches above the street, her head down, speaking to the passing ground in bitter tones. She seems to hate everything, but most of all she hates ambulances, for every ambulance she sees is the one that took her daughter away. If I park long enough in the area of Forty-fifth Street and Seventh Avenue, inevitably I'll hear a pounding on the back doors and Doris calling, "Marie, Marie, it's Mama. I'm going to get you out." Then she walks around to the front. "You've got my daughter; she's in there," she'll say. "You give her back." The first few times I saw her, I tried talking to her, but her hatred was uncompromising, exhaustive, a mother facing her child's killers for the first time. "You give her back," she yells, picking up her bags to follow as I drive away.

2

Larry climbed through the back doors and sat in the chair at the stretcher's head. He reconnected the Ambu-bag to the tube in Burke's lungs and squeezed. One of the EMTs sat at Burke's side, searching the arm for a blood pressure. I hung the IV bags, hooked up the oxygen, and plugged in the EKG wires that had come off during the four-flight carry-down. The machine beeped out a record of the heart's stubborn knocking, a perverse cable from the pale-blue face whose open eyes pointed blankly at the ceiling. Twice I tried to close them, but the lids rolled back.

When the daughter stepped in I grabbed her arm and turned her to go, saying she could follow behind us with her mother, but she refused to leave. I'm always bad with the consoling part. I can start an IV in the back of an ambulance bouncing down Seventh at sixty, but my words of sympathy always sound so empty. I tend to look more stricken than the family. The best I can do is keep them from the dying, and Burke's daughter had seen too much of that already. I pulled her out, and though she fought me, I held her arm and shut the door. "Help your family," I said. "They need you more. Help yourself." I left her there in the green halo of the streetlamps and the oily rain sweeping in from Ninth Avenue.

Into Forty-third, silent through the gray steam rising, no lights, no sirens, only the slow ticking of Burke's EKG and the rhythmic slap of the broken wiper, a dirty mop on the front glass. I felt like I had been upstairs in Burke's apartment for days, like the rest of the night would stretch out through every remaining year of my life.

I made a right on Tenth. No rush, I thought, but when I saw the daughter drive up behind me in an old black Ford, I turned on the lights and sirens, pressed down on the gas. The emergency room couldn't do much for Burke, but it was important for the family that it look emergent. I stared straight ahead, trying to think only of the road in front of me, the simple job of taking the patient to the hospital.

I needed to concentrate because my mind tended to wander on these short trips. It was the neighborhood I grew up in and where I had worked most as a medic, and it held more ghosts per square foot than any other. If I wasn't careful I could stop at a red light and forget where I was going, disappear into the past: a young boy climbing the elms in Clinton Park, a young man carrying a stabbed hooker out of the Smiling Eyes Pub. Lately I had been disappearing a lot, missing turns. I even took a couple of patients to the wrong hospital. Larry had sent Captain Barney three transfer requests in three weeks. He told him I was crazy, though that is a relative term and I considered Larry one of the strangest people I'd ever met. I just needed a few slow nights, a week without tragedy, followed by a couple of days off. I wanted to deliver Burke, give my condolences to the family, and never see them again.

Get through the rest of this shift and forget it, see the new day in at the Blarney Moon bar.

I was born in the same hospital I was taking Burke to die in, Our Lady of Mercy, Fifty-sixth Street between Ninth and Tenth, but those who worked there, or were unfortunate enough to be treated there, called it Our Lady of Misery, or simply Misery. My father, who was also born in Misery, never referred to the place as anything except the butcher shop, following an appendectomy in which the surgeon left a sponge under his colon. Three weeks after surgery, my father returned in agony and was immediately reopened. He spent the next two months in Misery's critical care, a stay that was anything but miserable, for he had fallen helplessly in love with the night nurse, Mariah Horan.

My mother often told me of the night they met. In details only a nurse could love, she described his thin feverish face and pale weakened frame, comatose from shock and so close to death, she claimed, the priest had been called. Neglecting her other patients, she stayed with him through the night, her hand rarely leaving his burning forehead, tracing with her fingers in his damp skin the sign of the cross. She came from a long line of Irish faith healers, peasant physicians who made house calls with Bibles and beads, and as she sat next to my father she spoke the prayers learned from her mother, a mix of Latin, Gaelic, and King James that sounded in my young ears like the kind words of a dinosaur queen. In the morning he opened his eyes and they were gray and without shine, but he was alive, and when he saw her he smiled and said, "Who'd ever thought they'd let me in heaven."

That was my favorite part, because my mother always laughed, something she rarely did. "And do you know what he called me?"

Of course I knew. He called her the angel of his resurrection.

She loved to tell that story while preparing my bed, mechanically pulling down the crisp creased sheets and softening the pillow with three quick punches. She was born a nurse, had as a young girl nursed every stray child or animal, left her job at Misery to nurse me and my father, and never quite stopped, and as she leaned over to feel my forehead and whisper good night, it was easy to see the angel he fell for that morning, her eyes glittering blue-white like Niagara, her cheeks flushed as if just christened, her hair bundled up over her head like a Greek madonna. "It was a long and difficult recovery," she said, "but I never doubted. Every day I cared for him I loved him more."

Such was my mother's power in those moments I would not have been surprised if the room had filled with the fluttering of doves, the songs of a hundred harps, and every night in that music she wrapped the earth in my blanket and secured it under my chin. In the grace of a child warm under the world, I slept easily, through the blaring of the night streets outside my window, the screams of my parents' pitched battles outside my door.

My parents fought often and ferociously, and it was not uncommon for my mother to leave my room after her sweet declarations and begin a blindsided verbal lashing of my father so intense you would think she had just found him dancing naked on the coffee table with the widow from next door, swigging whiskey out of the bottle and throwing up on the cat, instead of doing what he did every night: sit in the green recliner, sip gin from his '64 World's Fair glass, and watch television reruns: *Father Knows Best, My Three Sons, I Love Lucy,* and his favorite, *The Honeymooners.* During her attacks he never rose or yelled or took his eyes from the screen, but when she had worn herself to tears he would counter with a piercingly detailed summary of her faults – small-minded hysteria, religious fanaticism, poor dishwashing technique – his voice rising to describe mercilessly her stifling presence, right down to her hairy toes, climaxing with calls for divorce so grim they seemed irrevocable.

I was proud of how well they fought. On our street it was defined as romance, more plausible than any candlelit dinner. All our neighbors fought, and my friends and I were skeptical of those who didn't, like Dupa Dan's folks, who were known Communists and antiwar agitators. Through the cramped rows of walk-ups, cries of anger and crashing glass were as common as sirens. Almost nightly the thin walls in our kitchen thudded with the smashing of our neighbors' crockery. The Corcorans were smashers, my folks were screamers, and every day my friend Jimmy Corcoran and I tallied up their scores. It was all a game to us, a game because sooner or later they always made up, the storm passing sometimes as quickly as it had come, my mother still crying but smiling, my father holding her in his chair, stroking her hair: "I would die if I left you, angel. I could never do that."

Born to a poor family in the Bronx, my mother was raised on miracles. By the time she became a debt-ridden mother in Manhattan, she could find the marvels of God almost anywhere. She had shown me the Last Supper in a hardware store window, the Lord ascending into heaven in the spin cycle of a washing machine. She once found an entire Nativity scene in the bottom of a Slurpee, yet the great miracle she had waited and prayed for all her young life, the meeting and saving of my father, left a long and unremark- able wake. How could something so grandly brought end in the bent figure of my father – the same chair, the same television shows, the same dwindling gin? She had expected her faith to be tried, was ready for any infidelity, violence, or bankruptcy the Lord would choose to send – anything, that is, but the trial of dullness presented by my father.

So she invented his betrayal, searched daily through his drawers and his wallet, sniffed his clothes for perfume, checked his neck for lipstick. She accused him of affairs with every woman in the building, the local hairdresser, a bus dispatcher, a crossing guard. She even for a time suspected him of secretly meeting Audrey Meadows, who played Alice on his favorite show.

My father came home from work every night at five- thirty, and every night he would quickly change from his bus driver's uniform into a pressed clean suit in which he would eat dinner and retire to his recliner, drinking until he passed out at midnight. His routine was evidence enough of his fidelity, but my father rarely denied my mother's charges and often enjoyed encouraging them. At dinner he would casually refer to the height of his passengers' skirts, and he could go on at length about the widow's lingerie hung to dry outside our kitchen window.

About once a week he would rise from the table and announce that he needed a walk. Preparations for these excursions could last over an hour as he showered, shaved, and changed into his best suit. He stood before the hall mirror and stared at the figure in the glass, a man of obvious wealth and industry, of power over many, a man who was perhaps on his way to the club for drinks and talk of the world and then to his table at the Plaza, a discreet supper with an actress friend.

He was handsome, the handsomest man in the city, my mother used to say, but before his weekly walks she refused to be in the same room with him; acting as if it was their final parting, she banged the pots against the sink and cursed the cat. She told him never to return, to go to his women and let them endure his faithless love for more than one night. She said this though she had followed him enough times to know he never walked farther than the corner bar, to talk baseball with Pete the bartender.

I lived for the few hours between dinner and the gin he disappeared in at eight. He might come home snarling, knock me around for a C in math, but there was always the chance he might step through the door laughing at some joke he had heard at work and couldn't wait to tell. Some evenings he poured attention on us. He'd prop me on the thin edge of his knee and tell me stories of my grandfather, an Irish immigrant who made good, at one time owning three liquor stores, an entire building on Fifty-second Street, a house and horse in the Catskills, and who drank all his good luck away and gave what was left to his friends. He spoke of the years when there was nothing his father wouldn't give him and years when there was nothing to give, and yet, rich or poor, he always spoke of the city as a child's dream, a fenceless playground of construction sites and demolition zones. When my mother finished in the kitchen, he'd grab her and pull her into his arms, toppling us all to the floor. He'd smother her protests with kisses, and afterward, standing and laughing, he'd grab my wrists and swing me over her, around the room, my arms stretching out until I felt the wind of my feet pushing down the walls.

But the nighttime always came, and with it the sickness's inevitable return, my father staring at the television, irritable to any intrusion. When the bottle was half drained, he closed the door completely, walled up in his chair to relapse in the history of his failure and the disease he blamed for it. The doctors at Misery had declared his recovery complete. My father did not agree. The first forgotten sponge might have been removed, but he believed the space it left was still infected; though perhaps less septic than the surgeon's mistake, it nevertheless sapped his will and energy, leaving a lingering malaise from which he could not rise.

He had wanted to be a pilot, had left Fordham his junior year to join the Air Force, had just flown his first time alone when the appendix forced him down. He was given a medical discharge, and after spending six more months in my mother's care, she told him she was pregnant. Driving a bus was the first job he could find. Then the bills came and the baby's cries, their first arguments. He felt the fever's return, fed, he believed, by that hole in his side that had first led him to her and which he began filling with gin, the hole growing larger so that by the time I was nine he needed a quart and a half a night. Hours he sat, sipping and staring. In his clean pressed suit he looked like a shell-shocked duke. My mother sat on the couch not far from him, yet so withdrawn was she in her own life never lived, she could not have been further away. Some nights I would sneak from my bed and sit between them, watching TV for hours without being discovered. The television volume was always turned up, and still you could not drown out the street, the horns and sirens, the drunken threats and laughter, the breaking bottles.

The first dead person in my life was my grandfather. He died behind the counter of a store he had once owned and then just worked in. I followed my father there after the cops called. He said not to look, but I was already beside him. The old man lay on his back, appearing more angry than dead, more alive than Burke, though they were both about the same age and Burke's heart was still beating. No medics then. The undertakers at Buckley's were called. Took him up the same street I was taking Burke but continued past Misery and up out of the city to Gate of Heaven Cemetery in Westchester. My father sat in front of me in the limousine, stared out the window for the whole trip. "No one came," he said. "He worked his whole life in this neighborhood and a handful of old women show up. Where were the Reillys – he practically put that kid through school – the Marinos, the Treinans? There was nobody he wouldn't help if he had the money, and now he's broke and dead and no one gives a shit. Everyone we knew is gone. There's nothing in this city for us. Christ, you gotta speak Spanish to get a cup of coffee."

We left that year for a bus stop forty miles upstate. My father wanted space, and our house was a castle compared to the four rooms we shared in Hell's Kitchen. From the first day, we trod warily through the place, almost at pains not to disturb the oppressive size, the silence that hung over it. My mother spent more and more time at the church. She organized canned-food drives and rosary picnics. My father wanted more space. He bought his own bus and started a one-man company, giving tours of the country to German tourists. The shelves in my room were soon filled with souvenirs: a miniature Alamo, framed pictures of Indians and outlaws, Old Faithful, the Golden Gate Bridge.

My father left on a Pony Express tour and he never came back. He called a few times, inviting me to his new apartment in San Francisco. I used his toothbrush until the bristles wore out, then I burned it in the backyard. The space surrounding me felt like a museum, deadwood. The frontier was back in the city; life lived and fought for every minute. In the fields behind the house I imagined I was Diamond Jim Brady strolling down Broadway. I would never be like my father, never curse my life with regret. I wanted to go back to the city, fight it out where he had given up.

I was nineteen when I decided to become a medic, drive an ambulance. Perfect. Save lives and see the front lines, help the people who had stuck it out in the city I dreamed about.

At the time, I believed the only way to avoid regret was to wrap my life completely in the present, in a succession of quick, kind acts, and no job seemed more suited to the moment than medic. Only much later did I realize I had chosen my parents' careers, a bus-driving nurse, a nursing driver.

I was good at my job; there were even periods when my hands moved with a speed and skill that were beyond me and my mind worked with a cool authority I had never known. I would scrap with depression, I drank too much, but every once in a while I participated in a miracle, breathing life back into a young asthmatic, holding a tiny just-born jewel in my hands.

But in the last year I had started to lose that control. I'd always had nightmares, but now the ghosts didn't wait for me to sleep. My wife left. I drank every day. Help others and you help yourself, that was my motto, but I hadn't saved anyone in months. It seemed all my patients were dying, everything I touched turned to shit. I waited, sure the sickness would break, tomorrow night, the next call, feeling the bottom fall away.

The steering wheel vibrated when Larry started the suction, and I listened to the pump's whine as he worked it deep into Burke's throat. Larry was coughing, and the smell of Burke's dying filled the front. It mixed in with the garbage decay from the river grates and the sour taste of the rain, and it moved out into the night, rising like a gas through the starless air. My eyes were closing and I could feel my hands shaking; they shook almost all the time. I looked in the side mirror and saw the daughter's Ford stopped just behind my bumper. Her eyes made it clear she had a good view of Larry wrangling with the old man's fluids. Taxis passed me. I looked up. The light was green. No idea how long I'd stopped.

I fled up Tenth then. As I passed the building I grew up in, I heard my mother's voice. He's having a seizure, she says; put something in his mouth so he doesn't bite his tongue. I can see my father looking for something, anything, finally stuffing a pack of Lucky Strikes between my teeth. An old woman lives in that apartment now. She is lonely and sick and calls a few times a year. When I climb those stairs again I almost expect to see my nine-year-old self on the floor, my head in my father's hands. The old woman tells me about her bad heart and her sons who left her, and I have to turn down her television because I can hear my father screaming at it. She is afraid only of dying alone, afraid of the mess it will leave, of the smell if no one finds her right away. She is a ghost, alive but a ghost, like the woman in the project building across the street who gets drunk and throws herself in front of the taxis on Tenth because it was a taxi that killed her son there. None have hit her yet, but she is a ghost, in a building full of them, living and dead, like the man who fell fifteen floors onto the low cement wall that lines the front. He crushed three cinder blocks, and every time I pass the spackled patch I see the man twisted over it. Behind the wall is an eight-year-old boy shot in the head. It takes only a glance to bring back the small face with a hole in the middle, and then I always see Jimmy Corcoran's face there, as if he died that day he split his head open on a rock, in the same spot, before the building went up, when it was an empty lot where we played Man on the Moon.

Jimmy is still alive, but not by much. Every few weeks he overdoses in DOA Park. He never recognizes me, and I don't tell him who I am. I call it DOA Park because of all the junkies I've pronounced dead there. On bad nights I see them all together in the northwest corner, near the statue of the forgotten man. They sit or lie in a circle on the ground. Sometimes Jimmy is with them.

And they always ask me, What have you changed? It's obvious to me now. What in the end can you change here? Of all the people I went to rescue, it was only those lost I thought about. The boy shot on his bicycle, the girl Rose who I helped to kill and who follows me through every shift. A hundred more. Sometimes the whole damn city's crying – in the bars, the drunks on the floor, the men shot near the doors, up the stairs, the ODs in the hallways, the back rooms full of heart attacks and strokes, on the roofs, the women raped and screaming – a chorus of abandonment.

And above that, over the taxis' horns and the wails of my siren, the steady tones of Burke's heart beeped from the monitor like a countdown to the world's end. Everything else was broken, but Burke's heart kept going. A nearly perfect machine, it needed no other controls, nothing but the food and air which Larry provided every five seconds or so with a squeeze from his bag. In this way it could fire itself eighty times a minute, one hundred thousand times a day, every day, working the reluctant body along. For without the brain, the body was in revolt. The liver was backing up poison into the arteries. The kidneys, seeing that load, had taken the day off. Suffocating limbs spit toxins, which in the feet and hands slowed through sick blue ponds. In the brain, the dead cells were exploding like sap in a fire. Their acidic remains bled down the spine and into the trunk. The stomach was backing up too, pouring its holdings into its master, the now useless head. Green fluid seeped over Burke's lips. It came up faster than Larry could suction it, rising from the nose and tear ducts, filling the eyes and running in slim streams down the cheeks.

I was called to a cardiac arrest in a building on Fifty-seventh Street, an old man who had just stopped breathing. We found him on the kitchen floor and hooked him up to the monitor. He was flatline and I started CPR and after a minute he reached up his arms and clasped them tightly around my throat. I stopped and the arms fell back to his sides. I started again and again he reached for my throat. I stopped and they fell. Eventually I had to get one of the neighbors to hold his arms while I did chest compressions. His rhythm on the monitor never improved, but it took almost half an hour for him to lose the strength in his arms. We pronounced him then.

3

The emergency waiting room of Our Lady of Mercy was a white-lit cement box painted yellow and decorated with the framed playbills of old Broadway shows. Four rows of six plastic chairs faced a television set chained to the ceiling. Under the TV and to the left was a door, a desk, and a guard in dark glasses who controlled the door from a button in his desk. The guard screened entry into the treatment area and kept the patients from attacking the triage nurse, who was always being attacked and who sat in a glass-enclosed cubicle just behind the door. At her small table she asked each patient a few questions, took pulse, blood pressure, and temperature, and assigned him or her a number, one, two, three, according to urgency.

It had been a bad night and the crowd was close to riot when I brought Burke's stretcher through. The waiting room usually reached its breaking point around eleven, when the sick families and workers from the afternoon backed up into the drunks and assault victims of the evening rush. All the seats would be taken then, and the bleeding, cursing spillover leaned against the walls or sat on the floor, getting up every half hour to ask the guard if their name had been called and then pacing in the back, through the standing knots of families and friends, or going out to the parking lot to throw up and smoke a cigarette.

The Misery regulars were often the least patient. They'd wake from a four-hour nap screaming for attention, and if they didn't get it they would slide from their seats in dramatized seizures or stumble forward to the triage desk clutching their chests in the desperate hope of raising their status. If they saw an asthmatic taken inside, they approached the nurse with a series of unsuccessful wheezes. The nurse only reminded them of the inconsequence of their condition. Their ailments, they were told again and again, hardly merited a priority three, and all threes had to wait until all twos and ones were cared for.

The guard was no more helpful. He had taped a white square around his station and placed a sign on his desk: "Please Stand Behind White Line. Thank You." With his dark glasses on and his arms crossed over the great wall of his chest, the guard ignored everyone outside the line. To those that crossed he growled, "Don't make me take my glasses off." He always gave them the option of not making him take his glasses off, for if the shades did have to come down, someone would be bounced, off the floor, the wall, even the street. A good bouncing could keep the crowd quiet up to an hour.

We brought Burke in slowly. The two IV lines, each one connected to an elbow, were tangled in the EKG cables that wrapped twice around Larry before reaching the monitor on his back. To avoid pulling out the lines, Larry had to hold the IV bags behind his neck, his face just a foot above Burke's mottled belly. I led the stretcher with one hand and with the other squeezed the Ambu-bag, which kept disconnecting from the tube in his lungs. I stopped in the entrance to reconnect it and to pull up the sheet bunched around his ankles.

"Let's give him a little dignity," I said, tucking the sheet under his chest.

Larry spoke into Burke's midsection. "Where you gonna find some to give?"

Two lacerated Russians scrambled out of our way, dragging off a third whose nose bent strangely over his cheek. Three young children ran up to the stretcher, straining to see Burke's face. Their pregnant mother called them back. Dear God, a Filipino woman said, and then the only sound was the snoring of Mr. Hand, a regular at Misery, who was stretched across four seats. Everyone else watched in quiet dismay as we wheeled Burke toward the door. They knew that this man with all his cables and tubes was one of the much discussed though rarely seen priority ones. They stared at the eyes that could not close, the skin white as an old kitchen stove.

Griss the guard sat at his desk reading from a television guide lying in the half-open top drawer. "Hey, partner," he said, looking up, his brown face wide and lined like the base of a tree. "Your man does not look well. They're not gonna appreciate you inside."

"Nobody loves me, Griss."

"Griss is only telling you there's been a few catastrophes tonight. Things are backing up."

"They're bad all over," I said, and pulled Burke's sheet up again.

"Telling me."

The street doors opened and the Burke family rushed in, hoping some miracle had occurred during our drive to the hospital – Mr. Burke now standing by the guard, asking to sign out and go home. When they looked upon the stretcher it was as if he died again for the tenth time that night.

"Griss," I pumped the Ambu-bag. "We better go in."

"All right, partner. Whatever you say."

He pushed the button and the door swung open, striking the bandaged feet of a man lying on a stretcher against the wall. "Yow," the man screamed, and we moved inside. Griss reached out his arm and blocked the family. "You can't go in there, folks."

The bandaged feet were the first of four pairs of casted, bandaged, or in some way restrained feet that lay upon the four stretchers in the hall. The nurses called the area Skid Row and put the worst-smelling patients there, the farthest point from their station in the treatment room. This form of triage infuriated the triage nurse, whose cubicle opened to the right of Skid Row, making it a natural gas trap.

Triage Nurse Constance held her surgical mask close as we wheeled Burke past. "That's right," she said, "just keep moving through. Don't even slow down." Then she turned back to the thin, nervous-looking man seated before her. "Sir, you say you've been snorting cocaine for three days and now you feel that your heart is beating too fast and you would like us to help you. Well, to tell you the truth, I can't see why we should. If I'm mistaken here, correct me, okay?

Did we sell you the cocaine? Did we push that cocaine up your nose?"

The last stretcher on Skid Row held a dark-skinned young man. His hands and feet were tied to the railings with straps of cloth, and his chaotic mass of black dreadlocks swung back and forth over his face as he pulled feverishly at his restraints. "Give me some water," he cried, his eyes wide and dry like those of a starving child. I could hear him trying to smell us. "For God's sake give me some water."

"Shut up," said an old man one stretcher down. His feet were swollen purple, like prize-winning eggplants. "God-damn civilians," he said, staring at the ceiling. "Quiet down there."

I nosed Burke into the treatment room, and the nurses were quick to ignore us. Three of them huddled together around the doctor, who was bent over a textbook behind the waist-high wall of the nurses' station. It appeared as if the staff were under siege by a battalion of shriveled old men and women lying on a field of white sheets. Only two slim paths led from the station to the twelve critical care units that ringed the room.

"Don't take another step," yelled Nurse Lucia Crupp, who could avoid us no longer. "We're on diversion." She waded toward us through the stretchers. "We can't accept any more patients. Your dispatcher should have told you."

"Everyone is on diversion," I said.

"Not like this. Take him to Episcopal. They're probably just finishing their tea now. Wondering what's on the telly tonight, I bet, or getting ready to start the hangnail rounds."

"I got him at Forty-third and Ninth. You're the closest."

"Where will I put him, Frank? Look. Tell me."

"He said he wanted to come here. He said the nurses in Misery give the best Foleys in the city."

"Please. What I'd like to do to you I won't say. All right, give me one minute, I'll kick someone out of slot three."

When Lucia left, the new nurse, the one who never spoke, came up. She picked up Burke's hand and stared at his palm. She shook her head and mechanically took Burke's pulse and blood pressure, looked into his pupils, listened to his lungs. She walked over to the doctor, who was now asleep on the book. She pulled his elbow, but he didn't stir.

While Larry unraveled himself from the IV lines, I did my best to ignore the man tied up beside me. "Excuse me, sir," he pleaded, "excuse me. You are a very kind man. I can see that right away. You are the kindest man in the world, the most true. A man like you could not refuse a poor sick dying helpless man a small cup of water."

"I can't," I said. "I have to stay with this patient."

"Get me a drink of water, damn you. I need water."

"Shut the hell up," cried the other man. "If it wasn't for these dun feet I'd go over there and kick your ass."

The nurse had given up pulling at the doctor's arm and begun shaking his head from the shoulders.

"What." He leaped from his chair, the side of his face flattened by the book. "Call a consult." He twisted his head until each side cracked, and then he sat down. "What is it, Milagros?"

She pointed at Burke.

From his chair the doctor made a quick summation of

Burke's condition. He noted the cyanosis in the lips and fingers, the pale, mottled skin, the Ambu-bag, IV, and EKG. He concluded that Burke was a critical patient needing immediate care, and so he returned to his book and began again the same page that, because of interruptions, he had been unable to finish all night. Milagros shook him.

"What? What is it?"

She pointed at Burke.

"Goddammit." The doctor slammed the book closed. "Guys," he said, walking toward us, "what are you doing to me? I thought we were on diversion. I can't deal with this shit. We're all backed up here. I haven't sent a patient upstairs in days. Christ, would you look at him. He's gonna need the works. What's wrong with him anyway?"

"You should know," said Larry. "You pronounced him."

"You. You told me he was dead. You said he was flatline for half an hour."

"He got better."

"I hate pronouncing people dead over the phone." The doctor walked around Burke, striking his reflex hammer uselessly at the elbows, knees, and feet. He flashed a light into Burke's eyes. "Better, huh? They're fixed and dilated. He's plant food."

Nurse Crupp returned. "We stole a stretcher from X-ray. There's no pad on it, but I don't think he'll mind. Put him in unit three, next to the overdose. Respiratory says they're out of ventilators, but I know the sixth floor's been hoarding. I sent Odette for it."

We moved Burke over to the stainless-steel stretcher top, his pale form shining silver and white. The doctor and I watched as the nurses dressed him in a gown and hooked him to their machines.

"He's our lowest priority now," the doctor said. "There'll be no extraordinary measures taken. He shouldn't even be here. All this technology. What a waste."

On the monitor over Burke's head the beats came in regular bunches of two or three, followed by a wide-spaced aberration that carried no blood and made no sound. The doctor watched from the foot of the bed, holding Burke's ankles tightly, pushing down.

I always thought of Dr. Hazmat as the doctor I would have been. For two years I left work at seven in the morning to sleep in my car two hours before chemistry class. Tired as I was, I loved those bloodless days in the lab, burning magnesium, memorizing the cold numbers on the blackboard. I never finished. The grades were good but the dream was gone, unraveled over long nights at work, bringing patients into emergency rooms like Our Lady of Misery, watching doctors like Hazmat learn the limits of their tools.

"Come here," Hazmat said, and pulled my arm. He pointed to a middle-aged man lying in unit six. "I've got a first-time heart attack here, forty-five years old. He should have gone to the CCU ten hours ago. He needs catheterization, venous central pressure monitoring, EKGs every thirty minutes. I couldn't do it here even if I had the time, but the CCU's full. There's three bodies up there like the one you just brought in."

"Over here," he said, walking down to units ten through

twelve. Three AIDS patients stared back, shrunken white men, pale, brittle, dry. The IV lines ran up from each hand like puppet strings.

"All advanced cases. This one in twelve is filling up with fluid. His lungs are whiting out and I am going to have to intubate because the kid's mother won't sign the Do Not Resuscitate. She thinks she's murdering him by signing, and she's right. I've found that mercy killing doesn't translate well into Spanish. I tell you it's a sin to tube this kid."

The doctor spun me around to face two stretchers, a man and a woman lined up against the nurses' station. "Sepsis and pneumonia," he said. "Each needs a week in house medical, but they're homeless and uninsured and upstairs won't give up the beds. I'm supposed to break the infection here, twenty-four hours IV antibiotics, and then send them to the streets with a prescription. I guarantee you they'll be back in two weeks, probably needing an ICU bed too, which of course will be full. And look over here." He pointed to two men and a woman lined up in the corner. "Three more ODs from the latest killer junk that's been going around. They call it the Red Death." From his pocket he pulled out a thumb-size plastic tube with a rubber stopper at the top and a red skull and crossbones printed on the side. "You must have seen these."

"I've been out for a few days," I said. "Sick."

"You're sick a lot, Frank."

"It runs in my family."

"There's been at least three DOAs since the stuff showed up two days ago. It's a mix of heroin and I don't know what else, some kind of amino acid maybe. The lab's checking it out. The stuff is so strong you don't have to shoot it; you can snort it, smoke it, they're even drinking it mixed with grain alcohol. You might have to use up to ten times the usual amounts of Narcan to wake them up, then watch out because they're liable to go nuts on you."

"Water," cried the man tied to the stretcher. "Water, water, doctor man, water."

"Is that one of them?"

"No, that's Noël; he's just crazy." I followed Hazmat over to Skid Row. "Please," Noël screamed. Hazmat pulled down on the man's eyes, pushed up on his chin. "When he first came in I thought he might be an OD. He was completely unresponsive but didn't wake up to the Narcan. Vitals normal. No signs of trauma. It turns out Nurse Crupp knows him, said he's a local nut that used to live in the alleys and was a regular off and on, but she hasn't seen him in years. She thinks he was in jail. Anyway, he seized twice and almost coded. I really had no idea until the bloods finally came back. His sodium level was like a hundred. Normal is one thirty-five. I gave him a hypertonic solution, slowly – they go flatline if you bring the levels up too fast – and he woke up like this, screaming for water."

"Oh, Doctor," the man cried, "you are the most greatest. So kind and smart. If you please, you could give me one cup of water. This is all I need."

"Will you shut up," yelled the man with the purple feet.

"I was reading some old journals and I think I figured it out. Psychogenic polydipsea. It's a very rare severe obsessive-compulsive disorder, an unquenchable thirst. They will drink out of toilet bowls, anything – antifreeze, urine. He drank so much the kidneys were taking out salt to pull the water out, diluted his system. I called the Psych Department. They don't believe me, but they're sending someone over. I might even write something to the *Journal*."

"I am dying, Doctor. You must help."

"For God's sake, Doc, give him a cup of water," the man with swollen feet said.

"I am helping you, Noël," the doctor said. "You could die if you drank more water."

"Give me some water you son of a bitch. Fuck your mother, shithead. I need water."

Milagros came up silently from behind and pulled the doctor's arm. "What is it?"

She pointed at Burke.

Burke's monitor started ringing like a fire alarm. The irregular beats had broken down into a quaking line. Nurse Crupp stood next to him, searching for a pulse.

"Dammit." Hazmat hesitated a moment, staring at the green screen, then he headed toward Burke, giving orders as he walked. "Nurse Crupp, start CPR. Milagros, get me an epi. Odette, wake up Dr. Stark. Tell him I need a blood gas, stat."

The doctor grabbed the paddles next to the monitor and began charging them. "Clear," he yelled. "Clear." I pulled my stretcher out of their way, piled my equipment on it, and headed for the door. The entire staff was working on Burke, and only I saw the old man with the swollen feet climb up on his infected arches and, crying with pain, begin to untie the obsessive-compulsive.

"Bless you, sir. Bless you," Noël moaned.

"Shut up," said the old man.

I moved around them and down the hall. The triage nurse waved to me. She was interviewing a man with a wide bleeding gash over one eye. "So you get drunk every day and you fall down. Tell me why we should help you when you're going to get drunk tomorrow and fall down again."

I struck the metal button on the wall, and the door swung open just as Noël struck me from behind, sending my stretcher into Burke's family, who were still standing, waiting near the door. We moved together toward the wall as Noël pivoted on his heels, retreated, and then screamed when he located the water fountain in the back of the room, near the statue of Our Lady. He ran for it, his gown flapping crazily behind. Throwing aside a small child, he began drinking in short deep gulps, snorting like a bull just let out of his box.

As I watched Noël drink, I felt the family, one by one, turn to me, the eyes of wife, son, and daughter asking the same question.

"He's very, very sick." My stock reply.

Noël finished at the fountain with a loud gasp, an intrepid belch. "I *know* him," Burke's daughter said, and began walking toward Noël. "That's Noël. Noël." I deftly cut her off. "We better go outside," I said. "Quickly, quickly." I herded them through the doors, feeling the wind rush past us as Noël exploded, the first in a flooding wave of spasmodic eruptions that sent anyone who could walk or crawl into the parking lot with us.

"Is there any chance?" Burke's daughter asked.

I shook my head. "I guess there's always a chance."

Through the ER doors I watched Griss the guard rise slowly to his feet. He removed his glasses, folded them, and carefully placed them in the breast pocket of his jacket. Suddenly the doors broke open and Noël came flying through. He landed on the cement at our feet and bounced up to go back inside, but Griss filled the doorway.

"Noël," Burke's daughter called. "Noël." She ran over to him and put her hand on his shoulder. He jumped three feet. "Noël, it's me, Mary, from Forty-third Street."

"Mary, Mary, Mary," he said. I wasn't sure he recognized her, but he enjoyed saying her name. "Mary, Mary, I'm so thirsty. They won't give me anything to drink. Please, Mary."

"I'll get you some," she said, and Griss swung aside for her when she went in and again when she came out, a paper cup in her hand.

"I wouldn't give him that," I said, but Noël was already holding the cup between his fingers, sipping gently.

"Thank you." He sipped again, like he was tasting God. Then he walked to the corner of the lot, watching us.

"The doctor seems to think he's suffering from some rare disorder."

"I don't think it's that rare," she said. "He grew up on our street. He's had a rough life and he's a little crazy from it, but that's no excuse for not giving someone a lousy cup of water." We watched the crowd limp back into the emergency room, Mrs. Burke at their center. The daughter turned to me. With the rain on her face I couldn't tell if she was crying or just biting her cheek. The words I wanted to say were trapped somewhere in my left chest. I could hold

45

her hand at least, touch her shoulder. I fumbled for a tissue and pulled out an unpaid phone bill and, while looking through my other pockets, was finally saved by Noël, who stepped forward and, head bowed, handed Mary the empty cup and said thank you.

"My father's dying, Noël."

"Oh Mary, Mary, Mary," he said, and hugged her clumsily, his shoulders bobbing, his nose jabbed in her eye. Exactly what I should have done. He started walking and then stopped. "I died tonight, Mary, and I was the happiest ever. Now I must die all over again, and I wish for the day I've never been born." Then he turned and ran five steps and stopped, ran five steps, stopped, and walked down the drive. I finally found the tissue, though it was too late, and too dirty. "I better go look after my mother," she said, and walked to the doors and turned around, "Thanks for everything." She went inside. I looked down the street at Noël crossing the sidewalk, his gown flapping open behind as he disappeared in the dark line of parked cars.

About every few days after my call for Rose, the girl I helped to kill, Larry and I would be dispatched to a young woman in cardiac arrest. All of these calls would be within a few blocks of where I found Rose, and they would all go the same way: I drive like a maniac to get there, sure I'm going to find Rose again, in her yellow raincoat, a tragic, apneic heap on the curb, but every time I pull up to the scene, the streets are empty. I check the sidewalks, stairs, and doorways. I jump out and look under the bus. "There's nothing here," Larry says. "False alarm, I guess. Probably someone sleeping who moved on." "She's here," I say. "You just can't see her." Larry puts the bus in drive. "Sure, Frank."

4

The night had begun badly and I had little hope for the rest of it. My ears rang when I thought of going to another call, and I felt that lump growing again in my middle, a liver-size tumor twisting up against my heart. So I took a long time restocking, changing the oxygen tanks, replacing the dirty airway equipment, running through new IVs. I poured half a bottle of alcohol on the stretcher and worked it into the corners and underneath the rails, around the wheels. I threw a clean sheet over the pad, carefully tucked in the corners.

"Come on, Frank," Larry yelled from the front seat. "The Chinese close in five minutes. You know what happens if I don't eat."

He walked around to the back and helped lift the stretcher in. Larry became catatonic if he didn't eat once an hour. "Beef lo mein," he said. "It's been on my mind ever since I woke up. What do you think?"

"I think the minute that food hits your mouth we'll get a job."

"Why do you have to talk like that?"

I pulled into Fifty-sixth Street, past the brick church and its bare pedestals, the rectory, the funeral parlor, the empty lot ringed with razor wire. Most of the restaurants on Ninth were shuttered, and the homeless had set up house under the dark awnings. Only the smoke shops were still open, one on every block, lit like nightclubs.

"Turn here," Larry said. "The Chinese are down Forty-sixth. Here, here. You missed it."

I stayed on Ninth until Forty-third and then made a right. The stoop in front of Burke's building was empty and on the fifth floor the light was on and I could make out a darker light moving through it, like a curtain rippling in the still air. I stepped out of the bus and walked around to Larry's side, then across the street, to get a better view. From the other sidewalk I saw Burke clearly, a pulsing white form circling the room, soundless fury. I slapped myself several times in the forehead. You're sick, Frank. You know that? The pain in my side suddenly doubling me over.

"Hey ambulance man. What you looking at?" Two whores stood in front of an abandoned brownstone, like they had just stepped out for some smokes and forgot their keys to get back. The skinny one was pregnant. "Pretty soon you'll be coming for me," she said, rubbing her belly stretched out big and brown below her yellow shirt. Next to them, in the shadow of a steel door twisted from its hinge, three men fought over a thin flame. Larry put his head out the window. "Frank, why are you trying to kill me?"

I opened the driver's-side door, grabbed the wheel tightly, and pulled into the street.

"Some partner you are, Frank. I could have walked there faster. I'm starving, and you stop to talk to hookers. You're making me nuts. If that's what you're trying to do, it's working, dragging me down with you into nutville."

With my foot off the gas I let the bus idle its way to

Tenth. I looked up at the rows of shades that never rise, yellower every year, like jaundice, liver failure, a slow death. "Hey Larry, you ever have the feeling you were dreaming, except you knew you weren't?"

"Oh Jesus, not now, Frank. Let's just drive very quickly over to the Chinese who close in two minutes."

"Your eyes are open, you're standing up straight, but what you see doesn't fit right with what you know is there, like the locks have been changed on the doors to perception, you know, like you got extra eyes in the back of your head but they're looking inside."

"Please, Frank," Larry said, and then he howled and slammed his ear against the dashboard and left it there. "Oh no – I just remembered something."

"What?"

"I'm so stupid. I had beef lo mein last night. I can't eat the same thing two nights in a row. And oh God, it's two o'clock right now, the last open Chinese in midtown, what the hell am I gonna do, Frank? Too much pressure. What are you getting?"

"I'm not hungry."

"Oh, I forgot. You don't need food."

"I eat. I just haven't had my coffee yet."

"No wonder you're hallucinating. Coffee and whiskey. Whiskey and coffee. Lucky you're not dead with that diet. Wait, I've got it." He clapped his hands twice. "Half fried chicken and fries. The chef's special. Let's go hurry up. Come on."

I made a right and stopped, the avenue jammed tight with Jersey johns trying to squeeze into Forty-fourth where the girls waited, chests out, mouths open – the busiest strip in the city. The pimps stood in a group on the corner, under the gas station's lights. In their long coats they posed and shadowboxed, watching the traffic pile up.

I hit the sirens, and the johns jumped at once, but they kept their place when they saw an ambulance behind them and not a patrol car. If you don't carry a gun, nobody cares. Larry got so upset I thought he might hurt himself. He punched the dashboard, the windshield. He turned on the lights, twisted the siren knob back and forth from yelp to wail to hi-lo. "This is an emergency," he said. Larry was very strict about using the sirens only for emergencies. I tapped the bumper of the taxi ahead of me, and grudgingly the cars made a lane for us.

While Larry went in to order, I rested my head against the side window. I closed my eyes but Burke's empty eyes floated in, forcing mine to open – half asleep, half watching the street. One of the freelance hookers waved to me from her office on the cellar steps. She looked like a laundry worker just finishing her shift. An old garbage picker walked by, head bent to his task, sifting the waste already searched and sold and thrown away.

Noël appeared on the corner of Forty-ninth, walking toward me down Tenth. He had exchanged his hospital gown for a suit of army-issue camouflage, rejoining the army of midtown crazies who walk the streets in survival gear while muttering to friends in hell. He seemed to have outgrown his thirst, a more conventional madness settling in as he walked against traffic, down the center lane, waving his arms above his head, scattering the windshield washers, screaming the cars out of his way. When he had passed, the washers returned, followed by the pockmarked junkies who always wandered these lanes waving pieces of stolen slump gold, broken watches, knives rusting in their packages. It was cash only in the doorways of Forty-seventh, ten dollars a hit.

In the mirror I watched Noël's green camouflage turn left into the yellow-lit ashes of Forty-fifth, and from that place a girl appeared, a teenager, tripping over her high heels as she walked toward me. I couldn't see her face, but I knew the yellow raincoat she wore, the black stockings with a hole in the knee where she fell down once because she couldn't breathe. It was Rose, the girl I had helped to kill. We all make mistakes, but some things cannot be forgiven.

I hit the horn three times, and when Larry looked over I waved to him and pointed to the radio. He held up one chubby finger and then returned to telling the cook how to fry his chicken. Rose was getting closer. Maybe it wasn't Rose. Ever since the call a month before, it seemed like all the Spanish girls in the neighborhood had started wearing yellow raincoats, a fashion trend that was killing me. Better not to know. If I looked again, regardless of whether it was her or not, I would have to relive the whole call, and I could not do that. I crossed my arms on the steering wheel, and holding my breath I pressed my forehead on my hands until they were numb. One of the first things you learn on the job is how to block out the bad calls. In the same way that cops fence off a murder scene, you wall these memories up in the deepest cave in your brain. I used to be an expert, but lately I'd found some big holes.

Anything could trigger it. The last month belonged to

Rose, but there were a hundred more ready to come out. Something as simple as that strung-out junkie on the corner, shaking his cup for change. It might be the arms or the shirt, the lines in his face, the eyes like a junkyard doll, but suddenly I know, it's in my head, and once it starts there's no stopping until I reach the screams at the end. I have to climb those stairs again, have to stand in that sunless back room checking for a pulse on that same kid, dead, wearing that stupid shirt but looking years younger, his arms clean except for one bruise. I walk through the cluttered hall past the bedroom with a Christ shrine in the corner and three children sleeping in white, folded over each other like cubs. I walk into the kitchen, where the mother waits for me, looking at me like I'm going to say her son has a fever, he'll be fine in a day or two, but I have to tell her again – years later, and it's worse every time – tell her that the son who refuses to get out of bed will never wake up. He has passed away, I say, I'm sorry. But that doesn't stop the screams, the pain exploding from her.

These spirits were part of the job. I always knew that. I had worked Hell's Kitchen for years, and it was impossible to pass a building that didn't hold the spirit of something: the eyes of an unloved corpse, the screams for some loved one. In the violent eruption of life that is death, all bodies leave their mark. You cannot be near the new dead without feeling it. I have seen even the quietest night passing fill a room the next morning with a dense fog of life's remains, and after the air has cleared, the mark lingers, in a pillow that never regains its shape or a stain on the wall that never comes clean.

I could handle that. What haunted me now was more savage: spirits born half finished, homicides, suicides, overdoses, and all the other victims, innocent or not, still grasping at lives so abruptly taken away. Rose's ghost was only the last and most visible of many who seemed to have come back solely to accuse me – of living and knowing, of being present at their deaths, as if I had witnessed an obscene humiliation for which they could never forgive.

It was a sickness, of course, the mind playing tricks. That's what I told myself, for that was the only way out. I'd been down before and always came back, but never before had I been so closely tied to someone's death. There were times when Rose could look as real to me as Larry. It had been easier when I had people to talk to. My wife before she left. My first partner, Tom Walls, before he went crazy in his own way and I had to leave him. On the outside I felt like old wood, but inside I was a mass of shoddy wiring, sparks flying, a flash fire waiting to happen. When Rose came closer, when, without opening my eyes I could tell she was standing next to my window, I felt one of the wires go. I threw on the lights and sirens and charged into traffic. Halfway up the block, I was trying to push a taxi through the light when Larry came running up, banging on the window.

"Where's the call?" He put his food on the dash, climbing in.

"We don't have a call."

"Where were you going?"

"I thought I heard a cry for help. In the distance."

"Are you drunk?"

"I'm not drunk."

"I told you the last time I'm not working with you drunk." He tore off pieces of fried leg as he spoke. "It can't go on, Frank. I'm not one of those rookies who think you're some kind of legend. That shit happened years ago."

"Look, I'm not drunk. Anyway, working with me drunk can't be as bad as working with you sober." I stopped in front of the deli on Fiftieth. "I'll get you a beer."

"I'm not kidding, Frank. Captain Barney says they're going to terminate you."

"When, man, when? They keep promising. What else do I have to do – kill my partner?"

"That's not funny."

I bought a coffee that was too hot to drink and I stood on the sidewalk, the cup warming my hands. I took one sip and the red lights started flashing – Larry's signal we had another job.

"What is it?"

"I was just starting on my fries."

"What's the call?"

"Cardiac arrest."

"Jesus."

"I know."

"That's two in a row."

"I know."

I drove furiously fast, probably because I hated going so much, and hated Larry for not minding so much, and hated the dispatcher too, for giving me this call. All dispatchers, in fact, were messengers from hell, brimming over with evil.

Eighth Avenue a wreck of concrete volcanoes, moonlit craters. Burning-hot coffee ran down my arm and I drove faster. Larry soon gave up grabbing his food from the air. He moved into his emergency response position, crouched on his seat, one hand on the roof, one on the windshield, yelling "Christ" or "Shit" after every bump.

The building was a massive prewar hulk on Central Park South. I yanked the stretcher through the front doors, past the groggy doorman, into the oak-paneled elevator. I dragged Larry and the stretcher over the thick carpeting of the twenty-eighth-floor hallway. Grabbing the airway bag I sprinted the last twenty feet, dreading the door opening, thinking this might be the call that breaks me. If they scream, I'll cry and piss on myself, everything spilling out.

I could hear groans on the other side of the door, like a grief bomb had just gone off. An old woman opened, stinking of it. She covered her mouth, then her eyes.

"He just stopped breathing," she said.

I had to push her out of our way. "Where is he?"

"To the right, in the back room. Oh God, Richard."

I passed three rooms, scattered with Victorian furniture, a television, portraits of spaniels. By the time I reached the back room I was holding my arms blindly in front of me. "Where?" I yelled.

"He's on the bed."

The bed hastily made. I pulled back the covers. Nothing.

"No, no, he's under the bed."

Larry and I squatted down, searching.

"I don't see him."

Larry looked up. "Maybe he's in the closet."

I sat on the bed, exhausted. The woman was pulling suits from the closet and throwing them on the sheets next to me.

"He was just here. He wasn't breathing."

Larry pulled at the pillows, peered behind the paintings. "He really gets around for a corpse."

She threw down another pile of suits and I grabbed her hands and made her sit on the bed. I saw the pictures of her with her husband on the dresser. He probably died years ago and you could tell by her face it was as real to her now as on the day it happened.

"It's all right," I said. "He's gone now, and there's nothing more you can do."

"No, no. He was right here."

"No, he's passed away. You know that." I put my arm around the wide shoulders, felt like crying with her. I knew all about traumatic stress syndrome. Then the toilet flushed.

"Oh my God, he's in there," she shouted, and the three of us backed away from the bathroom door as it swung open. There stood Richard, alive and well, black socks and white boxers.

"Marge, what the hell is going on here?"

"You stopped breathing, Richard. I couldn't get you up."

"I was sleeping."

She pointed to me. "This man told me you were dead."

Richard scratched himself. "Look, I'm fine." He pounded on his chest. "I hate to bother you gentlemen like this. She gets upset now and then. I'm sure you have more important things to do."

He led us down the hall into the large living room, Marge wrapped tightly around him. She was a big woman and he must have been over eighty, but he held her easily. I thought he might challenge me to an arm wrestle.

"This used to be a great place to live." He pointed to the paintings over the fireplace. "The city's changed. We used to go for walks in the park, night, day, anytime. A taxi up to Harlem, catch Basie's orchestra. Now we're afraid to step out the door. I feel like a prisoner in my own home. It's very stressful on Marge."

Marge looked up from the couch. "The doorman tried to poison me."

"It's true," Richard said. "He's very clever." He walked over to the window and pulled back the heavy blue curtains. The glass had been covered over with cereal boxes held in place by silver duct tape. "They keep the searchlights on us all night long, back and forth." Larry peeled back the corner of a box of cornflakes. We looked down on an empty horse-drawn carriage, a man walking his dog.

"They let anyone live in this building. The people upstairs are not from around here, I'll tell you that." Richard was walking angrily in a circle, his hands raised over his head. "There's a flood coming through the ceiling – feces, urine, blood. No one will help us."

Marge stood unsteadily and walked to the corner of the room. "Richard built this to stop it." She pointed to a great funnel made of aluminum foil, six feet tall, which fed into a plastic portable toilet.

"Sit down, Marge. Remember your heart."

She had almost forgotten. Slumping to the couch, she hefted up her left breast. "Oh, the pain! Richard, please, get a pill."

Richard brought over a bread box full of medications. He took a pill from each container and held a handful out to her.

"Wait a minute," I said. "You can't just give her all those."

"Believe me, it's the only thing that works."

The pills were mostly laxatives, vitamins, antidepressants. I picked out a Valium. "Here, just give her this."

Larry grabbed the Valium and put it in his pocket. He took out the EKG monitor and started hooking Marge up.

"Larry, come on – let's go." I was starting to feel like a prisoner myself. I checked the ceiling.

"Frank, she's got chest pain."

"She's got everything," I said. "Ma'am, what does the pain feel like?"

"I don't know."

"Is it like a pressure?" Larry said. "Is it like an elephant sitting on your chest?"

"Yes," she groaned.

"Is it a fluttering pain," I said, "like a bird flying in your chest?"

"Yes."

"Or a burning pain, like eating lit matches?"

"Yessss," she cried.

"She's got the yeses," I said. "Not much you can do for that."

But Larry had committed himself. He was a medic. A woman had chest pain. He set up the IV kit, wrapped a tourniquet around her arm, and wiped the skin with alcohol.

"She hates needles," Richard said. "She just needs the pills and she usually does quite well."

"She needs an IV, sir, in case we have to give her our

medication." Larry grabbed the woman's left arm. "You're going to feel a pinch."

Marge screamed like a beaten seal, and with a nimbleness that belied her great size, she yanked back with her left and drove forward with her right, catching Larry just above his ear. Daunted but determined, he went in again, just above the now freely bleeding mark of his last assault, and this time the right hook brought Larry to his knees. By then she was bleating so loudly I was sure the spotlights would come on. Richard and I watched Larry go in for the third time. Both combatants were breathing hard. The woman had lost some blood and Larry was still reeling from the last blow, but I knew he'd never give up. His was a higher cause. He reached for a fresh needle. Gracefully he darted toward her lacerated left arm, but at the last second he pulled back and dove across her. Sending his shoulder into her chest, pinning her to the couch, he thrust for the untouched stream of blue that ran up her right arm. She gasped and swung, but it was too late. Larry hit the vein and amidst her last ear-piercing cries he held her arm tight and taped the IV line into place.

Richard dressed quickly: yellow slacks, green bathrobe, blue fedora. "We have to go to Episcopal Memorial. Her doctor's there."

"They usually don't accept nine-one-one patients."

"They'll take us. I practically own the place."

By the time we reached the hospital, Marge's chest pain had dissipated and her only complaint was of the punctures to each arm. The emergency entrance was locked and I had to go around the corner to knock on the waiting room windows. The entire staff was there, spread out in the empty chairs, watching a television drama about beleaguered emergency medical workers. After a few minutes, one of the nurses came to let us in.

She kissed Marge on both cheeks. "Mrs. Foster. How have you been?"

Mrs. Foster pointed to her arms, and the nurse shook her head sympathetically. She led the stretcher into one of the six empty rooms lining the back wall. Then she waved us out, closing the curtain. "I'll handle it from here. I think you've done enough."

Two doctors came in. They shook hands with Mr. Foster and slapped him on the back, talking about the new surgery wing under construction. I sat on one of the other beds, waiting for Larry to finish the paperwork, for the nurse to return our stretcher. I listened to the television, voices arguing about how to save a pair of Siamese twins. A ringing noise mixed in, my tinnitus returning, everything moving unbearably slow. I needed to lie down.

The bed was clean and soothing. It made me want a doctor, oxygen, medicine, and, most of all, to hear my heart beating calmly on the new machine above me. I imagined taking off my uniform and putting on the simple hospital gown. I'd lie there and wait for the nurse to come and take my blood pressure, pulse, and temperature. The doctor would follow, eyes tired from too many hours, and I would be sullen at first, uncooperative, but her dogged profession-alism would win my confidence and I'd tell her of the ghosts that followed me, the pains that found a new home every night, the unexplainable madness that made me keep com-ing in to work. The doctor would listen sadly, and behind her the specialists would come, to remove my blood and trap my urine. Afterward, I'd wait, doze off, wake, think about my death until the lab results came back and the doctor returned to tell me that every procedure had been exhausted and nothing significant found. My problem was probably stress-related, perhaps psychosomatosis. Nothing serious, of course, and further tests would be done to rule out every possibility. Thank you, Doctor, I'd say. Glad to help you, sir, she'd reply. Then the nurse again and one shot that didn't really hurt that much at all, for nerves, and I'd walk out on my own with a menu of references in my pocket, more specialists to consult tomorrow, and then a taxi home, one beer, and a sleep like winter's son.

"You can't sleep here." The nurse was shaking my shoulder, pointing to the stretcher, waving us out. "This bed is for patients only."

Back in January, the month of fires, Larry had picked up a burn call while I was getting coffee. I was so angry I gave him a hell ride over there, but I felt no better for it even after I hit eighty-five on Twelfth, with Larry standing on his seat, his back pressed against the cab's roof, mumbling, "Oh Jesus, Jesus, Jesus." We pulled up as the fire trucks were leaving. I drove into the park behind the baseball fields, toward the lights of the police car. The cop had taken out the yellow death tape and was roping off a clump of bushes. In a clearing in the center, a large pile of old clothes and paperback books still smoldered. A black arm was sticking out from the bottom. The fire had burned it so thoroughly in parts that the skin had stretched open, showing the cooked white meat beneath. Larry and I pulled off the books to reveal the charred body, the whites of the eyes burned yellow. "There's a can of gas over here," the cop said. "Someone must have lit him up and then piled those books on. I'm going to Aruba next week." Larry went back to the bus for his camera. He kept a scrapbook of DOAs. The guys at his volunteer fire department loved it. "You want one?" he said as he clicked off three shots. "No, thanks. I'm fine." The man's eyes had already seared a picture in my head. I picked up a book that was lying at my feet. Fishing the Great Lakes, *by Robert P. Gulliver. I carried it back to the bus.*

5

It was three in the morning, and still the calls came in faster than the Manhattan Central Board operator could give them out. "Fifteen Boy, you got a pedestrian struck by a taxi, 320 West Fifty-eighth Street, apartment five B on the fifth floor. Must have been driving through the kitchen. Oh, wait – it says here that he was hit yesterday. Fourteen Young, you're going to the cardiac arrest at 235 West Sixty-third Street, apartment ten Charlie. Eighty-five-year-old male that no-body's seen in six days and there's a bad smell coming from the apartment, so you can rush right over there. Thirteen Victor, I hate to do this, but I have to take you off that meal break. At Forty-fifth and Lex, in front of the shelter over there, you got a forty-year-old male in a wheelchair com-plaining of leg sores, vomiting, rectal bleeding, and seizures. Enjoy. Come on, units, update your signals: Thirteen Zebra, forty-eight minutes in the ER. One-Three Charlie, Twelve Adam – I'm holding jobs here."

We were Thirteen Zebra that night, but the dispatcher would not get a signal from me until after coffee. Somewhere in his blue screen something horrible waited for me, capsized and bug-ridden. I stopped in front of the bagel shop around the corner from Episcopal. One coffee, black, no sugar, I said and said it again, but the owner's son just stared, as if I'd asked for a piano. He was still upset about a call we'd had in that store over two months before, a middle-aged customer who had dropped dead on the floor. In a rush to start the IV, Larry used his scissors to cut through the man's coat and in so doing broke paramedic rule number eight: Never cut a down-filled coat. Immediately the feathers were sucked from the dead man's sleeve and into the huge fans that are designed to move the hot air away from the ovens. Within seconds, a feather blizzard was blowing through the little shop. Feathers swirled into our eyes and mouths. They covered every corner, every bagel. They drifted into vats of cream cheese and bags of flour. Ahmed, the enormous Iranian owner, claimed he was still finding feathers.

"Please tell me," he said as he carried the coffee around his son and placed it on the counter, "why you should cut the coat of a dead man."

I should have gone somewhere else, but this was the closest coffee and the best. "I really have to go. We're very busy."

"Take my blood pressure. Please. My head is killing me." He began to roll up his sleeve.

"No," I said. "I can't stay. Go to the hospital."

"Please, who will look after this? My sons, they are too stupid and lazy. All they think about is skinny women and Corvettes. Business is already very bad from these feathers."

I walked out before he finished. I'd heard it before. His blood pressure was always incredibly high, almost incompatible with life. Every time I took it, I told him to go to the hospital, and every time, he told me all the reasons he couldn't go. If it wasn't his sons, it was his wife, the weather, his gout. He was a tough old guy, though, and I liked anyone that refused to go to the hospital.

Larry was sleeping, so I turned down the volume of the ambulance and police radios and sipped at the steaming coffee. Five minutes, I thought, I'll take five. I closed my eyes, but Burke's eyes returned, so I stared at Larry's head, which, except for the small bud of the nose, formed a perfect sphere. In the six months we'd worked together I had watched him fall asleep dozens of times, and I still marveled at the transformation. While awake, Larry's body crashed across earth with the grace of a butcher in full armor. I always thought the problem was in his neck, which was as lean as a runway model's, and given only that support, the features of his great skull seemed to wax and wane in the sway of mysterious cranial tides. This constant buffeting inclined Larry's head naturally toward the closest support – a window, a wall, the steering wheel. Once he was at rest, the shifting ceased, his trunk deflated, his head rounded, and his face took on the benign fulfillment of a baby at its mother's breast.

More than anything else, I wanted to sleep like that, to close my eyes and leave this haunted city, to drift, far away, in the sun, across a glacial lake walled with pine. To wake up in the morning lazy with sleep and close my eyes again and dream back to a clearing on the edge, a log house, a fire, a wide soft bed, Mona. It had been months since I was in that house, more than three weeks since I'd seen my wife.

* * *

Mona used to say that meeting me was like getting hit by a truck. Actually, it was a station wagon. When I first saw her I assumed she was dead. The motorcycle was bent and twisted gruesomely beneath the wagon. She was lying about thirty feet away, not moving. But as I walked toward her she raised her head and looked at me and I saw that she was not only alive but pretty, and generally intact too, except for the part of her leg that bent where it should have been straight. I cut up the leather pants to expose it, though she screamed at me not to. It was the most beautiful broken leg, long, white, and smooth, and bent gracefully where the fractured edge of her fibula tried to push through her calf like a new joint, but far prettier than a knee or an ankle. I hesitated to splint it, keeping my hands near the break, staring at the angle and the strange new beauty it gave her, until she sat up and watched with me. "Straighten that out," she said. First I fell in love with Mona's leg, then I fell in love with Mona.

She told me she was a dancer. In the back of the ambulance she made me promise to shoot her if I thought the break would keep her from dancing again. I was useless for the rest of the night, bandaging headaches, splinting heart attacks. After work I went up to her room, bringing pillows and painkillers. "The doctor told me I don't have to shoot you."

I told her the story of how my parents met at Misery. I helped her down the hall and showed her the nursery where I was born. She talked about Ohio. In my mind it became this heavenly cemetery of empty silos and broken-down factories, a little girl dancing in the weeds. Then the painkillers set in and I was witness to a miracle, Mona sleeping, so beautiful I nearly fell off the chair.

Two mornings later I helped her home in a taxi, and that day I shopped for a boot to make up for the one I cut off at the accident scene. Looked all over town until I found a size 15 extra wide, which just fit over the cast. I brought books and peanut butter sandwiches. At work that night I saved a cat, found him mewing under the bed of an old woman who had died alone. I cleaned him up and gave him to Mona. I told her he was a medicine cat, trained in Aztec healing.

Her doctor said the cast needed to stay on for at least eight weeks. By the end of the first month I was bringing her meals almost every night. After one candlelit dinner, sandwiches and wine, three long kisses, we couldn't wait any longer. I pulled off the big boot. With my medic shears I started cutting her old jeans, over the cast, the thigh, to the golden-red curls between her legs, blazing like a sunrise, another miracle. I wanted to be slow, so careful not to hurt her leg, but when I kissed her again, when I tasted her breast in my mouth, felt the muscles in her back straining to dance, I forgot all else but pulling that sun to me, pulling up against the damn cast that was like an anchor hooked on a mountain, the sun fighting to rise, tugging, straining on the chain, leaping, twisting in the air.

Her family owned a summer house on Lake Superior, and when the cast finally came off we drove west to celebrate, two weeks on the lake, our Shangri-la. I remember those days as a blurry collage of perfect moments, every one a blissful alignment of leaves, water, earth, and Mona's face, now turning into one big rusting heap in my mind. The only pictures I recall clearly are from the night we got drunk together. We drove out to the local bar, twenty miles away, named the Edmund Fitzgerald. The exterior was shaped like a ship's bridge, and inside the walls were crammed with pictures of famous ships lost at sea, all the frames askew, as if shaken during a heavy storm. Ed, the bartender and owner, claimed to have been captain of six different ships. The locals said he'd never made it out of the boiler room, but he wore a captain's hat, and late that night we asked him to marry us. It came out more like a commandment than a sacrament. "You, Frank Pierce, take this woman to be your wife." "I will, Captain." "And you, Mona Olearkick" – trying to read her name from a card – "Oleerazak . . . Oleoracrack . . ." "Olejarczyk," Mona said. "Yes, you, take this man to be your husband." "I will, Captain." "Dismissed." We were together barely two years. Little more than a maiden voyage.

The last time I saw her, Mona said that my work was killing me, and that my death was killing her. It was the same morning I had helped to kill Rose. Just one of those days: a woman had come into my life to die, another had left to live. Through it all they never became jealous of each other, and in the last few weeks they had learned to share me, to haunt me in shifts, Rose with coffee in the evening, Mona with a whiskey straight up in the morning. The harder I tried to forget them, the more they stayed in my head. Mr. Burke and the gallery of ghosts were little more than a diversion. I tried quitting, tried getting fired. I worked double shifts for one week and then used up all my sick time the next. I imagined myself in other jobs, seeing other women, though mostly I dreamed about sleeping, one eight-hour, unmedicated, dreamless slumber, drop my head and good night, the way Larry did. On slow nights I'd watch him sleep for hours. I tried to imitate him, my head in the same position as his, our breathing in sync, snoring in the same key. I strained to focus upon life as a series of interconnecting eating and sleeping points. I listened to his stories, wanting to know all the details he attended to when not eating or sleeping. I worked hard to overcome the fact that I disagreed with nearly everything he said.

Larry carried his life in his wallet. The first night we worked together the wallet was out and when we shook hands I came away with a picture of his young wife in a white sweater, standing next to the white fridge, white kitchen shining behind. This was quickly followed by the first of at least ten photos he carried of his children, his favorite the one that showed both kids sleeping upon an angry-looking Labrador. Soon I knew all about his boiler problems and what termites did to the resale value of a two-story colonial in Bayville. I knew about his sick father and his mother who ran away when he was seven. He had even shown me his amazing assortment of licenses – to drive large trucks and forklifts, to sell commercial real estate in Brooklyn, to carry explosives in his trunk, to kill and skin Canadian moose, to donate his kidney after he died to a cousin in San Diego, to marry people in wartime.

Larry had filled me in on most of this in the first two days we worked together, and after getting that information out of the way, he had devoted nearly every talking moment to the one true love of his life, the Bayville Volunteer Fire Department. He spoke passionately about the camaraderie of men who risk their lives together. He told me what they ate, what porno movies they watched, what type of Twin-sonic lights everyone preferred for the new pumper coming in May. Larry had always assumed that being a medic automatically enrolled me in the sacred brotherhood of fire-killers. It didn't; I hated fires, and when he told me for the fourth time about the "big one," the four-alarmer of '91, I blew up. I cursed all fires and firemen. Since then our relationship had been strained.

"Hey, Larry." I reached over and banged on the window next to his ear. "Get up."

"What?" His head sprang from the door.

"Turn it off."

"What?"

"You know what. The radio."

Larry reached deep into his bag and pulled out the personal portable fire department channel scanner that he had promised never to bring to work when working with me. Through the static I could make out a woman's voice: "Ladder Four, respond to a ten-twenty-two four-flight residential, 417 West Fifty-second." I reached over and turned it off.

"Let's do it," said Larry. "It might be a good one."

"No. No, I told you. There's no such thing as a good one. People get burned up in fires. They can't breathe. Their homes are destroyed."

"I know. That's what we're there for. Now come on, Frank." He went for the ambulance radio on the dash. I grabbed the antenna. We both pulled. "Don't push it, Larry."

"You're burned out," he said. "You're scorched."

"No, Larry, I'm still burning, and if you get any closer I'll burn you."

The dispatcher broke it up. "One-Three Zebra," he called. "Zebra Three, I need you."

I let go of the radio and Larry pulled it to his chest. "You see," he said, "he's giving it to us anyway."

"Zebra, are you there?" the dispatcher said. "I'm holding an unconscious at Forty-six and Ten."

The radio fell to the console between us. "Forty-six and Ten," Larry screamed. He looked at his watch. "Oh no, it's three o'clock. That can only mean one thing."

"Mr. Oh."

"It's Mr. Oh. I'm not answering it."

The radio lay on the dashboard. I had no intention of answering it.

The dispatcher spoke again. "Answer the radio, Zebra. You know it's that time."

"Four times this week we've had him," Larry said. "Four times. Aren't there any other units out there? Don't answer the radio. I'm not going. He'll give it to someone else."

"So we won't answer it."

"Thirteen Zebra. One-Three Zebra. Ten thirty-three hours. You're going out of service in two seconds."

Before he started working with me, Larry had never been put out of service for not answering, but in the last three months we had been put out three times. Larry stared at the radio and then at me, and knowing I wouldn't answer it, he picked it up. "Look, Frank, when I say don't answer it, that means answer it. I mean you can do that for me at least." He keyed the mike. "Three Zebra."

"Yes, Zebra. You'll be driving to the man who needs no introduction, chronic caller of the year three straight and a shoo-in for number four. The duke of drunk, the king of stink, he's nine one one's most frequent flier, Mr. Oh."

"Ten-four," Larry said, but when I started the ambulance, he grabbed my arm.

"Don't go," he said. "I'm telling you. Not this time."

I waited, and we watched a woman pick through a garbage can on Broadway. Two minutes, longer than I had ever waited for Larry. "All right," he said. "We'll go over there, make sure he's just drunk, and then we won't take him."

I parked in front of the liquor store on Forty-sixth. A man stood on the curb, waving to us and pointing frantically toward Mr. Oh, who lay curled on his side in front of his wheelchair. Another man bent over Oh, trying to revive him, and a group of concerned alcoholics, Oh's friends, surrounded him with their wheelchairs and their three-legged seats made from abandoned dining room furniture. They drank from the communal wine, glancing worriedly from Oh to us to the draining bottle, and then the man at the curb came up to Larry's window and began tapping it. Neither of us made any move to get out.

Larry pointed at Oh. "Someone's going to die because of that bum, going to have a heart attack and the only medics in the area will be too busy taking care of Mr. Oh."

"Relax," I said. "It's a street job, easy, except for the smell.

We'll just throw him in the back and zip over to Misery. At least he's not really sick, that's how I look at it – no blood, no dying. He's just drunk."

"It's not my job to taxi drunks around. I'm not taking him to the hospital."

"They'll just keep calling for him."

"I don't care. Four times in one week is the limit."

Most of our patients in that area were beating victims, routine sicks, drug overdoses, and drunks like Oh, and even after four years on the job Larry was still mystified by the nightly abuse of his lifesaving talents. The good people in his hometown of Bayville would never consider calling an ambulance for a man like Oh, drunk every night. Ambulances were for emergencies. Medics saved lives. Through every minor call, Larry complained, he made speeches, he lectured his patients on their responsibilities in the 911 system, but he always took them to the hospital. Mr. Oh was different. Oh made Larry crazy.

"He's bad, mister," the man at the curb said. "He ain't eaten nothin all day. He's seizing and throwing up and he keeps passing out."

Larry raised his hands. "So what's different about him today?"

"He says his feet hurt."

"Well, why didn't you say so? Let's go."

The man kneeling over Mr. Oh looked up. "I can't find a pulse," he said, moving his fingers over Oh's neck and groin. "But he's still breathing."

"Looks like we're just in time," I said. "Would you step aside, sir."

Oh looked as well as ever. He wore his rainsuit, a black garbage bag with holes cut for arms, and over his head a clear plastic hat secured with a rubber band. His pants rested in the familiar position around his knees, and the white globes of his ass shone eerily next to the blackened face and hands. Even while sleeping Oh smiled, nodded his head, and murmured over and over the word that had become his name: "Oh, Oh, Oh."

"He's sick," said a man missing most of his teeth. "Please, you gotta help him."

"He's drunk," said Larry.

"Just take him to the hospital, will you? I mean look at him."

"Oh look at him," cried a woman as if it were Oh's last moment. "Look at him, look at him, look at him."

Larry glared. "There's nothing wrong with him. He drank too much and now he's asleep. I'm not taking him."

A man in a badly worn pizza delivery uniform stood up from his wheelchair and took three steps toward Larry before tottering back. "I'll be honest with you," he said. "Oh had a couple of drinks tonight, but wine only, and he keeps throwing that up. Now we can't wake him."

I bent over Oh and shook him. I pinched him behind his ear. "Good morning, Oh," I said, and he opened his eyes and smiled wider, "Oh."

"He's fine," Larry said. "He can walk to the hospital tonight."

"Walk? Are you crazy?" said the woman. "He can't walk. He's in a wheelchair."

"Don't start that. I've seen him walk. He walks better than me."

I crouched next to Oh and waited for Larry to give in. The script was the same for all Oh calls. Larry argued against taking him, then insisted on walking him until, failing at that, we were forced to take Oh to the hospital, wheelchair and all.

Oh could walk. Many mornings, at the end of our shift, Larry and I saw him leave Misery pushing his wheelchair before him like a shopping cart. He did not walk fast. At full speed it could take him over an hour to travel one block, but that was his style and not his handicap. Every day he made the pilgrimage from his bed at Misery to his evening engagements at Forty-sixth, a total of ten blocks in twelve hours. Along the way he begged change from drivers and collected cans, which he exchanged for beer. He napped. He ate cookies. He chatted with his many friends along the route. When I worked days overtime, I spoke with Oh and was amazed to hear more than the one syllable he conversed with at night. He spoke slowly, as if choosing each word from a list of thousands. We discussed the drug problem in the schools and the many ways of getting hit by a car without being badly hurt. He usually reached Forty-eighth or -ninth before he took to his chair and began dropping syllables. He pedaled himself the last two blocks, and there Oh started drinking seriously, quickly losing his vocabulary and all sensation in his legs. When the liquor store closed, his pants began their descent, and by the time they reached his knees, Oh was beginning his own descent, slowly, gracefully, the fall to the sidewalk lasting five minutes or more. Then peace.

Unfortunately, Oh slept so deeply he always appeared to have just taken his last breath.

"Get up," said Larry. He pulled twice on Oh's arm. "Oh," said Mr. Oh. Larry put on his gloves and tried to pull up Oh's pants. Unable to do that, he put his arms around Oh's waist and with great effort hoisted Oh to his feet. Oh's legs provided little support, and while barely holding the man up with one hand, Larry tried again, vainly, to raise Oh's pants. Oh's friends surrounded Larry, cursing him.

"Goddammit, he's going to walk," Larry said, hoisting Oh again. Oh would have had trouble with his pants up; with his pants at his knees, the attempt was ridiculous. They took two steps and fell. "Oh," they screamed together. I grabbed Oh's chair and positioned it behind him, and as Larry lifted him for the third time I shoved it forward, clipping Oh behind the knees; his white cheeks dropped neatly in. We wheeled him to the bus.

"Good luck," the crowd yelled. "Get better."

Larry covered Oh's body with a sheet. He put an oxygen mask on himself and plugged it in. "Let's go already."

I turned on the lights and sirens. Oh's stink made it a true emergency. "Faster," Larry called out, and faster I drove, swerving and cutting against the hooker traffic on Tenth. When the smell reached me in the front, I opened the window and pushed my face out into the wet and cooling air. "Faster," Larry yelled again. "Faster," I screamed, racing to Misery.

Most of the sick people in Misery's waiting room had gotten sick of waiting and left. I wheeled Mr. Oh through, hoping the Burkes would be gone too, but I quickly found their backs in the first row, with the usual assortment of drunks, hypochondriacs, and mugging victims scattered behind. The drunks gave Oh a hero's welcome. Oh smiled and nodded. Griss the guard was less friendly. "Get that stinky-assed motherfucking bug-ridden skell out my face." I pushed Oh down the hall and waited at the entrance to Nurse Constance's triage stall. She was taking a man's pulse and speaking to his hand while the rest of him retched beneath her desk. "You drink too much. This is your body's way of telling you to stop. Listen to your body. It knows more than any doctor. The biggest favor I can do is not register you. You'll thank me later."

The hand she held grabbed the table and tried vainly to pull the rest of itself up. "Look, lady," came the voice from below. "I just need something to eat, a sandwich, anything, and I won't bother you again."

"I would have to register you to give you something to eat, and my conscience just will not let me do it. Good luck. Griss," she yelled to the guard. "Griss, this gentleman wants to leave." She stepped out of her stall to allow Griss in, and when she saw Mr. Oh she put her hands on her hips, shaking her head. Constance was from Florida, blond, big-eyed, and mean. She considered about one percent of the cases presented before her to be true emergencies. The rest she believed suffered from moral ineptitude manifesting as twentieth-century anxiety. No hospital in the world could cure that. She tried to set them straight before turning them away. She spoke against weakness in all its forms – drug addiction, suicide, anal fixations – lectured her patients until they wandered away in confusion or went for her throat, but she had no patience for lazy drunks like Mr. Oh. She typically threw them out without taking a pulse, and so there was no explanation for the love she poured on Oh. Whenever we brought him in, Constance became like a heartsick mother, spoiling and cajoling Oh, pinching his cheeks and rubbing his matted head until they both blushed. Oh worshiped her.

"He looks so pale." She sighed. "You're not eating enough. You need more fiber."

"He's wasted," Larry said, and pointed to his report. "That's my diagnosis: shitfaced."

"I know, but we're working on that – right, Oh?" Oh smiled and nodded. "He just needs a bath and some food and new clothes. Take him to the back and see if you can find him a stretcher."

"She's nuts," said Larry as we wheeled Oh down the hall. "That's why he comes here every night. She encourages him."

Larry cursed Constance's uncharacteristic generosity, but everyone, no matter how burned out, had moments of compassion. I saw Larry cry when we pronounced the Duke, Bill Dolan, in the back of the Venus Cinema. We were called to that back row every night for a month, yet Larry loved him. He looked like a midget Mickey Rooney and told stories of his adventures in the merchant marine, the girls of Bangkok, Manila, Saigon. Griss the guard had thrown Bill out of Misery dozens of times. Griss threw out all types of people – old women, children, accountants – yet he regularly lent money to a local crack addict. Griss tried to help the kid off dope; he fed him and found him clothes and let him sleep in the waiting room three months straight, until he caught the kid stealing. He nearly killed him. Dr. Hazmat set the boy's arms without ever touching him. Hazmat didn't like touching anyone and always wore two sets of gloves; but he took the gloves off for kidney failures. He held their hands, told stories of his youth. He never explained why. Odette the orderly gave canned sausages to worried mothers. Nursing supervisor Crupp once bought makeup, a dress, new shoes, and a wig for an old woman dying of cancer.

"Don't you dare put him there," cried Nurse Crupp. She ran to us and stood between Oh's wheelchair and the empty stretcher. "This is my last stretcher. The only open one in the hospital." She spread her hands flat on the bed and smoothed the sheet's lines. I looked over to the stall where Burke's body lay exposed, the skin sallow and exhausted. Except for the sink and rise of his chest, the groan of the ventilator, he appeared ready for the coroner's wagon. I walked to his side and covered him with a sheet.

Nurse Crupp bent over Oh. She grabbed his pants with both hands, pulled up once, hard. "We're too busy tonight to look after Mr. Oh. This is not a shelter. We actually have some sick people here this evening. He'll have to wait outside."

"No way, man," Griss explained as he waved Oh's chair toward the door. "Not even in the corner. Griss cannot abide that funk tonight."

*   *   *

I parked Oh outside near the ER entrance, and together we stared at the newly returned moon. Oh smiled but the moon did not smile back. It pushed a March breeze through the April night and it appeared to bring bad memories for Mr. Oh, who fell from his chair in one graceless slide. I lifted him back, wrapped a sheet under his arms, and tied each end to the chair. He was asleep before I finished.

I figured I had enough time for a smoke and a coffee, a moment of peace before the dispatcher hit us with another job, and while I stood in the cool air, waiting for Larry to finish his paperwork, Burke's daughter walked up the driveway. She opened a pack of cigarettes and searched for a light. I looked around for Larry to come out, thinking it would be better to go, to volunteer for a call rather than hear any more.

The match shook as I held it before her, the pained lines around her mouth. She inhaled deeply and coughed twice. "It's my first cigarette in a year," she said, and coughed again, so hard she had to bend over. Then she stood straight and took another long pull.

"The first is always the best," I said.

"It's this waiting that's killing me, not knowing, you know. It's really hard on my mother. I've been talking with this doctor, and he doesn't think my father's going to make it. He says he was dead too long, that after six minutes the brain starts to die and once that goes close the door. I know you got there as fast as you could and everything, but I was just thinking it would be better if you could tell . . . isn't there some way you can tell when it's too late? I can't remember now, but it seems to me like he must have stopped breathing more than six minutes."

"Yes, but you never know," I said, though I knew.

"I mean, if he was dead I could deal with that. It would be hell on my mother, but we'd handle it."

I shrugged. "Well, at least he's got people around him. He's not alone, with no one."

"I'm not so sure," she said. "I probably shouldn't even be here. My father and I haven't spoken in three years. He was a great man, my father; nobody he wouldn't help, unless you were his kid; if you were his kid, he could be very tough. Do you really want to hear all this?"

I nodded and she turned away. After a few steps she crushed her cigarette on the ground and pulled out another. She searched her pockets again for a light. I lit another match. "Thanks." She coughed. "When my brother called to tell me my father was having an attack, when he first locked himself in the bathroom, all the way going over to their place I was thinking how I was gonna tell him what a bastard he was. I didn't care how much pain he was in. Then when I got up the stairs and helped move him to the bed, I thought of all these other things I wanted to say."

"Even when you say the things," I said, "there's always more things."

"Well, right now it's my mother I'm worried about more than anything. You know, they won't let her see my father. What kind of rule is that?"

"Go home," I said. "Take her home. Get some rest. Not going to find out anything more now."

"That's what I told her, but she won't leave until she sees

him. If she could see him just a second, then I could take her home."

Mrs. Burke smiled sadly when I told her she could see her husband. She pulled back some loose hairs and smoothed the wrinkles of her dress. Side by side we walked down the hall into the still crowded treatment room. A man with a fractured skull screamed for a sandwich and a cigar. Another yelled for painkillers. Burke's wife waited while I fixed the sheet around his shoulders and wiped the green bile from his face. I stepped back. She moved up to his face and stared into his eyes a long time before jumping back suddenly, almost knocking me over. "That's not my husband. Where is my husband?"

"This is Mr. Burke," I said. "I brought him in."

"Well it's not *my* Mr. Burke." She pulled aside the curtain of the stall next to her husband's, looked in, then moved around the room, checking each bed. "I should know. I've been married to him nearly forty years."

Nurse Crupp held up the Foley she was about to insert. She pointed it at me. "That is your husband, ma'am. He's very sick."

I grabbed Mrs. Burke's elbow lightly. The joint felt soft, like wet cardboard. If I pulled, the arm would come off easily. "Please, Mrs. Burke. They'll take care of him. We should leave now."

"No, no, I have to make sure someone is there for him. He needs me. He's all alone."

She began to cry, *Ah, ah*, a terrible sound, but she let me lead her, my hand on her back, to the waiting room. Burke's son was sleeping on the daughter's shoulder. "He wasn't there, Mary," the mother said. "They won't let me see him."

I wanted to forget Mrs. Burke, her damaged daughter, her dead and dying husband. I wanted to buy her flowers, apple pies, golden novenas. The smoke shop across the street was out of novenas. Its owner, a mad Brazilian who worshiped Dolly Parton, catered to a very selective buyer. One wall of the small store was covered with pornography, the other with razors, baking soda, and butane. A refrigerator in the back stocked malt liquor and eggs. In the front, carefully arranged in a locked glass case, was the owner's collection of exotic porcelain pipes. "Everything is on sale," he said, waving his hand in a circle.

The coffee looked like it had been cooking for days, caffeine gravy. I took two sips, set the cup on the counter, and pointed to it. The owner shook his head. I pointed again. "Come on, Manny, super unleaded, fill it up." He pulled a liter of Scotch from under the counter and poured two shots into the gravy. I bought a box of artificial chocolate doughnuts and walked up the drive to the ER. After leaving one doughnut in Mr. Oh's lap, I took the box inside and gave it to Mrs. Burke, still crying in her daughter's arms. "Thank you," she said, and gave the box to her daughter who shook the son awake and handed it to him. Quietly he started eating.

Rose, the girl I helped to kill, haunted not only the streets I worked but my memory as well, altering it, making it hers. Though the call itself had happened only a month before, I began to believe she was the victim in other calls, from years earlier. For example, in my first year on the job, Tom Walls and I were called for a shooting on 107th and Columbus. Thinking back on it now, I know it couldn't possibly have been Rose, and yet the pictures in my head are so clear, the bus racing faster and faster up Amsterdam, the sirens pounding the corners, pulsing, the lights like a shield, the middle lane a chute rising behind. Tom turns against traffic down 107th and I see the glowing raincoat, black shoes pointing from below. Someone must have covered her, maybe the young cop roping off the corner. "You don't need that," the sergeant says, pointing to the bag I hold. "One in the head. We got the kid, her boyfriend." I look over at the boy, handcuffed, leaning on the car. His face pressed against the blue hood, he is crying her name, Rose. He definitely says Rose. I keep walking – there's no way I can stop – the cop's voice in my ear. "We found him here still holding the gun and kneeling next to her. The son of a bitch was kissing her." Closer, I notice the black stocking torn at the knee, blood and gravel dotting the white patch. Above that, the coat covers all but her left hand, chubby, a girl's hand, with two silver rings and shiny red nails. The detectives are already there, dark-blue trench coats, milling around like in the movies, talking about angles and entries and what a little hole the .22 makes. The coat is so bright, difficult to approach, but of course I do. I pull back the hood and her eyes are open but dark, I remember, and behind them the blood still leaks from near her ear. I remember Rose. Oh Rose.

6

I got back to the ambulance to find Larry sitting in the driver's seat. "Time to switch," he said. "I wheel, you heal." I walked around to the passenger side. It was four o'clock in the morning, the noon of our night tour, Larry's turn to drive.

When working with Larry I always drive the first half of the shift, the busiest, and hope the second half will be slower – the less patients the better. My biggest problem with not driving is that whenever there is a patient in the back, I am also in the back. The doors close, I'm trapped. The old-timers used to tell me that the longer you work this job the longer your stethoscope. I wore the longest on the market, and still I could hear, under the pulse, the heart's fortune-telling wail. Through the bubbling air in the fluid-choked chest, a terrible silence. No instrument can block that.

Questioning patients exhausts me. Whenever I can, I wrap them in sheets, head to toe, a small opening for the face. If they're not critical, I turn the lights low, lift up the stretcher's back, and sit behind, out of sight. Then I can talk to them comfortably, professionally detached, like an analyst. So tell me, sir, have you ever had any medical problems? Very good, now let's talk about allergies.

There are fewer patients in the early morning, but they're

generally sicker, and the worst ones always seem to be the last, just before dawn, just when you've been lulled into thinking it might be safe to close your eyes for one minute and when you do this red light goes off on the dispatcher's control panel and the next thing you know your driver is pulling up at a flea market of mass hysteria. You can barely step out of the ambulance, so tired you can't feel your hands and your heart's frozen and your brain keeps stalling. I could trace about ninety percent of my nightmare calls to the hours between four and six. That's when I first found Rose, my swollen eyes watching her chest rise for the last time, my hands reaching for the airway bag with the dexterity of a newborn.

I gripped the dash as Larry crashed us into Fifty-sixth Street, then plowed down the center of Ninth. Through the demented radio static came a barrage of ambulance calls, the dispatcher striking units all around us. Terrible-sounding calls. "Thirteen Boy, go to the men's room of the bus terminal, Forty-two and Nine, for the man who set his pants on fire. Bad burns on both legs. Fifteen David, at 450 West Fifty-third, off Ninth, there's a woman who says a roach crawled in her ear. Can't get it out, says she's going into cardiac arrest. Thirteen Eddie, on the corner of Thirty-eight and Nine you'll find a four-car accident, three taxis and a taxi. One-Two Henry, at 427 West Forty-ninth, cross of Ninth, a report of a very bad smell. No further information."

"Larry, turn off Ninth. We're gonna run into one of these calls."

He pulled up in front of the diner on Ninth and Forty-seventh. "I'll be right back," he said. Like parking in a minefield.

"This a bad spot, Larry. Everyone's calling nine one one around here. Look inside – they're lining up at the pay phone."

"Relax, will you, Frank. I'm just getting a milk shake."

I placed both hands on the dash and waited for the Brazilian cocktail to kick in. Four in the morning is always the worst time for me, and this night especially, with the ghosts massing and the dispatcher attacking, the wisest move was to stay completely still. I lowered my face to my hands, but after ten seconds I was forced to raise my head and shake my arms to release the trembling. I took off my jacket and put it back on and stepped out of the bus and back in and lowered myself in the seat until no part of me could be seen from the street. The feeling unshakable, of people dying all around.

Outside the diner stood a group of theater types, tuxedos and pearls, drunk, kissing good-byes, sporadically laughing and crying. The tall blonde glanced at me and away; only a second, but I recognized that look, the way Mona used to turn to me at a party, the eyes rolling up, the help-me-this-is-so-boring look. Something so similar in her face too, the shape of her hair, but Mona had red hair, this woman gold, and Mona wouldn't be caught dead in an evening gown. I stared at her feet, her elbows, searched her right shoulder for the mole I used to know. It couldn't be her, and when she looked back to me there was no doubt. What a fool I'd been, following redheads for weeks, my head spinning at every one

that walked by, when all this time she'd dyed her hair blond.
How could I forget those eyes and cheeks, the swept-up
nose, those lips shooting sparks: Frank, I'm leaving. She
started walking down Ninth, turning back every few steps to
wave and toss kisses to the group, to me.

"Mona," I shouted, but she kept walking, a block away, a
right on Forty-fifth. I started after her, two hundred feet,
staying close by the crumbling stoops of the main hooker
block. A few cars still patrolled the street, searching among
the fast-dwindling market. The big moneymakers had gone
home and only the freelancers were left, women dressed like
housewives, some in robes and slippers, housedresses and
raincoats (none yellow, thankfully), out for a midnight stroll.
One of them grabbed her chest as I passed. "Help me. I'm
dying." Another feigned fainting, strictly an amateur fall.
"Mona. Mona, wait." I walked faster, closing the gap. "I'm
quitting, Mona. I was going to call you today to tell you.
That's it, finished." She quickened her walk. "I'm getting
another job. I want another chance."

An ambulance pulled up next to me, driven by a milk
shake. "Frank, what the hell are you doing?"

"I saw someone I know." I climbed in and pointed to
Mona. "That's her. Just stay behind, like fifty feet." He
pulled up next to her, close enough that I could nearly touch
her. "You're too close. Back up."

"Aw, Frank, that's not her."

"What do you mean?"

"You always do this. I met her at the Christmas party. It
doesn't look anything like her. Anyway, this woman's
blond."

"She dyed it."

"You're crazy. She looks like that hooker who was thrown out of the car – remember? – who broke her hip, her foot ended up next to her head – remember? – a few months ago, when everyone was throwing hookers out of their cars."

"My wife's no hooker, Larry." A small black car moved in front of us and slowed to Mona's pace, two feet away. As if in response, she swung her hips a little more, stepping higher. She turned to the man in the car and waved. Furious, I turned on the lights and sirens. The car pulled away. She saw me watching and held her coat tighter, walked faster.

"I told you it wasn't her."

"Just follow, okay? Do me this one favor." We drove slowly behind, a right on Tenth, letting her lead, her walk so much like Mona's, head cocked back slightly, right arm rising over and down, left eye on the moon. Almost together we passed the ravioli store, the Spanish pharmacy. The same car pulled up to her again and honked its horn. I recognized the driver as one of the tuxedos standing outside the diner. This time she got in. Laughing, she kissed his cheek.

"Follow that car," I said, but when the happy couple made a right on Fiftieth, Larry made a left on Fifty-first.

"Where are you going?"

"To the pier. I think you should try to relax, Frank." He circled the top half of DOA Park, the men sleeping in boxes, on the seesaws and in the crawling tubes of the playground. Two sirens hailed from the north, screaming in my neck. What sounded like gunshots near the gas station at Forty-sixth. More sirens. On one of the benches, two men sat. One was Jimmy Corcoran, my boyhood pal. The other was the man burned under the pile of books. He stood up and started to walk toward me, probably wanted his book back. Ashes swirled around him like strips of black cloth. "I'm not feeling well, Larry. I say we go back to the hospital and call it a night."

"You have no sick time, Frank. No time of any kind. Everyone knows that." He stopped at a red light on Twelfth, where a woman was lying in the street near the curb where she'd been thrown from a car, her hips shattered. One leg stuck out perpendicular to her side, the other had come all the way up parallel to her body, so that her foot was only inches from her face. She was staring at her shoe, crying. "You're right," I said. "That woman looked like the hooker who was thrown out of the car."

"I told you," Larry said, and ran her over. I closed my eyes and held my breath, bending over in the seat until she was behind me. "Take me back now, Larry, put me to bed; I surrender. We've done enough damage here."

"Relax, Frank."

"Mona told me to give myself up. That was months ago."

"I can't work like this, Frank. I'm saying it the last time." He drove past the aircraft carrier museum and the sightseeing ferries and made a right onto the pier's entrance and parked at the end, the Hudson surging below. He unwrapped the remains of his chicken and chewed loudly. "You take things too seriously, Frank. Remember that week you refused to turn on the siren because you said that every time you used it someone died? You got over that, right? I mean, look at us, sitting by the river, talking, eating, and getting paid for it too. We've got a good job here, the good life."

"You're right; it's great," I said. My body felt like I was plugged into the cigarette lighter and the next time the dispatcher said "Three Zebra" I would pop up through the roof, out into the water. "Tell me, Larry, do you ever think about doing something else?"

"Sure. I'm taking the captain's exam next year. And after the kids are all in school, Louise can go back to the post office, and I thought, what the hell, I'll start my own medic service. Out on the island the volunteer systems are becoming salaried municipal. It's just a matter of time and it's all who you know. Someday it's going to be Chief Larry calling the shots."

Chief Larry's head leaned over against the window and in seconds he was asleep. I watched two lovers holding hands on the pier's end. Behind them a pair of tugboats plowed upstream, their high, broad bows crushing the current and pushing it aside. I wanted to call to the thin figure standing in the tiny wheelhouse, to wave him over, ask him to sign me on. I didn't need money, just food and a bed. My bandaging talents, I thought, were little different from the skills used when roping in a tanker and tying it fast.

The radio was so quiet I kept playing with the volume to make sure it was on. After ten minutes I felt the muscles in my shoulders loosen up, the bone ends not grinding, the whiskey finally taking hold. I leaned back in the seat and closed my eyes and ran through a list of employment alternatives – lawyer, barber, dogcatcher – canceling each one until I came to my favorite, the one job for which I was perfectly suited: Hollywood consultant.

I'd be called in to supervise the special effects in every shoot-'em-up slasher/screamer. Whenever the campers were chopped up with axes, or the terminal cancer patient finally died, I'd be there, paid ridiculous sums of money to ensure that everything looked authentic. I imagined myself lying by the pool with a whiskey on one side, a beautiful young actress on the other. My assistant arrives with the latest blood samples. "Still a little too pink, Steve; a touch more iodine, I think. Oh, and Steve, could you get me another drink. You're the best." The girl takes her arm from mine and silkily she says, "One-Three Zebra, Thirteen Z." "Steve," I yell. "Get me a different girl too."

Tom Walls was my first partner, my first night on the job. We stood together at roll call while he complained to Captain Lisa for making him work with rookie milquetoast. After the captain left, Tom pulled me aside. He said there were times on the job when you had to kill or be killed, that he was ready to die when the time came, and that he wanted a partner who felt the same way. I told him I also hoped he would die when the time came. We got along immediately.

That night was the coldest in years and when I saw a man sleeping on Broadway I convinced Tom to stop. The man was wearing nine shirts and shook so violently we had to drag him to the bus. After that the others were easy. I was on a mission, and Tom loved missions. In one hour we had five homeless men sitting in the back of the ambulance, drinking coffee and discussing neighborhood trade wars. On our way to the shelter, the dispatcher gave us a call for an old man who had become dizzy on the toilet. Just let me die at Mount Sinai, he pleaded; my doctor is waiting for me. This man had prepared himself for death – he probably lived twenty more miserable years – but he could not have imagined the party that waited for him in the ambulance. They're medical students, I said, Canadians here to study our health system. The patient was not impressed. Ignoring the strange but sensible advice of these future physicians, he pulled the sheet over his head and refused to say another word. I couldn't blame him; no doctor should smell like that. We dropped off the old man and drove over the bridge to the shelter on Wards Island. Opening the back door, Tom called the roster. He lined up our brigade in the parking lot, and single file, right hand on preceding right shoulder, he marched them through the front doors and up the stairs and into the office of the bewildered security director.

Father Francis, Tom named me that night, and in the morning he had the captain make me his regular partner. I was twenty years old. We rode unit Ten Sam – Wham Bam Thank You Sam – General Tom and Father Frank. For three years we raced around the city, beating the cops to most shootings, picking up every job we could, especially kid calls – we'd cross Brooklyn for kids, even drive them home from the hospital sometimes, our fists full of candy. We prided ourselves on toughness too, thought toughness could fix the city. This is the frontier, Tom said, pointing to his chest. In Dodge City, the law starts here. When we picked up injured muggers, ailing wife-beaters, or any others who disrespected the law, Tom would pull me out of the back. Time for some psychological first aid, he'd say before closing the doors of the ambulance, turning out the lights, and delivering that aid with both fists. He always smiled afterward, even if he took a few shots. Justice administration was a tonic for Tom.

We worked West Harlem and Washington Heights – the highest murder rates in the city. Tom called them the streets of no joy. At least once a night Tom and I would be called to pick up another shooting victim, and at times the violence got so heavy they died faster than we could take them in. They opened small businesses, and bill collectors shot them. They came from New Jersey to shop, and merchants stabbed them. They leaped from buildings infested with crack-raised demons. They were bludgeoned by their johns or strangled by their pimps. Neighbors complained and chopped them with axes. Old friends called and cut their throats. They died in heaps of garbage, under splintered doorframes, on piss-stamped mattresses, in the trunks of Chevrolets; they died and their hearts kept beating for more.

Tom commanded the radio. "Give us some blood, Central. If you got any blood on your screen, give it up." We drove around the city like we owned it, and we pulled up to scenes feeling as if someone much more powerful than the dispatcher had sent us, like we were mid-level managers of destiny. No one dies in the back of this ambulance, Tom said. That's rule number one.

Even the worst calls had some kind of special light. We passed a fatal car accident on the West Side Highway, the sun just coming up, three dead teenagers lying in the road. Near one of the bodies I found a battered tin statue of Saint

Christopher, and afterward, at the start of every shift, I would reverently place the statue on the dash. I told Tom we were crusaders protected by the fallen saint, surrounded by a box of magic that saved us and those it touched from the powerful ill-willed fates of the ghetto. There were times when I was driving to a hot call, a shooting or a jumper, and I would feel the space around me charged with an energy that pushed everything before us. In those moments I felt invincible. I would fly through red lights without looking, knowing nothing could touch me. I knew who would live and who would die.

Tom liked the crusader idea but dismissed the magic. Magic, he said, had nothing to do with it. Hard work and dedication to duty made good things happen. Never rely on luck was one of Tom's commandments, like never say you're sorry, never take your eyes off your enemy. Most of these rules came straight out of Tom's favorite movie, *She Wore a Yellow Ribbon*. He made me a videotape though I had no machine to play it on. Then he told me if I kept driving through red lights without looking, he would have to kill me.

He refused to acknowledge our luck even after our greatest call – pulling two kids from a fire. We were driving by an old tenement when an explosion on the fourth floor showered the ambulance with glass. By the time we broke through the door, the kids were hugging each other in the corner, flames all around. The joy of holding that child in my arms, the two of us choking on the sweet Harlem air – sweetest thing I ever tasted.

*   *   *

General Tom and I had been heroes, maybe the best-known medics in the city, but after three years our luck went bad. Like farmers wading through a month-long crop-killing torrent, Tom and I drove to one bad call after another. Nothing went right: misdiagnoses, bad timing, fights. Captain Lisa suspended Tom two weeks for punching out a fireman.

I joined the medicaholics morning support group. After work we'd drive up to the South Bronx, to the Blarney Moon, outpost of hate and self-pity. I told the guys Crazy Tom stories and I drank too much and waited for the bad luck to pass. Tom reasoned we weren't working hard enough, driving fast enough. Fifteen minutes left in our shift and he was still yelling at the dispatcher: Give us your drunks, Central, your malingerers, your injury-faking accident victims. Instead of doing eight bad calls a night, we were doing thirteen.

Near the end of one particularly endless shift we were sent to 107th Street for a man shot. It wasn't a man, though, just a boy, hardly eleven, lying in the street next to an old bicycle. The cops there said he had been running drugs for a local business leader and someone shot him, then cut out his pockets. He looked like any boy who had hit a hole in the road, tripped over the handlebars, and was taking those privileged seconds of shock that are always deserved after such a fall, to let your back mix into the gravel for a moment, to be like a stone, before moving the fingers and feet, then the knees and elbows, and, sure everything works, climbing back on.

Only the small things about this kid were different. The

weak, rapid pulse, the grasping breath, the cold, clammy skin, the little hole in his side, under the stick of his arm. He was dying quickly and we rushed him to the bus. In the calamitous press of the rear compartment, as we pulled off his clothes and punched him with needles, forcing fluid into his draining arteries, he stared at the ceiling and bit his lip, trying to be tough like we told him he was. Then he turned over, threw up the blood the bullet had brought into his belly, and died.

When I was eleven, I liked to steal apples. Every week in autumn I planned elaborate excursions over the hills to Mr. Wright's orchard. I always took more than I needed, often more than I could carry, and I would leave a trail of rotting apples up to my backyard. I doubt the old man ever noticed those few apples missing, but I imagined a small South American army imported with the sole object of bringing me in, dead or alive. The clumsy soldiers were rarely a match for my warrior cunning, yet there were times when I became too greedy, the bags weighed me down, and I would find myself holed up behind the abandoned Volkswagen at the bottom of Killer Hill, alone against a thousand guns. I always died valiantly, my pistols blazing, charging into the mouth of their fire. That was how I understood eleven-year-olds died before going home to dinner, not like 107th Street, where death was a hole in the road, spiritless and brief, like falling off a bicycle and never getting up.

For the rest of that night Tom drove without stopping – gas brake turn, gas brake turn – like a shark chasing his own cut and bleeding flank. The boy had broken rule number one: nobody dies in the back. As if to make up for this, he said the boy was a future perpetrator, that it was a good thing someone killed him before he could start killing others. I didn't say anything.

Tom came out with us to the bar that morning. I had seen Tom in a bar about three times in three years, and I had never seen him have more than a beer, but that day he drank with us, one for one, shots too. He told everyone the stories of our night, and when he finished the tale of the boy shot he repeated his speech on what a fortunate thing it was the boy had died. I was so drunk I could hardly stand, but I took a swing at him. I knew I had only one shot, and still I was off the mark, barely connected. I tried to go for him low then, but he was already on top of me. Incredible how fast old Tom could be when he wanted to. He had both my arms pinned on the floor around my ears. I just lay there waiting for the damage. And then he let go. He rubbed his chin and started to laugh. "Well, what do you know, Father Frank. It's about time." He stood, still laughing. "Hey, did you guys see his face? There was murder in the father's eyes. Just one piece of advice: If you're going to sucker-punch some-one, you damn well better knock em out."

The night after his death the boy rode by us, circled the ambulance twice, and continued up the block. At first I refused to acknowledge him, letting my eyes pass without recognition, the way I would if the Pope were eating in the same restaurant, seeing him without looking, and like a celebrity, the boy wanted to be recognized, the loneliness of his special position. As he came around the ambulance for the second time, staring directly at me, I nodded my head and he rode away. Something broke then, some basic understanding of the world that I had always taken for granted, that had been tested so many times before by the job, had finally snapped, and every time I saw the boy in the weeks following, sitting on his bike waiting for us when we pulled up to a call, I felt it snap again, like a funny bone striking inside my chest.

I requested a transfer, and Captain Lisa moved me down to Station Misery, midtown. More bad luck and depression followed. A cold, sodden winter. For the first time in my career I didn't look forward to coming to work, no longer hoped to make a difference. When I walked down the street I saw only the beggars and the takers, the beaten and the taken. Lovers always fought. Babies only cried. I wrote a resignation letter; ordered my transcripts from the university; called my cousins in Chicago.

I was as close to leaving as I'd ever been, but that week I saved a young man having an allergic reaction. I slipped a tube between his vocal cords just as they were shutting for the last time. One minute he was a corpse and in the next, Bob the college student, the crazy dreamer. A string of good calls followed, culminating in the greatest call of all, the meeting of Mona, red-haired, oily-eyed, wildly practical Mona, she who pulled me from the flames to place me on her mantel. Two years later she was begging me to quit, but when we met she said I had the most important job in the city. I was a lifesaver, the reaper's reaper.

Walking with Mona in the light of those first months together, I thought I had shaken off the boy's shadow like a bad cold, but he showed up again, in a Hell's Kitchen alley once, and again riding that same bike through an East Side parking lot. Other ghosts followed, some only distant figures in the half-light, from calls forgotten, others terrifyingly familiar, stalking, confronting. Yet there was no question of leaving them, no matter how shook up they left me. We were kin. Even while wrapped in one of Mona's life-giving embraces, I still felt the clinging moss, the clumps of wet earth. I was damaged goods. Just quit, she kept saying before she left, and we'll find some way to start again. I had quit a hundred times since, and still I kept coming back, as if I was too weak and too heavy to climb free, the job holding me like gravity.

"Zebra," the dispatcher called. "One-Three Zebra."

I opened my eyes and stared at the radio, wondering how it spoke, and why to me.

"Zebra, answer the radio. Come on, I've got one for you."

In the zebra cells in the old zoo, if you stood just far enough away, the bars became the stripes, the stripes, the bars. It looked as though the zebra could get out, nothing holding him, and yet he'd be a prisoner wherever he went.

"One-Three Zebra, pick up the radio." The zebra trainer's voice, terrifying. "Pick up the radio and push the button on the side and speak into the front."

I did as I was told. "Zebra."

"Male bleeding, corner of Forty-two and Eight. No further info."

"Ten-four," I said, and banged on the window next to Larry's head. "We have a call, Chief. Somebody's bleeding, Forty-two and Eight."

BRINGING OUT THE DEAD

It took half a minute for Larry to open his eyes and find the ignition, his hands slipping off the key. Finally I reached over and turned it on and we bucked backward, then forward, then reversed at fifty miles per hour. "Brake," I screamed.

Putting aside all the other reasons I preferred to drive, the most important was that for every moment I drove, Larry didn't. He was an awful driver: poor judgment, blindness – he didn't like wearing glasses – arrogance. You gotta drive this way to keep these Fords from stalling, was how he described the chaotic pedalwork that jerked us spastically through midtown. He had adopted Tom Walls' two-footed style, in which the right foot remains pressed on the gas while the left brakes to regulate speed. Walls was a master of this, the fastest in the city. He would wait for a red light with the engine screaming at six thousand rpms. When he took his foot off the brake, the bus leaped forward like a dying salmon. He drove that way to shootings and sick calls and to the Spanish coffee shops for double espressos. After driving with Tom for a while, I knew I would die in a flaming ambulance wreck, and yet I found some comfort in knowing he could drive. With Larry, death was no less certain, but his monumentally lousy driving devalued my death, made it worth no more than one of his sneezing fits, which he seemed to have only when behind the wheel.

"God bless you," I said, as we narrowly missed a garbage truck.

"Thanks."

We came to a jawbreaking stop in the middle of Forty-second Street and I jumped out, jumped into traffic just happy to get out, but when I saw our patient I jumped back in. We needed no further information. It was Noël, running toward me, his face soaked with blood.

"Noël," I yelled, but he kept coming, bent low with his arms spread out like a linebacker. He had sliced up a tire and fastened the pieces with string over his shoulders. Tin soup cans circled his wrists and ankles. One hand held a broken forty-ouncer, the other, a stringless violin. "Noël," I cried one last time, and then I locked the door and rolled the window up moments before his face struck it, almost breaking both. "Kill me," he cried. "Kill me, please." Blood clotted in his hair, matting in large clumps to his scalp. Bright-red blood dripped from his ears and ran freely down his neck. He beat the glass, yelling between blows. "You must kill me. No one else will. Please help."

The blood on the window where his face struck formed strange buglike patterns, and through the stains his eyes glowed, just as when I first saw him screaming in Misery, the outer limits of lunatic suffering. Suicide was his preference, but he looked ready to kill if his own death didn't work out. Again his forehead hit. I saw the glass bend, and sure that it would break, I reached for the bat behind the seat. "Noël, don't."

Larry yelled into the radio for help, anyone that might come – medics, police, firemen, coastguardsmen, wrestlers, hypnotists.

I held up the bat. Noël nodded and pointed. He wanted me to hit him with it. I tapped the window. "Drop the bottle."

He put his fiddle under his arm, and with two hands he

pushed the jagged edges of the bottle toward his neck. He held it there, the glass pressed against the skin but not breaking through. He sighed and threw the bottle down.

"You see, I cannot do it myself."

I rolled down the window. "Can I get you a glass of water? You look pretty thirsty."

"I have come out of the desert."

"You've come out of the hospital, and you should go back."

"I was lying in the desert, dying of thirst, and Mary Burke came to me and gave me water."

"You were tied to a stretcher, hallucinating, begging for water."

"And did you give me some?"

"The doctor said it might kill you."

"Thank you so much." He picked up what was left of the bottle.

"Look, we can't kill you, as much as we might like to. It looks bad, medics killing people in the street. Someday you'll be glad we didn't. You've got some bad chemicals in your head, Noël. There's medicine in the hospital that will fix that."

Noël stepped back and shook his whole body, like a dog just out of the rain. "No, no, no medicine." His arms wrapped to his back, his eyes closed tight, those long, blood-soaked dreadlocks whipped around his head. I closed the window fast as I could, but the warm drops landed on my face and arms.

"He got you." Larry handed me a box of tissues. "He got that bad blood all over you. Hey, watch out with the bat."

A crowd had gathered on the sidewalk, Forty-second Street regulars, all bleeding in their own ways, yelling. "Off him." "The man begging for it." "Take him out." One of the kids on the corner fired a few rounds from his finger. "I'd know how to kill that mother. Pop like pop." Noël took hope with that and ran over, spraying blood everywhere. The crowd panicked, fled down the subway stairs, the kid leading the retreat, and Noël was left standing alone. He returned to the street, jumping in front of cars in hopes of at least breaking a leg, but the traffic, now backed up half a block, moved too slow to hit him. He lay down on the double yellow lines, crossed his arms, and did not move.

"He looks familiar," Larry said.

I put the bat away before hitting Larry with it. "Of course he looks familiar. He was strapped down in Misery when we brought that arrest in. The one screaming for water."

"I think he wants something a little stronger."

One of the local merchants, a Chinese man who sold martial arts weapons, Jesus clocks, and carry-on luggage, tapped on my window.

"That guy's crazy," he said.

"Do you really think so?"

"Sure. Two weeks now he's coming into the store trying to wreck the place. Last Tuesday he came in, started throwing spears, banging luggage; he broke four clocks, almost killed my nephew who is going to Princeton next year. Tonight he comes in he says he's sorry wants me to kill him, but I say no, bad for business in the store and besides I have a bad back. So this crazy man breaks a bottle of beer over his head, blood and beer all over. Now I have a headache, backache, and I cut my finger on the glass. Maybe I should go to the doctor. Look."

"You need some stitches," I said, and then, as the man still waited: "You better get a taxi, get you there faster than an ambulance. Need at least a tetanus, then you gotta figure the man's blood might have been on the glass, that's the big time, AIDS, hepatitis A and B, about a million other things too. You need the works, man. Probably better just cutting the hand off right here."

The first cops drove up, eyes half open, heads low, resting on the doorframe. The driver badly needed coffee. He weaved into Forty-second and nearly ran over Noël, who slapped the pavement, frustrated when the wheel missed his skull. Still, New York's Finest had beaten and threatened him so many times in the past, he must have been thinking that finally his killers had arrived. Joyfully he leaped up and ran over to them. "Please, men, you must kill me."

The driver never rolled down his window. Experienced and uninspired, he looked down the row of old marquees, broken bulbs, and crooked three-word titles like *Horny Leather Orgy, Black End Chaos*. He must have considered the paperwork involved in killing Noël, the minimal paperwork involved in driving away, and all the paperwork possibilities in between. Slowly he spoke through the glass and I could tell he was giving our patient the I'm-here-to-protect-you-from-yourself speech, because Noël began shaking and screaming halfway through, and by the time the officer reached the taking-the-ambulance-to-see-the-psychiatrist part, Noël was in a full rage, his bloody rain dance spraying the car's windows and doors. Without

never missed a fight. He pulled up and in one motion jumped out, put the bus in park, and skidded to a halt. Thick blue smoke rose from the wheel wells. He must have come from Brooklyn.

"Father Frank, what do you know." I saw his backslap coming and sidestepped it neatly. "Everything all right? Larry sounded like he was being beaten with his own radio. Hey, Larry, everything okay?" Larry snored loudly in reply. "You better check his airway. I've got the same problem with my partner, Medic Grunt." Tom pointed to the still smoking ambulance, to the passenger seat where the Grunt slept soundly. "Weird kid." Then Tom shoved Noël against the door. "So this is the guy you called for."

"Yes, but it was nothing. A little noise. You know how Larry gets carried away."

"Whoa, looks like you already did a number on him. Still bleeding. Didn't leave much for me." Tom pushed Noël again. "You give my friend here any more trouble and I'll kill you."

"Yes." Noël smiled. "At the hospital."

"Mmm. You know, Father Frank, there's something very familiar about this guy." Walls placed his face two inches from Noël's. "He looks just like a very bad man I took to the hospital about a week ago. A man who had been holding two priests hostage with a screwdriver and who had to be beaten over the head by the police and then strapped down at the hospital."

Noël wasn't smiling. He stepped slowly back and up into the ambulance, Walls right behind. "I knew the fathers wouldn't press charges. I told him that if I ever caught him making trouble again I'd kick the murdering life out of him."

"It's not worth it, Tom. He's surrendering."

"No prisoners," Tom said, and stepped into the back. He turned around to me. "Don't worry, Father. Just a little psychological first aid."

"Don't do it, Tom. Not in there. You'll make a mess of it."

Tom Walls swung, missed, swung again. Noël ducked. "Stay still, dammit." He swung and missed. "That's it." Tom took off his jacket and threw it on the ground and lunged, throwing all two hundred twenty pounds of his bald-headed, Brooklyn-born, America-loving, wounded-in-Vietnam-and-now-serving-his-country-in-the-streets-of-New-York body on top of Noël.

The two bounced against the back wall and fell between the stretcher and the bench. Walls held Noël down with one hand and tried striking with the other, but his hands kept slipping in the blood, his fists glancing off harmlessly, and all the while, under him, Noël was scrambling wildly. "No, the pills, at the hospital," yelling to me. "Tell him about the pills, man, the pills."

I had seen Tom administer enough psychological first aid to know there was no reasoning with him; you either pulled him off or waited for his storm to pass. In the few years since I left Ten Sam, Tom's cause had turned more fanatical, his rages more explosive. No one knew whose throat his hands would reach for next. I heard he'd killed a man uptown for shooting at two cops. He flooded the man's heart with epinephrine and called it a cocaine overdose and the coroner backed him up. Other medics were afraid to work with him, and he frequently ended up working with Medic Grunt, who now walked up next to me to watch the fight. Together we stepped in to pull Tom back, but he broke free and swung again, still hadn't damaged enough of Noël. Justice was no longer important to Tom, only punishment, random and complete.

"Let go of him, Tom." I pulled as hard as I could, but he had wrapped Noël in a bear hug, and in that violent embrace the two rolled back and forth, striking their heads against the stretcher's wheel. Noël was still bleeding. His blood covered the floor and bench. It stained Walls' white arms and hands and left three red fist-size blots on his white shirt, making Walls look more a victim than Noël. I think they would have held each other rolling like that until morning if Larry hadn't stuck his head through the small front window and said, "There's a double shooting three blocks up the street, Forty-five and Eight, confirmed. What do you say?"

"We'll do it," cried Tom.

He released Noël, who scrambled to the chair against the back wall. "At the hospital." He trembled. "You told me at the hospital."

Walls and the Grunt jumped out, the bus already backing up as I closed the rear doors behind them and cleared off the stretcher and set up my IVs. Noël crawled over to the chair at the front. "Man, first you say you can not kill me, then you will kill me but not here, and then this crazy man comes to kill me."

We came to a stop a few seconds later. "Stay here," I said, and jumped out, pulling the stretcher behind. On the corner the dark coats of the crowd soaked up the smoke shop's electric light. "Move it," I yelled, pushing my way through the cordon of legs. "EMS," Larry cried beside me, swinging the trauma bags before him. Two cops stood against the inner wall of the crowd. They held open a plot of sidewalk, about the size of a Buick, on which two young men lay. Someone in the crowd shouted, "Man just walked up and shot em. Not one word. Is that cold," the voice already sounding far away, everything outside the circle closing. The victim on the left held his belly and wore the quiet incredulous look of the gutshot. The other stared up at the lights from the cigarette ads, trying to be cool, like he simply chose that moment to lie there on the sidewalk, but he had the look, that damp grayness, of someone about to die, so I fell to my knees at his side, felt Tom Walls next to me taking care of the other.

"Where you hit?" I felt a strong pulse at his wrist, a good sign. I took out my shears to cut his coat, but he pulled his arm away. He looked up at me and then past, calling someone behind: "Come here. Come here." Painfully he pulled off his coat and held it up. Two arms reached over my shoulder and grabbed, lifting it over me. "You gotta get him right. It was the Outlaw did this. He's working for Cy. You take em both out." Something dropped from the coat and bounced off my shoulder to the ground; two small vials of white powder rolled against my shoe, the red skull and crossbones. A hand appeared and they were gone.

"Where you hit?" I said.

He looked back at me, then pointed to his chest. "I'm all right."

I started cutting the shirts, two at a time; he wore four. "Where you hit?"

"I'm gonna blow his ass up, man, I know where he does his business. I'll kill him."

I didn't have to ask a third time. I cut away the last shirt and saw the hole like an oozing birthmark just under the left clavicle. I sealed it with a plastic dressing.

"You hit anywhere else?"

He was trying to see the wound. "Look at that shit. He put a hole in me, man."

I rolled him on his side to check the back. Nothing. The bullet still inside. Larry slid the backboard in behind him and we laid him on it and strapped him down and lifted him up to the stretcher.

Walls was just rolling his patient. "General Tom," I called to him as Larry and I moved out through the crowd. "I'm going to Misery. You better take yours to Bellevue."

"Okay, Father, you take yours to heaven. I'll take mine to hell. Come on, Grunt, let's move em out."

Larry and I put the stretcher in the bus, and I jumped in. The doors closed. I placed an oxygen mask on the man's face. In the ceiling light's glare he wasn't more than eighteen, a kid, pale and cold. Sweat rolled from his forehead and down his face. He pulled off the mask. "Why does this happen to me, man? I never hurt nobody. I'm just trying to make a living, you know. I don't want to be shot."

"You should have taken the pills," Noël said. I had forgotten about him.

"It's all right," I said. "You gonna be all right."

117

I put on the stethoscope and listened to his lungs, to the gurgling blood in the left, hemothorax. I grabbed his cold wrist and searched for the pulse, now rapid and faint. God but he was going fast.

"This is one crazy city, man. I'm quitting, know what I mean? I'm going into the army, where it's safe. Leaving these streets. I had it. I don't want to die."

"*I* want to die, I'm the one."

"Shut up, Noël." I wrapped a tourniquet around the boy's arm, found a vein, and wiped the area with alcohol. Then I reached into the needle box and pulled out the largest, a fourteen gauge. I held it over the vein, waiting to feel the rhythm between the bumps of Eighth Avenue and Larry's mad swerving.

"You're going to feel a stick in your arm. Don't move."

"Oh Jesus, I don't want to die."

"You're not going to die."

Noël grabbed my arm. "What did you say?"

"Shut up. You're going to die and he's not. Got it."

I plunged, bull's-eye. I advanced the catheter, plugged in the IV and opened it wide. I taped the tubing into place.

"Hold my hand," the boy said.

"I can't. I have to do your other arm."

"Just hold my hand, man."

I passed the taped arm up to Noël and pushed the boy's hand into his. "Hold this. If you let go, I swear, I won't kill you." Noël held on.

I grabbed the boy's other hand. No pulse. Face so gray, crying, just enough blood to do that. I put on the tourniquet and set up another IV. Again I pulled out a needle and searched for a vein. Bull's-eye. I never miss. We pulled into Misery as I finished taping the arm.

"It's all right," I said. "We're here."

No answer. I looked up at Noël's face bent over the boy, his mouth pressing down on the boy's in a long deep kiss.

Larry opened the back doors and we pulled at the stretcher. "Noël, let go."

A kiss that was no longer a kiss. "Noël, let go." I had to pull him off. The boy dead, Noël screaming, knocking me down as he jumped out running.

"He's not breathing, Larry. Call a code."

We rushed the dead boy into the emergency room.

I once saved a man who had dropped dead while he was running to catch a train. Seconds after arriving on the scene, we shocked him back to life, and a few hours later I heard he was awake and talking. I didn't see him then, but a few days later I decided to visit him upstairs at the hospital – this was back when I wanted to see patients afterward, see how they made out. When I got there, the patient was arguing with the nurse, so I introduced myself to the man's family, who were all standing around the bed. "Why is he so nasty now?" was the first thing the man's son said. "I don't know," I said. "Is that normal?" he asked. "My father used to be such a nice guy, and ever since this happened he's been so angry and mean to everyone." "I don't know what to tell you," I said, and as I walked out I heard the patient yelling at the nurse: "Listen, you bitch, I told you I wanted another goddamn pillow. Now get it."

7

I wrote the paperwork in the early-morning quiet of the waiting room. From inside the treatment area I heard the surgeon asking for a scalpel, then suction, rib spreaders. He was cutting open the boy's chest to clamp the artery and force fluid into the empty heart. It never worked. I filled in the boy's name, age, and address from a court summons I found in his wallet: jumping the turnstile. He also carried a fake ID from the College of Times Square, an institution of which most of the dealers on Forty-second Street were proud alumni. I found business cards from two lawyers, a DJ, a Bronx dentist, a fishing license three years old, a few scraps of paper inked with numbers and names. I tried to imagine him fishing on a stream and couldn't.

I gave the wallet to one of the cops standing outside the trauma slot. Nurse Crupp signed my sheet and then returned to Odette the orderly, to help her zip the green plastic around the body. They stepped carefully around the blood that covered the floor and ran in thin lines under the curtain and into the slot in which Burke lay. I drew aside the divider and stared at the product of my night's work, my luck bad for months, death running up the score. I pulled the sheet up from Burke's feet and wrapped it around his shoulders. I checked his EKG leads and IV, and then I went outside for a smoke.

"Look." Larry pointed a thick yellow-gloved finger into the open light of the ambulance doors. "There's blood everywhere." He donned a surgeon's mask, cap, and goggles. He wrapped sheets around his legs, torso, arms, taping the ends to the gloves at his wrists. He grabbed the mop and jumped inside.

A taxi pulled up, and the bleeding store owner from Forty-second Street stepped out holding a red cloth around his thumb. He bowed. I waved back. The emergency room doors opened and closed. A third-floor spotlight buzzed on, and in its flicker Burke's daughter appeared, standing only a few feet away, a cold spirit, white and shivering in her brother's jacket. I offered a cigarette.

"You shouldn't smoke," she said, and took one.

"It's okay. They're prescription. For nerves."

"You should get another doctor."

"It works better with a little whiskey."

"That's my brother's cure. He's passed out inside."

"See what I mean?"

We smoked. I stared at the line of five broken ambulances in the corner of the lot – flat tires, busted windshields – then I looked at her face: the grief dents, the sad, colorless lips. I thought of the pictures on her father's wall, the queen of the prom. I never went to the prom. Maybe if I'd known her then . . . a kiss behind the bleachers, a midnight drive to the beach, dancing in the morning tide that drops us off in a different place from this.

Larry jumped out of the ambulance, waving his mop wildly. "That's it. I can't do any more."

She laughed once, less than a second. "That boy was shot, wasn't he?"

"Yes."

"He's dead, huh?"

"Yes."

"You want to know something? I think this place stinks."

"It's Misery."

"And my father, did you see him?"

"No."

"It's crazy in there. I get the feeling they haven't looked at him in hours. And what's wrong with that doctor? He keeps mumbling, poking himself in the eye when he talks to me."

"He's working a double shift."

"Well, it doesn't look very professional, let me tell you. Thing is, I'm not used to being the responsible one. I'm used to being the fuckup. The one on the stretcher in there – that's supposed to be me. Hell, it's been me. With my parents crying out here. I got a lot of guilt, you know what I mean?"

"I know what you mean."

"And my brother's helpless even when he's sober. Now, my other brother, Patrick, he's the one who should be taking care of all this, the perfect son."

"Is he coming?"

"He's dead."

"Sorry."

"Forget it. I'm just going nuts, that's all. My brother passed out, my father in a coma, and now my mother's going crazy, ever since you took her in there to see him. And she's the one I'm here for. If it wasn't for her . . . You know, she doesn't believe my father's inside. I tried to take her in after you did, but she won't go. It's like she's in a trance."

"I know how she feels." We watched an ambulance drive into the lot and back up to the ER doors. Two EMTs pulled out a man not breathing, another OD. One of them squeezed the Ambu-bag while the other pulled the stretcher inside.

"How do you deal with all this, every night?"

"I go into a trance."

"I'd like to take my mother home; that's the best place for her now."

"Maybe some other place would be better. Like a neighbor's home, a neighbor who lives far away."

"I'd bring her home myself, but then who'll stay here? She's too flipped out to send alone."

I stared at my hands, turning them over. She crouched down and rubbed her cigarette out on the ground. I wanted to put her in my jacket, get through airport security, mail us both to a warm island. "Have you ever been to the Caribbean?"

"I think if she was home she'd be okay. All I know is she's going crazy here."

I stamped out my cigarette and looked up at the gray brick, thinking of Mr. Burke in the window, the fury of the nearly departed. "I don't know if home is the best place to be."

I went to medic school to drive fast and save lives, like the heroes on TV, who in an increasingly muddled world always worked for the quickest, clearest good. At the EMS Academy I learned how to recognize and treat about two dozen types of emergencies. Basically I could do almost everything an emergency room doctor could for such problems as heart attacks, heart failure, dysrhythmias, respiratory diseases, etc. Much of the training is repetitive – a rapid, simple diagnosis, a controlled, direct response. The street is a much more unpredictable place to work than an emergency room, and to prepare for the unexpected I was taught to act without thinking, like an army private who can take apart and reassemble his gun while blindfolded.

But shortly after they put me to work, I began to realize that my year of training was useful in less than ten percent of the calls, and saving someone's life was a lot rarer than that. I made up for this by driving very fast, one call to another – at least I looked like a lifesaver – but as the years went by I grew to understand that my primary role was less about saving lives than about bearing witness. In many cases the damage was done long before I'd been called, and there was little I could do to reverse it. I was a grief mop, and much of my job was to remove, if even for a short time, the grief starter or the grief product, and mop up whatever I could. Often it was enough that I simply showed up. Most ailments are side effects of other problems: the fear of going mad, the anxiety of being so alone among so many, the shortness of breath that always occurs after glimpsing your own death. Calling 911 is a fast and free way to be shown an order in the world much stronger than your own disorder. Within minutes, someone will show up at your door and ask you if you need help, someone who has witnessed so many worse cases than your own and will gladly tell you this. When your angst pail is full, he'll try and empty it.

My problem was that I had collected all this grief and had no place to put it. I was filled up, and every call I went to just poured over the top. In the last few years there were plenty of times when I'd had enough, but a good call eventually came along, to balance out the losses, reverse the months of misery. That's how I emptied my bucket, and until now it had always worked. In the past I would have gotten to Mr. Burke a few minutes earlier, and Rose would be thanking me now instead of reminding me how wrong everything had gone.

Last spring, for example, I'd had a March of tragedy, of blinding smells and deafening stains. Mona and I had begun to fight seriously. Then one night I was called to the Dynamite Club for an eighteen-year-old girl with asthma. She'd come with her friends from Long Island, and after dancing two hours she smoked a cigarette and stopped breathing. From the front doors I saw her lying on the dance floor, taking her last breath in a forest of smoke-filled silhouettes. I grabbed a tube and laryngo-scope blade from the airway bag and sprinted toward her, sliding the last fifteen feet, like Pete Rose into home, slipping the tube in perfectly. Two minutes later her eyes opened, her cheeks flushed; she reached up and grabbed my nose.

For weeks after, I couldn't feel the earth. Everything I touched became light. Horns played in my shoes; flowers fell from my pockets. I was still doing the same calls, but now the dead kept to themselves, the dying kept hope, and the dispatcher gave the worst calls to someone else. Mona and I stopped fighting and were married again, this time in a bar on Second Avenue. Two cops put Mr. Oh on a train to Virginia. It took him more than a month to get back.

Saving someone's life is like falling in love, the best drug in the world. For days, sometimes weeks, afterward, you walk the streets making infinite whatever you see. Time slows and stretches forward and you wonder if you've become immortal, as if you saved your own life as well. What was once so criminally happenstantial suddenly makes sense, a reason and order to every detail. God has just passed through – why deny it, that for a moment there, God was you.

Taking credit when everything's gone right doesn't work in reverse, when things go wrong. Although you might obsess for a time on what you could have done differently, the most important move after a catastrophe is assigning blame: the family was crazy, the equipment broke, the patient smelled, the guy at the deli took too long to pour your coffee. Spreading the blame is an essential medic survival tool as well as a valuable asset in any post-medic career. The god of hellfire is not a role most of us wish to play.

The girl in the Dynamite Club was my last save, and I'd had nothing but bad luck since, one year, a run no medic could match. Larry called me the black cloud, and how could I blame him? I was too busy gathering blame, collecting more than I could give, and, with each bad call, digging myself deeper into debt. I wanted to quit, to leave the mess I'd made, to give Mona a reason to take me back, but for another chance to have a chance I needed to leave on top, from a position of strength, not the sad-smelling figure

I'd become. I needed to save someone, restore the order, yet the more bad-luck calls I went on, the more I became afraid that the good call, if it came, wouldn't be the cure it once was. I'd come to hold myself responsible for too much, things I would have shrugged off easily years ago. Didn't I bring Mr. Burke back to life? Didn't the coroner tell me Rose would have died no matter what I did? It didn't matter. The old rules were little help. In the depths of five in the morning only one order remained: if I was willing to take the credit, I had to take the blame, not just for my actions but for my inactions, my accidents, my nightmares come true.

Mrs. Burke walked out of Misery on her daughter's arm. Half sleeping, she took my hand and I helped her up into the ambulance. "So kind of you," she said. "You're such nice boys. My husband is ill, you see, and I have to take care of him."

"That's right." I sat her on the bench and closed the door.

The daughter put her hand on my arm. "I got through to her once; I think she understood. She started crying, fell on the floor. I had to get that guard with the sunglasses to help me get her up. Then she went back into her trance. I don't want to go through that again."

"Let her dream," I said. "She's suffered enough and there'll be more to come. I'll take care of her." We stood only inches apart. "Thanks," she said, and squeezed my arm. I felt like a man accidentally released from prison.

As Larry drove I kept looking back to check on Mrs. Burke, who said nothing more to us. She sat with her hands in her lap, nodding and quietly talking to herself. We turned into Forty-third Street, deserted. I checked the top floor: lights off. Nothing inside.

"Would you like some coffee?" she asked. "I have some apple cake too, and if you want to wait, I was going to heat up a little soup for Patrick if he's up."

"I can't stay. Thanks." I helped her to the sidewalk, where she stood as if suddenly blinded. Then she walked up the street, passed her building without looking up. "You live over here," I said. I grabbed her arm and turned her back and escorted her up the stoop. She leaned against the front door. I had to hold her to keep her from sliding down. "I'm sorry," she said. "I don't know what's come over me." I stepped back and looked at the top floor. No way around it. I called back to Larry. "Hit the siren if we get a call." He was sleeping and did not reply.

She couldn't find her keys, so I searched through the black pocketbook, which must have weighed twenty pounds. Inside the dark hallway she seemed to get better, stronger, and when she started up the stairs I followed behind her plain blue coat, the rhythm of her big legs climbing. I saw her surrounded with shopping bags, piles of clean laundry, crying babies.

"Patrick grew up in this building. He lived here on the second floor when he was a child. Funny: I lived around the corner but we never knew each other; different schools. We met at a Saint Bridget's dance. He was the perfect gentleman, so handsome in his suit, and he knew how to hold a girl's hand. After we were married he wanted to live close to his family, so we took this apartment upstairs. You know, that first day he carried me all the way up." She stopped to laugh. "I was a lot thinner then."

I was glad she stopped, for I was having trouble catching my breath, the air so thick, hard to pull in; as we started up the last two flights, I noticed a buzzing in the dank hall. I thought at first it might be Larry calling me down with the horn, but I realized the sound came from above.

"All his family lived in the neighborhood, three brothers and two sisters, and Sunday dinners at his mother's everyone brought food or drink or music and sometimes we'd stay up all night dancing. They all moved out, though, a long time ago, to houses in Long Island. They didn't like coming back. His parents died. Our friends moved. Tell the truth, I wanted to go too, but Patrick refused. Said he was born here, worked here, and would die here. He used to think he could make it back to the way it was."

The light on the fifth-floor landing was out, and I thought maybe the buzzing was from the broken bulb, but the noise became deafening near the apartment, like a burst steam pipe, and there was so much smoke I could hardly see Mrs. Burke put her key in the lock.

"Patrick."

I covered my ears, the sound unbearable. She opened the door. More smoke, a pale silver light.

"Patrick," she called, "what's going on? This place is such a mess."

The buzzing stopped when she entered, like she'd cut a wire. The apartment appeared ransacked, furniture shifted, drawers pulled out. As if the firemen had come before the fire. "Patrick," she said. "Patrick, are you drunk?" The door closed, and behind it I heard another voice, a man's: *I'm dying, Joan. But I can't die.*

"I'm here, Patrick. I'm here."

I took the stairs two at a time and on the street looked up at the light in the top window, yellow, flickering, and what appeared to be smoke rising from the top floor.

I opened the passenger door and jumped in. "Hey, Larry, you see a fire up there?"

Larry stepped out and stared up at the sky for a minute. He climbed back in. "I don't see anything. You see a fire?"

"I don't see anything."

We drove out to the piers without talking. Too exhausted to care. The madness of the past years, of the past weeks, had grown by degrees. The ghosts that once visited my dreams had followed me out to the street and were now talking back. In a way, it all felt normal. Mrs. Burke was mad. Walls was mad. I had seen Noël suck the life out of a man. Larry never saw a ghost, but that made him no less crazy. He kept a scrapbook of DOAs, pictures of mutilated bodies. Why shouldn't I hear Burke, see a dead girl walking down the street? I was the reason they were there. Some sanity in that. It called for a drink. On the pier, Larry started snoring as he set the emergency brake. I watched the river rushing up from the ocean. I closed my eyes, and if the dispatcher called, I wouldn't have heard. I didn't wake until the sun was behind me.

There was a time when I didn't rush to the bar after work, when all I needed to get me drunk on the way home were thoughts of Mona's sleeping smile as I kissed her hello. I stopped at the West Indian's for groceries and sometimes the Korean's for flowers, and I always left a muffin or a bagel next to the bed before crawling in behind her. When she rose for work, I lay there watching her prepare for the day. "Tell me what happened," she'd say while brushing her long red hair, and she'd laugh at the crazy, funny stories, and after the sad ones she'd always kiss me. Then she would leave. It was about a year before I stopped telling her the sad stories; I had come to dread that brief embrace. I found roundabout routes to her bed, needing a break between covering up a DOA and feeling her warm body. I'd shower half an hour, trying to wash the night off me, drank a beer at the table, waiting for her to get up. "Tell me what happened," she still said, and I remember I wanted to tell her of the woman with the long red hair lying with a butcher's knife in her side and what trouble I had lifting her off the floor without her guts falling out. "It hurts," was all she said. "It hurts," again and again. How do you tell that to someone who's flossing her teeth? I began avoiding her in the mornings, making up late calls at work or errands I had to run. I drank every day, never going home, until the last morning I saw her and I didn't know how to stop her from leaving and she never came back.

8

Eight o'clock. The shift was over. I laid my head on the dash and listened to Larry warm up his car. He always left early, racing against sleep on that long drive back to Bayville. Every morning we worked together, as I gathered the radios and my tech bag and walked toward the garage, I watched Larry drive out of the lot, his windows open and the radio tuned to the black station he hated but that kept him awake, turning east on Fifty-sixth Street to the bridge to the highway to the queen-size bed with the roses and lace at the bottom and the warm broad curve of Louise's ass.

I put the radios on the desk. Captain Ed stared into his logbook, mumbling words I couldn't hear. The flame from his lighter circled two inches to the left of his cigarette, nearly igniting the thicket of eyebrows that swept down toward his ear. Mornings were very hard for Captain Ed. He had worked nights for twenty-five years, and in recognition of his thorough lack of ambition, self-discipline, and attention to protocol, the service had promoted him to station commander. The captain was out of practice with the details of his job. He was used to long nights tilted back in his chair, his boots on the desk, talking about boxing or the different ways to fry plantains, but as day commander he struggled to perform. He knew if he slacked off any more they would make him chief.

I walked into the crew room, Luther sleeping on the couch. I slapped his feet, and when he didn't move I sat on them. He groaned and bent his legs up, and together we watched the weather maps on the television. A thick patch of white that looked like pneumonia on a chest X-ray had consumed Ohio and western Pennsylvania and was eating its way toward us. On the other side of the room the morning crew filed in. They stood around the table and drank from extra-large coffee cups, careful not to stain their shirts.

Stanley walked in, followed by his partner, a new kid from the Midwest who had no name yet.

"I think she's calling us." The kid held out the radio.

Stanley grabbed it. "Well, she can call someone else for once. I'm not doing any more jobs." He lifted the radio over his head. "Good night, Dolores." He dropped it on the table. "You see, kid," he said, pointing at the morning crew, "you look like one of them. You can't work nights like that. When you go home today, I want you to wash your shirt with black coffee and use your pants as a pillow."

"Stanley, don't tell him that," said Suzette, leader of the morning crew. She sat at the table, wiping a spot from her shoe.

Stanley sat next to her. "Well, the kid learned some lessons today. He learned how to duck, for one thing. They send us uptown for a dealer shot twice in the head, a real piece of shit, got enough vials of Red Death on him to kill off a city block. I'm kneeling next to the guy, checking out the holes, when a bunch of rounds go off, sounds like a semi just down the block, and you know me, I squeeze into a crack in the sidewalk, and so I look up and there's this kid standing

138

like a statue called white boy, you know, like he's waiting for a bus on Fifth Avenue. Hey, kid, I say, for your information those are bullets flying past those big ears. So this piece of shit's got two in the head and still breathing, but I know he's going down thirty seconds tops, and when the kid comes running with the backboard I tell him to put it back. You should have seen the look on his face. That was lesson number two: Sometimes even the ones that have a pulse you have to let go. I mean the man was dead."

"Don't you listen to a word he says," said Suzette.

"You can show him the way it's supposed to be, Suzette. I'm gonna show him the way it is."

The kid stood there holding both his and Stanley's orange tech bags. He wasn't sure how to respond, so he just stood and kept smiling until Hector burst through the doorway, his hands in the air. "I am not working with this man anymore."

Veeber followed slowly, eating a kiwi, green juice running down both sides of his wide face.

Hector turned to Luther and me. "We get a call for a stabbing at the WestCheap, fourth floor. The elevator's out as usual so we have to climb and it takes us ten minutes because Veeber here has to stop three times to catch his breath. When we finally get upstairs I see the door to the room's open and I look in and there's this big fat guy sitting there reading the paper. He sees me and waves. 'I called,' he says. 'It's my wife. I stabbed her.' Like I was a plumber and she had sprung a leak.

"So she's lying on the bed, holding the holes in her leg, with one hand pointing at the husband, 'Ten years we been married,' she says, 'and every year he stabs me.' I take her blood pressure and Veeber goes to cut off her pants and I see right away it's going to be a problem. He gets halfway up her leg and the shakes start – you know how he gets around women – and by the time he gets up to her underwear he's shaking so bad I think he's going to stab her with the scissors."

"She was beautiful," said Veeber.

"She was not and that's beside the point," Hector said. We nodded in his behalf. He was a serious medic, and every morning he returned with another tale of Veeber's incompetence. Everyone liked Veeber, except when working with him. Veeber was all love. He'd give his last dollar, his last hour of life, joyfully to a total stranger. He was the worst medic I'd ever seen.

"So I have to cut off her pants and bandage her up and cover her with a blanket, and Veeber, he's sweating and wheezing all the way down the stairs. In the ambulance he goes to start an IV, but she gets sick watching the needle shake. She throws up, and Veeber, he's got that needle in his hand, he's starting to gag. I knew it was coming but I was too slow; he knocks me down going out the door. She's throwing up inside. He's throwing up outside. He can't go back. I have to start the IV, and you know how he drives, jumping on the gas at red lights, braking in the middle of the block."

"He learned how to drive from Larry," I said, and pushed Luther over for Hector to sit down.

"I had three stabbings last night, two the night before," Hector said.

"It's wild out there," Stanley said. "For two months I didn't see any blood, but last few weeks, man, the bullets been flyin'."

"A full moon," Veeber added.

"One of those three-week full moons," I said.

Luther opened an eye and raised himself on an elbow. "The CIA has been working with the Colombian cocaine gangs to stock the ghettos with addiction and violence."

Suzette stared at us through a mirror on the far wall. "Men been stabbing women long before the CIA got involved. Nothing new about that."

"Don't listen to a word she says," said Stanley.

"Actually," Veeber said, "aside from the assault, they made quite a nice couple. When we arrived at the hospital, the man was holding his wife's hand. She was cursing him but in a kind way, you know."

Hector stood. "You're crazy, man. Didn't you see all the vials on the floor? They were both stoned out of their heads. She told me she has three kids she doesn't even know where they are."

"She said she was trying to get them back."

"Look, my kids come first. What's wrong with this neighborhood is that the parents don't put the kids first. They think they got so many problems and so they're always getting stoned or drunk and then can't take what that's doing to their kids so they stay away and get more stoned. They don't understand the kids is the only thing what's gonna pull em out. You got to concentrate on the kids."

"You tell em, Hector." I stood up from the couch. "Now let's go get a drink."

He looked over to Veeber. "Yeah, man, I could use one."

Stanley slapped me on the back. "Now this is the product of a strong family environment."

"The best," I said. "My father was a bottle of Beefeaters and my mother was a box of Kleenex." I needed a drink so bad my hands were biting my pockets, my teeth formed fists in my mouth. Drinking used to help me over the bad nights, but since Mona went they were all bad. The one good thing about her going was it left a pain so strong it beat out everything else. Mona owned my mornings the way Rose owned my nights. I had only to start the process with a drink and a quick reprise of the day we parted and then sit back and watch her run the other ghosts out of town.

We headed up Tenth in two cars. I stared out the window and watched the morning grow. It often seemed to me that the sun rose on a foreign city, different from the one I drove an ambulance through. At night the walls went up and the gates came down and the fear chased everyone inside, except for those who spread it, those it caught, and those, like me, brought in to witness. I was always surprised when the new sun revealed a poor crumbling neighborhood like any other, full of people who wake up every morning and walk the familiar streets to the subways heading downtown or the school buses lined up on Fifty-third.

"You see that place?" Stanley's hand pointed to a row of brownstones. "I had a call there last week. At the top floor I go into this apartment, just a mattress on the floor, right, and three guys sitting around it so high they can't even move.

They're leaning over another one who's laid out cold dead as blue as this hat. They got something jammed between his teeth, and then I hear it, a blow dryer, they're turning it on and off, on and off. You know they all sharing this needle, but no one wants to do mouth-to-mouth. I pronounced him and the junkies were pissed off, but the man was cold, except for his throat – they must have been blow-drying it for an hour; second-degree burns on the tongue."

Luther lifted his head from the window behind Stanley. "I tell you one thing, you wouldn't catch me kissing no dead man. Of course if you find a nice-looking dead woman, that would be different."

The kid stuck his head in the front. "Did you ever do mouth-to-mouth?"

"A long time ago," Stanley said, "when I was just starting out like you. Never again, kid. Chances are you end up with a mouthful of puke. Remember you always got time to get a mask."

"I would do it if I had to. It's part of the job." The kid turned to me. "What about you? You ever do it?"

"Once, on a baby."

"Oh, babies," Stanley said, shaking his head. "Babies are a whole nother thing entirely."

We bounced quietly together along the neglected boulevards of upper Manhattan, dodging the abandoned construction sites and the black-bottomed potholes until a sudden closure of Third Avenue forced us to narrow streets bordering the river, streets lined with empty garages and the wrecks of stolen cars, streets that led us circling up to the soot-covered trestlework stretched across the slack water of the Harlem. Below us on the right lay the ruins of the South Bronx, the scattered bones of a neighborhood, brick from brick.

After we were married, Mona and I moved into an apartment on Fifty-first Street near Twelfth Avenue, a sagging brick square by the river. For the first week I didn't have my own keys, and early morning after work I would ring the bell over and over until Mona appeared on the landing, in her white dress, fast asleep, gliding down the stairs like a spirit from some ancient poem. She used to sleepwalk, and she always wore that simple nightgown because it looked like a dress and she was afraid of walking out to the street one night, waking up in a subway station. She would open the door, kiss me once, breathless, and glide back to bed. I could say anything to her then. "Mona, the house is on fire." "Okay." "Mona, you have to kiss me twenty thousand times." "Okay." All night at work I would think of her coming down the stairs, and even after I had my own keys I would ring the bell, waiting.

"Where are we?" I asked. The streets looked alike, blocks of windowless walls, empty lots heaped with ash and broken brick.

"The precinct is up ahead," Stanley said, "the bar two blocks from there."

The Blarney Moon had been getting cops drunk for over three decades. It was once a thriving neighborhood local, now it was the only Irish bar in the South Bronx, the only occupied building on the block, but happy hour still started at seven a.m. and the seats were always filled by eight.

"Ralph, give me a large and a small, please, a beer and a bourbon."

I downed the shot, ordered another, and looked around. The day laborers were finishing their beer breakfasts and leaving. The night crews took their places, drinking earnestly. Behind me, a group of about ten cops were talking up two Dominican girls one of the cops must have roped in on a traffic violation. The full-time drinkers were still working, Georgie the Russian, Don the Con, Damned Bob, but I could see in their embalmed lips, their open-coffin smiles, that quitting time was near.

Hector sat down next to me and ordered a beer. "How you doing, Frank?"

"I'm drinking to the ghosts this morning."

"That sounds healthy."

"You believe in ghosts, Hector?"

"Sure, man, and whenever I see one it always says the same thing. 'Time for a vacation, Hector.'"

"You got some good ghosts there."

"Go, man, take a vacation. You need it."

"Where am I gonna go?"

"Puerto Rico, bro. I got family down there take good care of you. The ocean, the sand, palm trees, the finest women in the world."

"Who's gonna take care of my ghosts?"

"Don't joke about vacation time, man. Everybody needs a

break. Even Superman takes a vacation. He's got a place outside San Juan."

"Yeah, well, you oughta know that I took Superman to the hospital not too long ago. Superman goes down to the subway and on the platform he starts to take off his clothes and he must have forgot his Superman suit because he had nothing on underneath. So he's naked and just standing there like he's waiting for the train and when it comes out of the tunnel he jumps on the tracks and stands in front of it with his arm sticking straight out like he's going to stop it, yelling, I'm Superman, I'm Superman. Fortunately, the motorman saw him in time."

"That wasn't the motorman. That was Superman's power."

"Yeah, well, Superman is in Bellevue now."

"See, he should have been in Puerto Rico." Hector stood and finished his beer. "I have to go."

"Come on, have another. You just got here."

"Can't. Have to take the kids to school. Look, Frank, you're going to hell, man. My family will put you up. I got three gorgeous cousins. Come on. Just say yes."

"Thank you, Hector, but this stool I'm on here is my vacation, Blarney Moon Cruises."

Hector walked away whistling, like he was attempting to imitate the sound of a falling artillery shell, and when he reached the chair by the door where Marcus was sleeping, he clapped his hands and shouted, "Bam," and walked out. Slowly Marcus lifted his head from the side of the jukebox. With his eyes still closed, he pulled out a handful of quarters and carefully fed each one into the machine. He pushed the buttons without looking, and then slowly lowered his head to its former position. Marcus worked the same shift as the rest of us, but he was always the first one to the Moon, and could usually manage five vodkas and a short nap before the serious drinking began. He liked to sit in the chair next to the jukebox, so that he could drop in his money without standing. Some mornings he would play "My Way" over and over until a fight broke out – the only black guy I ever knew who loved Sinatra.

Luther was passed out in the corner, his head resting on a copy of the *Irish Constitution*. Veeber was speaking to the kid about intestinal parasites. At the end of the bar, one of the Mexican builders had stopped talking and was knocking his friends one by one off their stools. The friends did not protest. After they fell, each one would stand up, dust himself off, and sit down only to be knocked over again.

"Ralphy boy, some iron slag from the pits, please, and a shot of kerosene."

It was the biggest bed either of us had ever seen. I had to cut a hole in the doorframe and then switch the door around on its hinges so that it swung out into the living room. The room was the bed, the bed was the world. Looking through the window all we could see was sky. On our rare afternoons together we took the bed to all the places we dreamed about. In the autumn we would lie there for hours with the window open, waiting for a leaf to fall in. In the summer we let the rain soak us. Announcements and other important news were always held for the bed. I told her about a baby I delivered, how its head was a soft jewel. We went to the hospital together, and the mother let each of us take turns holding it.

Next to me Slinkowsky was crying out of his glass eye and next to him the old woman who never left was crying too. Her wig had fallen back, exposing a scalp as bald and brown as a river stone. One of the cops fell down the stairs to the bathroom. Veeber started singing: "Yes, there were times, I've had a few, when I bit off more than I could chew." Marcus related a story from his first divorce to Stanley, who was in the middle of his second.

"Ralphy boy, Ralph Edward boy, over here. Let the spirits out. Pour the grave juice."

Every day, Mona went to the gym, and within a few months her bad leg looked as strong as the good. It wasn't. I can't get in the air, she said. A dancer has got to get in the air; it's the most important thing. The doctor told her to rest. He warned her it might never be the same. She worked twice as hard on it, and six months later she was in surgery, another cast. We spent our weekends on the couch next to a case of wine, Mona crying in the early morning. "You should have shot me when I told you to, Frank."

I told her that life was more important than lift, that sometimes a part has to die so the rest can live. She offered to shoot me. I looked through the want ads. I walked with her to the tiny theater that advertised for a public relations assistant. I went to a few rehearsals, opening night, the party after, standing in the corner waiting to go to work, watching Mona pirouette from one group to the other. By eleven o'clock I was telling gory stories to a circle of actors and writers who wanted to know all the different ways people died.

But I never told them about the woman with the knife in her side and how much she looked like Mona, how she danced in my sleep the way Mona once did, different places, different dances, but in the end always the same: she falls and I reach down and pull open the robe to see the hurt that no one lives through. It wasn't a dream I had often, but it always felt close by, like a dream behind a dream, like the knife I'd touch in Mona's back on those rare nights when we slept together, if I didn't take care not to put my hand there, where the steel wedged between her ribs.

Tell me what happened, she'd say, the mornings I still came home. Tell me what's inside. Talk to me, Frank. We have so little time. She was at the theater nearly every night. We had dinner with each other once a week. My job has really helped me, Frank. The world is so much bigger now that I can see beyond just being a dancer. There are many roles to play in life, Frank. There're many ways to play a role. But when you let one role play you, it chokes you. You're a medic, which is a good thing to be, except when it's strangling you, and Frank, I think you're going down for the third time.

She was going to save me. I needed to be saved. But the more she tried to get me to talk, the less I wanted to say. I didn't like how my feelings looked under the sun, so pallid and frail. I liked them locked in a vault, buried in cement, mined and patrolled and wired to explode when opened. Things will get better, I said; this bad luck can't last forever. She listed the classic signs of repression, the sinister virus of self-deception. My drinking and insomnia, the problems I had touching her, were symptoms of job-related stress. My refusing to acknowledge that was another. She cut out magazine articles. She bought large, heavy self-help books and threw them at me. Grow up, Frank, let it out, get over it and get on with life. Take some time off. Finish school. I can pay the bills for a while. You're screwed on so tight, Frank, that one of these days you're going to explode. Which is exactly what happened when she left.

"Ralph, a dying man comes out of the desert, and this is all you have to give. Where's the scorpion's sting, tumors of the brain and spine? Where's the witch's milk?" One of the cops jumped on the bar, punching the air. "It's as big as my arm. It's an oak tree, a battleship. I'll spin every one of you whore mothers on it like a top." The other cops blocked the door, trying to talk the girls from the Heights into another drink, but the girls had tightened up, and their frightened smiles only made everyone angrier. Veeber slept next to the kid passed out on the table in front of the comatose Luther. Stanley threw Marcus against a wall and was threatening him with a bottle. Marcus just laughed, singing, "The record shows I stood the blows, and . . ."

*   *   *

I was getting to the best parts then, the heart of the breakup, but the scene I wanted to remember most wouldn't come right – the trip back to the lake to save the marriage, the night I couldn't put my arm around her and got so drunk I fell off the pier, split my skull. For a moment the picture would be perfect, like the one of her driving me to the hospital with her eyes closed, one hand holding the bloody towel on my head, but when I turn around, Burke and Rose are sitting in the back seat and behind us the daughter Mary is driving the old black Ford and the people sitting at the bar look like corpses taking their last breath together and then they are dead, some of them days old and starting to smell. Everything swirling.

I'll try again. It was the morning after I helped kill Rose. I was drunk when I walked in and found Mona sitting on the love seat, calling a taxi. She had taken the day off from work to tell me. I imagined her waiting there those hours packing and repacking, putting on her coat and taking it off, practicing the words.

"I'm leaving."

"Good-bye," I said, and turned away. I walked to the bedroom, closed the door, not slammed. I went to the window and took out the first pane with my fist. I hoped she would leave then and not tell me why. She kicked the door. "I ask you to quit. You can't quit. I ask you to get help. You won't get help. Well I've decided not to wait around for you to kill yourself. You hear me? I've decided my life is worth more than your death." Left jab. Well put, Mona. Another kick to the door. "I tried, but you won't help yourself and I have nothing left to give." Right punch, bleeding on the left.

Then go. "You just gave up, Frank, on us, on yourself, everything. Well, Frank, you got me – I give up too." The taxi horn outside. Leaving. A beautiful speech. Left punch. I give up too. Her hands back beating on the door. "You bastard, who gave you the right to suffer? All the people you've seen so much worse than you. You let it die. Everything you touch. God I hate this place." Right hook again. Bleeding there too. The taxi horn. A broken vase. The front door slamming. Blood on the window and floor. Blood on the pillow and under the blankets, the bed we carried home together.

Veeber and Luther and the kid tackle Stanley to the floor. Marcus is standing next to me, laughing, and Ralph reaches over and grabs his collar, bending him backward on the bar. "You play that song one more time and you're hospitalized. I used to love that song." One of the cops has his gun out, pointed at Marcus, showing the girls how to shoot. "Ralph," I yell, "bring me my robes, the vestments."

Stanley's lying on the floor with his eyes closed. I pull off one of the red and white and brown-stained tablecloths and throw it over him. I grab another and wrap it around myself. Veeber and Marcus help me up to the bar. "Bless us, Father, for we have sinned." I raise my beer and splash the crowd. "May the Lord forgive you by this holy anointing whatever sins you have committed, amen. May the Lord forgive you by this holy anointing whatever sins you have committed, amen. May the Lord forgive you – "

Stanley gets up and grabs my legs, pulling me down to the floor, the robes covering my face and chest.

"Ralph, come on. Superman needs some more kryptonite."

Two weeks after Mona left I was called for a man under the train. I hate men under trains – the soaking filth down there, the bloody groaning pieces – and so I drove to the station with the usual loathing, my head pounding as I walked toward the crowd gathered near the first car, but when I reached them I found a man lying on the tracks, perfectly intact. The train had apparently stopped just before hitting him. "What happened?" I asked, and the woman next to me said the man had been sleeping on the platform and rolled over in his sleep, onto the tracks. I jumped down and checked him over – not a mark on him. I shook him awake and he looked up at me. "What happened?" he said. "You were sleeping on the platform," I said, "and you rolled over and onto the tracks." He raised his eyes and shook his head, exasperated, and said, "Not again."

9

I'm dying, the voice said to me. I opened my eyes. *But I can't die.* I raised my head from the living room floor. In the dark-walled void, nothing moved. *I am not dead,* the voice was in my head, *but everything I believed in is.* A voice I knew, sharp and white, the steam pipe in Patrick Burke's apartment. I crawled over to the kitchen and put my head in the sink. *If I have to die forever* – the cold water running over the words – *it'll not be alone.* I wrapped my hands around my ears, pushing in, trying to close the door inside. I took a deep breath and bent over and held it until I felt the door close. The clock on the wall said nearly twelve – I touched it with my hands to be sure. Dark windows told me it was night. A rough way to start the day – sick and out of sick time, crazy and out of crazy time. In the dirty clothes piled on the floor I found a uniform shirt with only two stains, black coffee on the collar, bits of blood clotted at the sleeve. I exchanged it with the shirt I wore, still reeking of the bar. In the bathroom mirror I stared at the writing on the cheeks, the inflating nose, the bricked-up mouth, Mr. Burke. *Let me be the first one to say, enough.* I squeezed my head again, breathed in deep, and held it until the pain stopped. I slipped out the door, closing it quickly to keep the voice inside. Then down the stairs. Only one hour late for work.

"Good morning, Captain." I stood on one foot in front of his desk.

Captain Barney looked at his watch. "Pierce, you're early."

"I shouldn't be here."

"What am I going to do with this guy?" He turned to Miss Williams, his secretary and confidante, who sat at a desk perpendicular to his. She did not look up and the captain went on. "Pierce, I was just on the phone with Borough Command. Out of twelve shifts this month, you've been late nine, sick four, and that includes the shift where you came in late and went home sick."

"I am sick, Captain. That's what I'm telling you."

"You're killing me, Pierce, you know that? You have no sick time, you have no time, period, according to Borough Command. I've been told to terminate."

"It's okay. I understand. I'll just get my things out of the locker."

"I've never fired anyone in my life."

"I'm sorry, Captain. Don't take it too hard."

He rested his head on the desk. Miss Williams glanced over. Then he raised his heavy eyes and stared at me a long time. The captain's face was an orphan's dream: lumberjack cheeks, fireman mustache, deep-blue eyes that cared but never cried. The face belonged on a billboard, smoking a cigarette in a sandstorm or warning home owners of lightning's danger. It was easy to see him like that, just a face, or to see just the rest of him, which was space. The captain had a butt the size of Staten Island.

"Look Pierce, nobody tells me to fire anyone. Shove it up the big one, I told em. Excuse me, Miss Williams. I'm not your goddamn washrag, I said. You want to fire him, come on over and do it yourself."

"You know they won't do it, Captain. It's up to you. You have to be strong."

"Pierce, I'll tell you something: You've always been like a son to me. You're working through a bad time now. I want you to know I'm there for you. But tonight it's out of my hands. We're in the middle of an emergency here. Everyone's called in sick. Larry, Veeber, Stanley. We need bodies out there. Our duty to the city. I had to put Marcus on Twelve Young. You know he's not supposed to work two nights in a row."

"You swore you'd fire me if I came in late again."

"I'll fire you tomorrow. Hell, even better than that, I might be able to forward you some sick time, a week, two weeks off – how about that? I tell you what I'll do. There's an all-night Polish place just opened on First and Twentieth. It was written up in the *Times*. The pierogies, if you get a chance, with extra sauce. Bring some back and we'll talk. I'll get you that week off."

The captain would take care of almost anything if you brought him late-night gourmet. He hated diners. I once crashed two ambulances in the same week and had to drive all the way to Brighton Beach for a brandied herring he described as a Caspian treasure.

"I don't think a week's gonna do it. Not for what I got."

"I'm sorry, Pierce." He handed me the keys, which clanged in my hand. I stood there listening to Luther screaming at the TV in the crew room. "Shoot the dumb bitch in the head, in the head, man." My face felt warm, my hands hot. I held my arms up in front of me; they looked like two sticks found on the beach. "I think it's a fever," I said. "I've been sick all day, sneezing, bleeding. I shouldn't be here."

Miss Williams frowned. "You should get some soup."

I shifted to the other foot. "Soup, yes, hot soup and rest. What about the couch? Luther's been on it for years. It's not fair. He's certified to work. He can go out there with Marcus."

Captain Barney laughed. "Luther work with Marcus? Did you hear that, Miss Williams?" She didn't smile and the captain went on. "Luther is much sicker than you'll ever be, and anyway I've already written up the log and Miss Williams has typed it. You know the rule."

The rule was that Miss Williams typed things once and once only. After typing, she placed the reports, errors and all – and she made many – into the box marked Outgoing. Eventually Luther would rise from his couch, pick up the papers, and drive them to a paperwork center in Queens, where the reports would be shuffled and evaluated. Special Queens clerks then converted these statistics into programs. More reports were written, then examined by more clerks. Professional copiers came and copied. Professional filers tried to outpace the copiers, running through the halls filing whatever they could find, then filing the copies. Department heads fought off incoming reports and praised themselves in memorandums. Professional defilers dumped rooms of files off the coast. Boxes of reports washed ashore in South Brooklyn, Battery Park, Jamaica Bay. Some found their way somehow to Luther, who returned them to Captain Barney. Often Luther would hand the captain a report he had sent off months before. The captain would sigh and shake his head and move the paper to the box marked Outgoing.

There were other rules about Miss Williams' typing – what she would type, the times she would type it – yet in my years at Misery I had never seen her press a key. Her typewriter was always covered, a permanent fixture gathering dust in the corner. I never questioned her about this; no one asked questions like that of Miss Williams, who was always at her desk with a smile, a kind word, a question about your family or your health. She was a grandmother who saw only the best in you and to whom you would gladly lie about missing church. In this rested her power.

I watched her grimace as she read her magazine, a tragic story of Somalian babies left to die on a desert plain. After reading, she would go over her nails again and then maybe have some of the chicken soup she always kept stewing in her bottom drawer. I pulled a chair up next to her, caught the gummy web of her perfume. If I can't get her to switch me with Luther, I thought, I could at least have some soup. I touched her arm. She looked up, tears in her eyes.

"Go on, Pierce, duty calls. Get out there. The city needs you."

"The city needs more couches, Captain."

"The order's in, Pierce. Right here. It's just a matter of time now."

Marcus was snoring in the driver's seat, his hands trembling even in sleep. Marcus was not supposed to drive because of the trembling and the tic in his left eye, which twisted his head to the side and blinded him for seconds at a time. He was not supposed to care for patients either, due to his religious beliefs. If God wants you, Marcus said, it's not for me to get in the way. Always a tough decision, to let him drive or not to let him drive. Fortunately, Marcus refused to do anything except drive. On most calls he even refused to do anything except sit in the driver's seat and keep the engine running. He had been a medic longer than anyone except Luther and worked only two or three nights a week. Most nights he and Luther spent their shifts watching TV in the crew room. Luther was due to retire in six months, and Marcus was being groomed for the position, though what that position was nobody really knew. "Twelve Young," Marcus said in his sleep. "One-Two Young."

I shook his shoulder, and he opened his eyes and looked over and winked at me twenty times before saying, "Oh my Lord mother man you look like hell. What were you drinking?"

"It's not just a hangover. It's like many hangovers, each adding something different. I've been hearing voices. Feel my head."

He placed a dark trembling hand over my eyes, slapping

me lightly. "It's only hot because you're crazy up there. Emotional overdrive. You ever notice how the people who tend to hear voices are all nuts? How many times have I said chill down or you're gonna die, like all these years I'm talking to myself. Too many circuits shortin and buzzin in that square head." Marcus demonstrated by turning his bad eye toward me and waving his bad hand over it.

"The captain almost fired me tonight. I'm on my way out. Anytime now."

"Nobody gets fired, Frank. Look at me. Only thing they might do is transfer you to the Bronx."

"I think the worst is over, mainly because I figure it can't get worse. It's like I'm floating in a big tank, suspended, like in formaldehyde, waiting to go to the lab. Then there's this constant buzzing too, and my fingers feel like they're coming unglued."

"Hey man it can always get worse. That's the thing. You can't change what's coming at you, only where you're coming from. Let the Lord handle out there, you take care of in there." His finger wavered over my nose. "You aged ten years since the last time we worked together."

It was two years since we'd worked together, the last year Marcus was allowed to drive, when he broke all crash records. I remembered sitting in the back of the ambulance treating a very bad asthmatic, Marcus driving us to the hospital. The trip took a long time, even for Marcus, who always stopped for every red light, and at some point I realized we weren't moving, that in fact we hadn't moved for the equivalent of at least five red lights. I looked out the door, to see Marcus picking up his Chinese food. "The place was closing," he said. "If I don't take care of myself first, how am I gonna take care of anyone else?"

Marcus came out of the second paramedic class, 1976, back when the knowledge gained from Vietnam was just starting to come together in a program for the city. There was only one medic unit for the upper half of Manhattan then, Eighteen Xray, and Marcus was known as the Xman. Like a comic book hero, the Xman was always there, charging through bullets and blood. No one in Harlem had ever seen a medic, much less a black medic, and they would never see one that good again. When I started working uptown and pulled off some job I thought was special, there was always someone telling me, Oh yeah, Marcus did that, only he did it like better. The Harlem garage had a wall called the Xwall, a memorial to Marcus, full of yellowing newspaper photos of the man climbing in from a ledge with a baby in his arms, starting an IV at the bottom of an elevator shaft, bandaging a hostage while under the hostage-takers' gun.

I never met the Xman. By the time I worked with Marcus he had already found Jesus and left Harlem and I hated him for what he'd become, the ex-Xman. Our first shift together he refused to tell me what unit we were. He slept in the park for three hours and then woke up suddenly, complaining about the diesel fumes, almost crashed three times on the way back to the garage. I didn't smell any gas that day, but in the past few months I had put the bus out for fumes a dozen times.

"Twelve Young," the dispatcher said. It was Dispatcher Love, whom we had all loved, each in his own way. "Let's go, Twelve Young. Answer the radio."

"Hey, Marcus, it's Love. I haven't heard her in months."

"She only works when I'm on. I make her wait, and it drives her crazy."

"Twelve Young," said Dispatcher Love, "I don't have time for your games. Now answer me, or do I have to come out there myself?"

"Give me the radio, Frank. I don't usually do calls before coffee, but I'm thinking it might just do you some good. Shake off those voices." Marcus held the radio in his good hand. "Twelve Young is here and I'm gonna take care of you, baby. Don't you worry bout a thing, yahear, cause Marcus is alive on arrival."

"I'm not your baby, Young. I'm not your mother either. You're going to the cardiac arrest inside the Graceland Ballroom, backstage entrance, 350 West Fifty-fourth."

"Ten-four, hon." Marcus put down the radio. "You feel better now, Frank?"

"I feel worse."

"That's good, man. I'm doing this for you."

Marcus stopped at every red light on the way. He stopped at every green light too, looking left and right to make sure no emergency vehicles were crossing. While watching him drive, you wondered how all his accidents happened, unless you saw him at the end of the shift, when it was time to go home, Marcus racing like a madman back to the garage, the only time he ever used the siren.

We pulled up and Marcus grabbed the airway bag and left me the other three heavier pieces. At the backstage door the usual collection of models and wrestlers waving us in and blocking our way. Bouncers shoving each other into the crowd, shoving the crowd into the medics. Out of the way – let em in. The usual hysteria.

"Let's hope we're not too late," said Marcus when we finally reached the door, "from you guys holding us up here."

A black-suited dwarf holding a radio led us through the smoke and broken glass down a hall full of standing overdoses to a small room packed with standing and sitting overdoses to the man not breathing on the floor. He appeared to have been dead for hours, but when I felt for a pulse at his neck it was bounding, and when I crouched down next to him I found out it was the makeup, blue and gray, that made him look so DOA. I took out my light and shone it on his chest, the breathing so shallow you couldn't see unless you knew how to look. I pulled back a greasy eyelid to reveal the flea-size pupil: heroin.

Marcus stood with his back to me, addressing the room. "Okay, what happened?"

One of the few who could stand – a young guy in a tattered white shirt that appeared to have been professionally torn – "It's like this. He finished the last song and dove into the drum kit like normal, and then he walked back here and just fell out. He's gonna be all right, right?"

"No," said Marcus. "He's dead."

"No way, man. We just signed our first record deal."

"He's dead and there's nothing we can do. Come on, Frank, that's it."

I stood and whispered in Marcus's good ear. "He's not dead. It's a heroin overdose."

Marcus turned back to the crowd. "As I was saying, he's dead, unless of course you people stop bullshitting me and tell it straight. Then if the Lord is willing, maybe we'll bring him back."

"He's just broke up with his old lady," said a man lying under the radiator.

"It's not a breakup," the woman behind me sobbed. "We're just seeing other people as like a test for getting married."

"I'm still waiting," Marcus said, "and this young man is still dead."

"She broke his heart," the voice under the radiator said, and that started off a round of slurred denials that left Marcus with his hands in the air. I couldn't wait any longer. I opened the drug box and took out the vial of Narcan and a syringe and withdrew 10 cc and rolled up the sleeve and tied the tourniquet and searched for a vein. Narcan is the junkie's worst nightmare, like a thousand cops sweeping through your body, closing up shops, confiscating every bag, needle, spoon, match, arresting anything that moves, until each cell in your body is sitting in jail shaking, sniffling, scratching the walls. Narcan is a medic's friend, the great resurrector, always a crowd pleaser, from corpse to standing in about twenty seconds.

"All right, all right, man, he's been snorting the Red Death. He's been on it for days now; he thinks he's in heaven."

Marcus brought his hands together as if to pray. He closed

his eyes and shook his head. "Okay, what's his name?"

"Riot."

"What do you mean, Riot? What kind of name is Riot?"

"I don't know. It's his name."

"It's Frederick," the man's fiancée said. "Frederick Smith."

"Okay Freddy – "

"It's Frederick."

"Okay, Riot, we're gonna bring you back. Now, every person here grab the hand of the person next to you and hold tight and pray, Come back, Riot. Come back to us, Riot." All eyes were on Marcus as he went around the room joining the hands of those who couldn't manage it. The Narcan resurrection was Marcus's favorite protocol, and he played it better than any medic in the city. I turned Riot's arm over and plunged the needle into a bulging line of blue under the elbow and pulled back on the syringe until the red rose up into the barrel. I popped the tourniquet off and shoved the red back in.

I gave Marcus the thumbs-up, and he raised his hands. "O Lord," he cried, "here I am again, to ask you one more time to give a sinner another chance." Marcus fell to his knees and laid his hands on Riot's chest. "Bring back Riot, Lord. Only you have the power, the might, the super light, to spare this worthless man. Though we are so unworthy, we beg you, Lord, just blink your almighty eye and please bring us Riot back."

And Riot opened his eyes and raised his hands.

"Frederick," the woman screamed and fell upon his face.

"Oh wow, man," the torn shirt said. "Oh wow, man."

Marcus stood and circled his arms out and in to his chest, out and in. "Rise, Riot. Stand up and start your new life." I closed the drug box and locked it, and Marcus and I each grabbed a hand and lifted Riot up.

"What happened?"

"You died," the fiancée said, and started punching Riot in the chest. "You died, you stupid bastard."

The torn shirt pulled her off. "You guys are awesome."

"Not us," Marcus said, and guided Riot to the door, his legs already shaking from withdrawal. "The first step is Love. The second step is Mercy." Through the hall to the bouncers on the street. We put Riot on the stretcher, and his fiancée climbed in behind.

He looked at her. "What happened?"

"Oh, Frederick, I love you so much."

"I love you too, Margaret," he said, and dropped into a trembling sleep.

"You see, Frank," Marcus yelled from the driver's seat. "The Lord takes care of everything."

"I think your partner's crazy," Margaret said, and slid herself next to me on the bench seat, our legs touching without touching. "But you're kind of cute."

On the television in Misery's waiting room, a bald, shrunken-hipped woman in golden tights reached over her head and back, grabbing her ankles from behind to make her body into a wheel. She rolled around the TV studio, gathering speed as she spoke, short phrases of generic inspiration, one for each rotation, followed by a pause as her face crossed the carpet. "Get involved." "Seek truth." "Be yourself." As we wheeled the stretcher through, I searched the rows of the rapt audience – mutant hangnails and rampant cellulitis, black eyes and bloody sputum. And no sign of Mary Burke. Griss the guard looked up from his anti-white-future journals.

"You know, pardner, revolution's gonna come when we least expect it, while the whole country sleeps."

"No one will know what happened," I said.

"Except that everything will be different."

"And exactly the same."

I left Riot with Nurse Constance and in the treatment area looked on the empty slot that I had come to regard as Burke's room. Three stretchers down the line I found Dr. Hazmat pumping clear fluid through a tube that fed into a nose. "That guy I brought in yesterday," I said, "the post-cardiac arrest. He's gone."

"You're not going to believe it," Hazmat said. He pulled out the quart-size syringe and clamped off the hose. "The guy's showing some cognitive signs. He started with spontaneous respirations this evening, and now he's fighting to pull out the tube. Had to sedate him. He's over in CAT scan now." Hazmat took off two pairs of the three or four sets of gloves that he wore. "I've been calling upstairs since I came on. They had room before but wouldn't take him because it didn't look like he'd make it through the day. Now he looks better, but they're overloaded again. Well, if they're not going to take him, they're going to pay for him. I'm giving him every test I can. Besides the CAT scan he's got thrombolytics, steroids, nitrodrips, heparin. Hell, I'll do a cardiac cath here myself if I have to. I've even had Milagros doing her hands-on healing."

"What do you really think?"

"Who knows. It's all lower-brain-stem activity, and the heart refuses to stabilize – he's coded eleven times since he got here – but let me tell you, this guy's a fighter. Every time the Valium wears off he starts yanking those restraints like the devil jailed in heaven."

"Does the family know?"

"I wanted to bring them in before, to see if he'd respond to their voices, but they weren't in the waiting room. It figures; the guy's daughter was in my face all last night, and when I finally have something positive to tell her, she disappears."

I walked back to the triage stall and took my temperature while listening to Nurse Constance lecture Riot. "So you put this poison in your veins and you stop breathing and now that we've got you breathing again you can't wait to say thank you very much and go back out poison-shopping. Well, since we saved your life, maybe you could do us a favor and stop breathing in another city next time. Don't slam the door, okay?"

The thermometer gauge rocketed up to 98 and hung there, searching for direction. I walked out to the waiting room. Still no Burkes. In the parking lot, I lit a smoke. My hands shook, but no more than usual, and the skin had puffed out some over the knuckles. Normal alcoholic-neurotic hands. Above me the moon was as pale and misty-eyed as on the night before, but the earth had turned over. Burke was fighting back. To die again, I thought, trying to feel worse. Death and more death, I said, slightly embarrassed by the naked longing that rose from the gut and that I'd pushed down so many times I almost didn't remember what it was. Hunger. I was starving.

For ten years, old Sal was known as the fattest, cheapest pizza man in midtown. He skimped on sauce, spice, and cheese and worked day and night to save money on help, and Larry and I were not surprised when we found him one night on the floor in cardiac arrest. It was one of those calls where everything goes wrong and the patient comes out fine. Sal was wedged between the oven and the garbage; we couldn't intubate; the defibrillator kept shutting off every time we tried to shock him. Ten minutes of bungling and we managed to spark him once at half power and his heart kicked in like it had never stopped. By the time we dragged him to the ambulance he was still unconscious but breathing on his own and fighting against the straps as if trying to get back to work. Three months later we went in for a slice and soda and found him working the overnights again. He stretched his arms around our heads and called out to the old men playing dominoes in the back booth. "Hey, what do you know, these are the guys that saved my life. Sit down right here. What you getting?" He threw the pizzas in and came back. "Now wait, you're wondering how I know it was you guys who saved me, am I right? 'Cause I was unconscious the whole time, right, and I was dead before that, but what you don't know is that I could still see, not with my eyes maybe but in here." He pointed to his ear and then to the floor behind the counter. "I was laying on the floor there and I knew my heart stopped. Everything went white and I could feel myself rising, real slow at first, like the fucking space shuttle, you know how it lifts off hardly moving, and then I'm up over the oven and it's like watching a movie of myself. I see you guys come in and thank you very much for that cracked rib that still hurts, just kidding, and then I was out shooting up through this like white space, faster and faster, everything getting bigger. I tell you it was the greatest ride of my fuckin life and wouldn't you know it I was dead the whole time. Then you guys shocked me with that machine and it was like, boom, the fuckin shuttle just blew up and I wake up on the floor and my chest is killing me. Crazy, huh?" He brought us over the pizza and Cokes. *"What a wake-up, I tell you really I don't know how I can thank you guys enough."* He gave us our change at the register. *"Hey, the Cokes are on me."*

10

"Stop looking like that," Marcus said.

"Like what?"

"Like you just screwed Dispatcher Love."

"I want to go to Forty-third between Ninth and Tenth."

"You're not listening to me, Frank. I know that look, that tonight's-a-new-night-things-are-going-to-get-better look. Marcus has been there, and he wants you to know, you're setting yourself up for a major fall."

"I already fell, Marcus. Too many times. In fact, there's no place I haven't fallen."

"I ever tell you about the time years ago I was on this ledge uptown, trying to talk this psycho inside?"

"Where the guy jumped, right, and you almost fell. No, you never told me this story."

"No, you never listened. Seventeen flights up, and I'm standing next to this nut on a two-foot little piece-of-shit stone. I didn't care; I'd go anywhere back then. Everything was going right, you know, nothing I couldn't do, like I could fly, man. And so the asshole jumps."

"And you flew after him and caught him just before he landed."

"You think this is funny. I was going, man, if someone on high hadn't pulled me in. I put all I had into saving that guy and when he went down I was so out of my head it was like I fucked up, I should go too, and yeah, there was this other part of me that had gotten away with so much in the past I thought for a second I can save him on the way down, this dumbass lowlife suicidal. The Lord pulled me in, and that's when I woke up."

"That's when you got that twitch in your eye."

"What twitch?" He turned to me, holding both eyes open as long as he could.

"Look, Marcus, I'm not out to save the world. I hit bottom, and now I just want to get back onto some middle ground where I can rest and get something to eat."

"I heard it all before, Frank, but the look, it don't lie. If you ain't gonna listen to me, then listen to Love. She speaks the truth. What's out there. What's always gonna be." Marcus pulled the radio from behind his seat and placed it on the dash and turned up the volume, the violent beauty of Love's voice: "Okay, units, I've got calls to give out. One-Three Zebra, you got a man trying to throw a woman and her dog off the tenth floor at 220 East Fiftieth Street. One-Four Boy, on the corner of Twentieth and Eighth there's an elderly female tied up in the trunk of a gray gypsy cab. Twelve Eddie, you're going to 55 West Thirty-three. In apartment Twenty-eight Adam there's a woman in a fur coat with her head in the oven. Sixteen Xray, take it uptown to One-two-five and Douglass. About halfway up the block there you'll find a pregnant female being stoned by a mob."

"It's not what she says," I said. "It's how she says it. I've heard she wears only black and works with a whip."

"She's more woman than you could handle." To Marcus

every woman was more than I could handle, and to demon-
strate, he began again the story of his blind date with Love, a
night that everyone in the service knew ended with a bottle
broken over his nose. Yet to Marcus that night was not an
end but a beginning, of a love affair never consummated but
deeper than any between two people who had seen each
other only briefly and with great violence. "She loves me the
way no woman ever has," he said, and turned to show me
the small dent between his eyes, upon which he could stand
matchbooks, bottle caps, syringes.

So much hope from such a little scar, and as we drove
down Ninth Avenue I thought of all the blind dates I'd been
dispatched to, the small tears each left inside, and the hope
too, though hope was the enemy. I couldn't help myself: it's
how this job makes you think – that the one who cuts you is
the only one with the power to save you, or the one you save
is the one to hurt you, or the one you hurt is . . . or they save
you and . . . If Burke lives, things will turn around, I prayed,
knowing full well what a sap I was for doing it, the lesson
never learned, and as I fought with these prayers I looked out
on the rest of the Ninth Avenue faithful, junkies crackheads
drunks, the homeless and the loveless, all praying too – that
the next score will fix them till morning: a new day, another
chance. Like praying for a safe to fall on your head. If I
survive this, O Lord, I'll be rich.

"Make a right here," I said when we reached Forty-third,
and I pointed to an open space in front of a hydrant across
the street from number 414. "I'll be right back." I stepped

out to the sidewalk and looked up at the moon-soaked clouds rolling over Burke's building, top-floor lights on, movement inside. I waited for the pain in my head, the voice behind the door, but the fear left me when Mary Burke appeared in the window, a broom in her hand, the motions of sweeping. I pushed the button for 5A, spoke on the intercom. "Hello, I'm Frank Pierce, from the ambulance. I brought your father into the hospital and I just learned some news."

"I'll be right down" – which was much better than Come on up, and from the sidewalk I saw the light go off and I was thinking how I should have said, I just learned some *good* news about your father, when the front door opened and she stood on top of the stoop, wearing a white sweater and a simple gray skirt like the kind Catholic schoolgirls used to wear. The makeup was gone, and for the first time since I'd seen her she looked happy, and I waited on the sidewalk, watching her step down, the black rain boot, the white curve of her calf. Three feet away, she said, "He's better, isn't he?"

"Well, the doctor says he's showing some movement. It's still early, might mean nothing, but I thought you'd want to know."

"I knew already. I knew when I was upstairs."

I stepped back and combed my hair with my fingers. Her eyes were like baby peas, her teeth perfectly crooked. "You look so different."

"I know. It's awful, isn't it?" She pulled at her sweater, looking down at herself in disbelief. "Night of the living cheerleaders."

"I think it looks good."

"I was going nuts in that waiting room, all day and tonight, and finally I couldn't take it anymore, and I came back here to check on my mother."

"How's she doing?"

"Sleeping." She turned around to look up at the fifth floor. "Exhausted like the rest of us. That's weird. I swear I turned the light off. She must be awake. You know, when I got upstairs it was such a mess in there, clothes all over, food left out in the living room. That's not like my mother, so I started to clean up; cleaning up usually makes me feel better. I put on another Sinatra record, and it was like I could hear my father talking to me. I mean, I haven't spoken to the man in years, but I remember from when I was a kid, the stuff he used to say to me when I was feeling down. You can't beat a Burke. Keep your chin up. Don't cry without a fight. Stupid shit like that. Anyway, I found an old box of my clothes, and I'm thinking maybe I shouldn't be wearing black, you know, no matter how bad we got along at the end there." She swung her arms as she talked, boxing with my right ear.

"Things have a way of never being over," I said, thinking how in a few hours everything that was over wasn't, Burke's dead body awakening, this reunion of father and daughter, the unfamiliar hunger in me. Pizza, I thought. I could eat a whole pie. "I was just going to get some food," I said. "Maybe we could."

"You know, I realized you can't kill my father that easy, especially once he puts up a fight about it – he'll fight forever. Like with me: hasn't talked to me in three years. Not that I had anything to say to him. But it's okay. Sometimes you have to put things behind you. He's going to be all right.

I believe that now. It's like we got another chance. I have to get back."

She ran out to the street, waving her hand up for a taxi, hips and elbows and shoulders moving at the same time in different directions. A black limo passed slowly, the driver leaning out the window, his hand dragging to the street.

"Be tough to get a taxi here," I said. "We can give you a ride if you like."

She looked at me as if seeing me for the first time, and I tried to straighten my shoulders, my perpetual stoop. "Okay."

I opened the back doors and she stepped up and in, the faint smell of cat fur. When I got into the front she put her head through the small window that separates the cab from the rear, Marcus looking at me and then at Mary in the mirror. "Who's that?"

"She's the daughter of a cardiac arrest I brought in last night. I told her we'd give her a ride back to Misery. Her father's showing signs of improving."

"Oh, Frank, you got it so bad, so much worse than I thought."

"And I'm hungry, too. We need to get some food after this."

"God help us, he's hungry too." Marcus shook his head, and that rare state in the ambulance, hope and hunger and disbelief working together, must have lit a bright-red light on Dispatcher Love's switchboard.

"Twelve Young, One-two Young, for the cardiac arrest."

"'I'm hungry too, Marcus. I'm hungry too, Marcus.' You see what happens," Marcus said. He keyed the radio. "Hey,

Love, howdyou know we were just about to eat? You afraid Marcus was coming out to your little basement to eat you?"

"You just try it, Young, you know what you'll get, right after you go to 757 Tenth Avenue, Fifty-two on your cross, in front of the video store, male in his seventies. CPR in progress."

I turned to the daughter. "That's only a couple of blocks from the hospital. You can walk from there."

"That's okay. I want to see it. This is cool."

Marcus kept the same pace up Tenth, pulled over to the sidewalk like he was going to buy a newspaper. Under a white sign a man and a woman bent over another man, a white sheet bunched up around the grossly swollen feet that had grown substantially since I'd seen them last, twenty-four hours before, the man who had set Noël free from Misery. I'd recognize those feet anywhere.

The couple, white and well-dressed, early thirties, looked up as Marcus and I approached. I bent down and felt the old man's pulse, strong and regular, saw the chest rise, then fall. "It's not an arrest," I said.

"He's alive?" the woman asked.

"He's okay."

"Well, what do you know – it really works," the man said, and wrapped his arm around the woman. "Susan, we saved him."

"You were doing all the hard work, Bill. I only had to breathe a few times." She turned to us. "We just took the CPR course."

"No kidding," said Marcus.

"Yes. We were driving home from an opening downtown, and while waiting for the red light here, I noticed how still the man was. I think it's just awful that people have to live like this."

I pulled the sheet over the old man's feet. He was holding his eyes closed. "Come on, open up," I said, but only after a great deal of nose pinching and ear pulling did he finally raise his head, squinting at the moon like its light gave him pain. "Will all you people just leave me the hell alone? I'm trying to get some sleep."

Susan bent over us. "Is there anything else we can do?"

"No," I said. "Thanks for everything."

"Good luck," she said to the man. "I can see that you're in very good hands now. Good-bye." She was walking away when the old man called out to her. "Miss. Come back. Please, miss. Hold my hand."

She was happy to oblige, wrapping both her hands warmly around the man's engrimed fingers, shaking them gently. He yanked her in close, the inner gases. He raised his head. "Kiss me again."

She pulled her hand back and stood quickly, smoothing her black skirt. "Yes well thank you, gentlemen. Let's go, Bill." We watched them drive away.

"That's incredible," Mary said. "They were just driving by."

"Incredible they didn't kill him," I said.

Marcus handed me the equipment. "We should follow them home to make sure they don't save anyone else."

The streets were empty except for two taxis slamming into

each other as they searched for fares on the empty sidewalks. The city that never sleeps had just taken a pill. Lights out, doors locked, shades pulled down over streetlights, skyline covered with night cream. I held the back doors open, but Mary Burke only stood there, confused. "He wasn't dead, was he," she said. "Just sleeping."

"It's not always so easy to tell."

"Yes, but you want to be sure about something like that."

"It feels much better if you are," I said, and she laughed, looking a little like Greta Garbo if she'd been a Marx brother. It was sort of beautiful, and when I reached the front seat I punched on the stereo, an old song from the sixties, and Mary started to mumble the chorus and I was tapping the dashboard and Marcus twitched to the beat, and soon the music was very loud and all of us were singing together, mumbling the parts we didn't know.

Nurse Constance was on a break and would not look up from her magazine because we might be patients seeking help and she was taking her break. In the treatment area only half the stretchers filled, but the nurses looked busier than ever. None of them saw us enter, or saw Mary Burke run to her father's side and grab his hand. "Dad, can you hear me?" I pulled the sheet up to his chest and stepped out, closing the curtain. "Open your eyes if you can hear me," she said.

Dr. Hazmat was standing near the thinnest of the AIDS patients, his hands high up in the forest of IV tubing. He squeezed the colored bags in turn, green white yellow, white yellow green, forcing the fluid in, as if searching for the right combination that would fill the gaps between skin and bone.

Dr. Stark grunted from the other side of the room as he attempted to relocate the shoulder of a man in slot ten. Nurse Crupp braced against the stretcher's far side, holding a sling wrapped around the man's chest while the doctor pulled his arm down and away.

"I can't dance with the devil like I used to," the man said. His red hair was singed, his red face boiling and full of steaming scars. "But I can't help it. I see him standing all alone there in the corner, I gotta ask."

"Hold him tight, Nurse Crupp," Stark said. He crouched low and leaned back, pulling the arm until his face turned as red as the man's, his eyes pulsed. "Come on, come on." He made a series of primitive noises, followed by an extraordinarily loud fart.

The man screamed, "That's it, she's in. Where do I sign?"

Mary Burke screamed too. I pulled open the curtain to find her kneeling on the floor. "He squeezed my hand. I told him I loved him and I said if he loves me to squeeze."

Dr. Hazmat came over, followed by Milagros. Mary yelled once more. "He did it again. He did it again," bringing Stark, Crupp, and the relocated shoulder to her father's side. "He's moving, Doctor. He grabbed my hand." Milagros examined Burke's feet, while Hazmat held his other hand.

"Move your hand, Dad. Come on, one more time," she said, and cried out again. "See, see."

"I'll be damned," said Hazmat. He checked Burke's

pupils. "Let's get another blood gas. It's movement, all right, but I'm not sure how voluntary."

"He hears me," said Mary. "How many times do I have to show you?" She turned to her father. "Open your eyes, Dad."

Patrick Burke's eyes, which had never really been closed, opened wide and shifted away from his daughter to the far right corners of his sight. Then the lower lids and cheeks shook, and the lips, as if talking some strange language, began to smack against the tube shoved between them. The head turned to the side, following the eyes, and the entire body was quaking tightly, back arched, arms yanking at the restraints, reaching up as if to pull out the wires and tubes. Green lights traced wildly across the EKG screen, then the alarms sounded, first the cardiac monitor and next the ventilator.

"He's dancing with the devil," the shoulder patient yelled, and started his own dance.

"Nurse Crupp, I need ten milligrams of Valium."

Both doctors held down Burke's arms, while his daughter stood behind them, dazed and tilted as if she'd nearly fallen from a train. Gently I put my hand on her elbow and guided her to the hall. "Why don't we go outside for a little while, wait there until this passes."

She took two steps sideways for every one forward, and at the door to the waiting room she leaned against the wall. "Why is he fighting like that?"

"He's wants to pull that tube out. It's pretty painful – that's why they'll keep him sedated – but it's a good sign for him."

"You sure? I know my father would hate to be tied down. He wouldn't even go to the dentist."

"That's how it's done, though. You have to keep the body going until the brain and the heart recover enough to go on their own." The door was open, but she wouldn't go through. I pulled on her arm, harder, so that my hand slid down and grasped hers, and then she went through easily. We reached the first row of seats and I helped her sit down, but she still held my hand, would not let go. I stood for a moment, not really minding that she was holding my hand, yet knowing how ridiculous it looked with me standing, and so I sat next to her but on the wrong side and we had to stretch our arms across each other and still she would not let go. I liked the clean slippery feeling rising up my arm to my chin, though I knew my hand wasn't really important to her – it was more like a ship's rail in a storm, or a glass of wine at a doomed wedding. "He's better though, right?"

"He's better."

She finished with my hand and dropped it. "Look, I'm sorry, but it's very important to me that he makes it. I mean, it's very important because just a week ago I was wishing he was dead. And now I want to hear his voice again, just once more – you know what I mean?"

"Sure," I said, though his voice was the last thing I wanted to hear.

I persuaded Marcus to drive over to Sal's Pizza, though I had to listen to him sing "My Way" three times; and then, in the pizza place, Sal shouting out, "Hey, look, it's the guy that brought me back to life." I tried vainly to dodge his bear hugs. I'd stopped going to Sal's because of that and had to keep telling myself it was worth it, the only pizza place open, thinking only of Mary and me sharing a pie. What prices we pay, having to listen to Marcus complain about the price of pizza and what ring of hell the Lord sends those who charge over a dollar a slice – Sal responding that he was going to heaven, not hell, telling me how he knew this, the whole story: the chest pain, the white light, the space shuttle rising. I lowered my head to my arms and closed my eyes, blocking out their voices, and finding the other voice.

Don't turn from me now. I know what you're doing.

"It's ready," Sal said, and I paid for the pie. "Here, take these, they're on me." He handed over two Cokes.

In the waiting room there was only Mary Burke and a trio of swollen feet. I sat one away from her and put the pizza box between us. "I'm not really hungry," she said, and then nearly bit my thumb as I handed her a slice. I held mine up, not eating, too busy watching her, a smooth-running pizza-eating machine, the perfect nose lowering, the soft angle of her fingers approaching, white teeth crashing down like a cannibal princess. I took a bite and handed her another slice.

She slowed a little while speaking. "My father was a great man, you know. There's nobody he wouldn't help. He took kids in from the street. He was always looking out for the neighborhood. You know that crazy guy Noël, who I gave the water to last night? He lived at our house for almost a year. A total stranger he'd do anything for. His own family, though . . . We were supposed to be perfect, and when we had problems it was like all of a sudden he forgot how to care, you know, like he just couldn't accept it. John got into drinking and I had some troubles with drugs, and then when my older brother, Pat, got killed outside a bar three years ago, my father moved into his chair and didn't get up. I mean, he's just retired and then his son gets killed – that was worse than anything. When my brother died, it was like *he* died, and then last night, when he grabbed his chest and locked the bathroom door, it was like he died again, and so I'm thinking maybe you gotta die a couple of times to come back, because when I'm next to him in there I feel that fight back in him, and something else too – what we had before all the problems started."

"It's probably best not to hope things'll be like before but to just hope for a new start. It's probably best not to hope too much at all, actually," I said, but she had that look, as Marcus would call it, and in her eyes I saw the reflection of my own look, and I wanted to hook those looks together, thinking our chances would be better to pull ourselves up or out or down, away, no past or future, just one long moment. I liked watching her eat and the Cokes were free. "It's good pizza, huh? There's nothing better than fresh-baked pizza at four in the morning."

"Not as good as Nino's."

"Do you remember that pizza place," I said, "Joe's, down on Tenth and Fifty-second, maybe fifteen years ago? When you ordered a pie it came with a little plastic madonna in the middle?"

"Yeah, or Saint Anthony. You from the neighborhood?"

"I grew up on Fifty-second. I went to Blessed Sacrament."

"Oh yeah. I went to Holy Name. Where'd you go to high school?"

"We moved out before that. Upstate."

"Like everybody else – right? – except us. Always standing on the sidewalk waving good-bye to the moving trucks. In the end, there was nobody left."

"I'm surprised we never met."

"Hey, Fifty-second Street was like upstate to us."

"You never played in Clinton Park?"

"Once in a while. That was like going on vacation. We mostly played in the Forty-fifth Street playground."

"We killed you guys in every sport invented."

"You wish."

She crossed her legs and uncrossed them and stretched them out and looked over at Griss like she was thinking she should go back inside. I wanted to be sitting in three seats at once, to watch her mouth, her knees, the back of her neck. She looked down at the pie and at me, and I handed her a slice dripping with cheese, which she gathered in her palm and deftly folded back over the crust. "Is it always this bad in here? I mean, how does anyone survive?"

"It's been bad lately, but it's always bad."

"How long you been doing this?"

"Five years."

"Wow, you must have seen some things, huh? So I gotta ask you – what's the worst thing you ever seen?"

"Lima beans on a pizza."

"God, that is bad."

"I don't like to talk about it."

"You must get a lot of overdoses. I bet you picked me up a couple of times."

"I think I'd remember that."

"Maybe not. I was a different person then. They told me I died once. One of you guys brought me back on the way to the hospital. That was a long time ago. I'm different now."

"It's what you do afterwards that counts." I looked out the doors, Burke's voice waiting for me in the parking lot. "And before it happens again."

She wiped her teeth with a napkin and stood. "Tell me something – does everyone you meet always spill their problems on you like this?"

"Everyone," I said. "It must be my face. My mother always said I looked like a priest."

"Right, tell me about it. My mother thought I was gonna be a nun because I ran away to a convent when I was thirteen. I didn't want to be a nun. I just wanted to run away. Always trying to escape. Sister Mary or Mary the junkie. Didn't matter to me." She looked over to Griss and back, her eyes on mine for the first time. "I better go check on my father. Thanks for the pizza. I owe you one. Maybe when he gets better, you know, when we're done with all this."

"Sure." I put my hand out, but she was already walking through the door. I gave the last slice to the guard. "Look after her, Griss. Okay?"

"You seem to be doing that all right."

"Look after me too, Griss. Okay?"

Tom Walls and I were once called for a woman in labor on Forty-second Street. The cops were already on the scene, and as we drove to the call we heard them on the police radio. "Rush the bus," they were saying, "rush the bus. The baby's coming out." Cops always become hysterical when a woman's about to deliver. I get the same way. When we arrived, however, the woman was sitting quietly on the sidewalk. She said the labor pains were still five minutes apart. The street was full of Forty-second Street crazies, so I placed a sheet on her. Tom wheeled up with the stretcher. I walked over to one of the four or five cops keeping the crowds back. "On the radio you guys sounded like she was about to deliver," I said. "She was," the cop said, "the baby was coming out. I saw its head. It looked around for a few seconds and then went back in." "You're kidding," I said, though I could tell from his face that he wasn't.

11

Marcus drove down Ninth at a walking pace, an old-man-with-a-cane walking pace, looking ahead as best he could, mumbling loudly. "Rule number one: Don't get involved with patients. Rule number two: Don't get involved with patients' daughters. You understand?"

"What about rule number three: Don't get involved with dispatchers?"

"You don't know the first thing about rule number three, cannot begin to understand the complexities of that rule. Come on, it's getting late: let's go look at the hookers."

Marcus made it easy to believe that cruising the streets looking at hookers was what we were paid to do. He answered the radio only when the mood struck him, which it rarely did. Don't touch the radio was rule number six, though Marcus said the numbers themselves were irrelevant and that rule number six was in fact the most important rule. He kept the radio behind his seat at the precise volume, he insisted, that he could hear and you could not. Only when Dispatcher Love came on the air did Marcus raise the volume above a mumble, and even then he would make her call a dozen times before answering, his favor to her. Three calls were his limit for the shift. He never did more than three.

According to Marcus, the best street hookers were to be found at Thirtieth and Park, hardworking and not too skinny. The most overpriced, who wore fur coats even in summer, at Sixth and Fifty-eighth. Crackheads on Forty-fifth, junkies around the corner on Eleventh. "Careful," said Marcus. "Don't ever call a junkie whore a crackhead; they get real mad." Transvestite junkies on Fourteenth, transvestite crackheads on Tenth, moonlighting housewives on Forty-eighth, preachers' daughters on Sixty-fifth, dog walkers on Fifth-third, and the raised from the dead on Forty-ninth, which is where he always began.

"Look at these women. You can't even tell who's a hooker anymore. What ever happened to go-go boots and short shorts? They wear anything now, walk out of the house with whatever they got on. And they don't even walk right, standing in the doorways like they lost their keys or something. Won't give you the eye either. Look at that girl there in the raincoat." He pointed down the street, though that wasn't necessary. I had been watching her since we turned the corner, the yellow raincoat, the black shoes. Who else? "Leaves you no idea what's underneath, not even a suggestion of what's there; could be a skeleton for all you know."

But I knew what was there, under the hood: Rose, in all her permutations. Appearing to show me how sick I still was, how cleanly I was being torn in two. I closed my eyes and tried to focus on Mary Burke, but her green eyes and sharp nose kept morphing into Rose. The problem was I couldn't remember exactly what Rose looked like, and so any young woman in a yellow coat automatically brought up the question, Is it her? I knew that if I could recall her features clearly, as painful as that would be, I could point out the differences one by one, but whenever I tried, a dozen pictures passed through, all of them different and all of them Rose, and I opened my eyes as Marcus drove by and watched her pull back the yellow hood, looking at me, stretches of sadness around her mouth. Then we passed.

"That's nice, though," Marcus said, "pulling back the hood like that as we drive by. There's a mystery to it, you know, you imagine all kinds of faces could be there, and then she shows you and so it's like half the face you wished for and half this other real fine thing."

"She's no whore, Marcus."

"We're all whores, Frank. But you know what I'm talking about, the way she looked at me."

"She wasn't looking at you, man, she was looking at me." Just because I was crazy didn't mean I was without rights. Rose may have been making my life miserable, but she was mine. I'd earned her.

"Take it easy there, Frank. A girl like that, you couldn't handle her."

But maybe I *could* handle her. If Marcus saw her and thought nothing of saying she was fine, then the problem was all in my head and could be controlled. A sickness. It would pass, the features would fade, as all the others had faded, Rose's grip over me failing as Mr. Burke walks out of the hospital with his wife by his side, his daughter waiting by the car, embracing him for the first time in years. And then a few weeks later I just happen to run into Mary Burke outside her apartment. She invites me to Sunday dinner at her father's, which has become tradition again and the whole family is there, John back together with his wife and kids, second cousins returning from Long Island. We toast miracles and miracle workers. I even tell them of the crazy voices I used to have in my head. Everyone laughs. We're all so much better now. I walk Mary Burke home, and on her front stoop I grab her by the waist and with my other hand pull her face close, kissing life. That's what miracles do: give us the time and space to forget we're condemned.

Unfortunately, the streets of Hell's Kitchen at four in the morning are neither the time nor the space for forgetting, are in fact the opposite of forgetting. Marcus drove in a widening circle, down Eleventh, then east on Forty-fourth, up Tenth, west on Forty-fifth, Eleventh, Forty-second, Tenth, and all around me I felt the widening gaps between want and need, desire and desperation. He drove so slowly I could hear the buildings sink, the sidewalks buckle. Men and women paced the corners like angels on fire. Yellow street-lamps flickered in my thumbs, Marcus's eye twitched double time, and in that hour of darkness, between the setting moon and the coming sun, many others were taking the time to fall apart. Dispatcher Love read out the list. "Fourteen Will, at 330 West Fifty-third, the Church of Jesus Son, for the demonic possession. Twelve Victor, you're going to Seventh Street and Third Avenue. On the corner there is a forty-year-old man hearing celebrity voices. Sixteen Xray, take it uptown to 521 West 135, apartment sixteen, for the elderly woman abducted by her cat."

"I have to go back to the hospital," I said. The sudden desperate need to see Mary Burke again, to talk and stretch our legs in the private shelter of our distress.

"I was headed for the Lap Club," Marcus said. "The dancers get off work at four-thirty."

"I really have to go, Marcus. I'm not kidding."

So Marcus shrugged and tilted his head a few times, like he respected the urgency in my voice, and slowly he drove up Tenth toward the hospital and then turned suddenly and without signaling, right on Fiftieth, toward the Lap Club, where the women leave work wearing little more than their socks and their ten-gallon pocketbooks and sometimes stop and wave at Marcus before getting into their taxis. Halfway up the block he was forced to a stop where an ambulance was parked, a cop car behind it. Around us empty garbage cans lay in the street like accident victims, their contents torn and exploded across the pavement. Marcus tried to reverse, but another police car had pulled up behind us. Two cops got out and ran past us with their guns drawn. They disappeared in front of the parked ambulance.

"Man, this is bad luck."

"You should have stayed on Tenth."

"But the girls are just getting out now. It takes ten minutes," he said. We waited and listened to the shouting from ahead – You got him You got him I got him – followed by a scream, as from a man being beaten with his own recently amputated limbs. Above the din I recognized Tom Walls' voice: Let me in there. Hold him down. The howling stopped, and the cops appeared at the side of the ambulance, followed by Walls pulling a stretcher on which lay a tied and beaten Noël. As they put him into the back of the bus I saw Noël's eyes open. The screaming again. Tom jumped into the back and pulled a sheet over the cries and punched into it. Then he closed the doors and ran around to the front and I heard the engine revving and the bus was around the corner.

By the time we reached the Lap Club the neon was off, the shutters were down, and the girls were on their way home or wherever they go. Marcus raised his hands and shook his head as if his best friends had just left him with the bill.

"I thought we were going to the hospital," I said, knowing how useless it was to tell Marcus where to go. He drove down to Forty-sixth and parked next to the paved island where Broadway met Seventh, the center of Times Square, nearly deserted now, the billboard faces looking fat and old without their lights. Marcus left to get coffee, and I closed one eye and with the other watched the signs switch off – the garage-size whiskey bottle quit tilting over the glass, the thirty-foot coffee mug spit out one last cloud of steam and freeze. In the accelerating darkness the voice returned – *I get nothing but lip service from you* – sounding both far away and very close, like an enraged subway conductor, the speaker in my head. *Just answer me one question.* My hands over my ears. *Why?* I took a deep breath and held it until everything spun around the hard darkened center of where I sat. I breathed out, and in the empty space, another voice, a dead girl's, another question: Why did you kill me, Frank?

"I didn't kill you."

"No, you didn't," Marcus said, "and thank you, Frank." He handed me a cup of coffee. "Though there's still a couple of hours left in the shift."

"Marcus, tell me something: how long have you been doing this job?"

"You were probably holding your mother's hand crossing the street the night I went on my first call."

"And in all that time you must have had your share of bad calls. You've told me some of them, you know, where you make a mistake or you think you made a mistake or maybe you did nothing wrong and still this terrible thing happens to someone and it really bothers you in a way that other calls, worse calls even, don't."

"I don't know what you mean. I can't remember anything like that happening."

"Right. Bullshit. You know what I'm talking about. The call you keep going over and over. It follows you around, faces on the street, in other people, voices in your head."

"And what do these voices tell you, Frank?"

"They say, 'Kill Marcus,' all right? I don't need shock treatment, I'm not that sick, just going through a rough time. You must have gone through some rough times; doesn't mean you're crazy. It's something you've got to go through every once in a while – am I right?"

"It doesn't mean you're crazy, Frank, no." Marcus raised one finger under his nose as he studied me with his good eye. "But it does mean you are fast beating a path to the bughouse. I want to tell you a story."

"I need a drink, that's all, and about sixteen hours of sleep. Let's open the bar." I reached for the bag behind Marcus's seat, but he grabbed my hand.

"One I've only told to Love and about fifty other partners I've worked with over the last ten years. When I was in the end of my running-around days, about as much time in as you got now, I was assigned a call for a forty-eight-year-old male diff breather, and it was late, I was tired, got the address wrong, I think it was Forty-eight and Eleven and I was at Forty-eight and Seven, whatever, you know how it goes. So I'm sitting there saying there's no patient here, and then Love gets on and tells me, in her special way, I'm on the wrong block, and when I get to the right address the guy had just stopped breathing. Who knows if I would have saved him or not, but I couldn't stop thinking about it. You see, my father died when he was forty-eight. I didn't know him then, hadn't seen him since I was twelve and only knew his face from pictures mostly of when he was young, and so this guy, well, it could have looked like him, it was him in a way, at least in my mind it wasn't hard to make it him. I'd drive back to the corner every night and after work, wondering how I made this mistake. I kept thinking about it, and sure enough, after that I started getting these forty-eight-year-old male diff breathers like once a week, and the weird thing is they all look like the guy who died, who I believed looked like my father. I'd hear his voice sometimes. I'd see him walking down the street out of the corner of my eye, you know, it was really freaky. For a couple of months it lasted, all because at four in the morning I got an address wrong, because I took a little too long to get to a call."

"But, Marcus, you go slow to every call."

"Now I do, sure. That's my way of dealing with it. Everyone's gotta find their own way of dealing, otherwise you become a son of a bitch like Luther or you go crazy like where I been before and where you're headed, Frank. What happens to others is God's will, nothing to be done about it. My father was going to leave me when I was twelve and come up here to die on Forty-eighth Street just before I could save him, so I could never have saved him. Love knows this, she understands, and if you come to understand, man, you can do this job forever."

Marcus talked on about the subtle differences between God's will and his own, how in tune they were, separate yet one. He used a number of analogies – football, prison, television game shows. I rested my head on the window frame and looked out on the near-empty streets, the crowds from earlier now sleeping in their hotel rooms, their cardboard boxes by the river. When the last billboard went dark, the hot dog sellers pulled down their umbrellas and packed up their sodas and buns. The blind man who worked the corner of Forty-sixth took off his black glasses and stood and folded his wheelchair. He put his cup in his bag and walked to the curb and hailed a cab. The crippled man who spent every night dragging his twisted foot and empty cup from driver to driver down Broadway's center lane had given up on the few taxis still running and was now running himself, limplessly full stride down the sidewalk, chasing one of the crack dealers from Eighth. The Reverend Scythe, who preached against all forms of vice from his sidewalk church on Forty-second, had closed up for the day and was sitting on the curb with a pint bottle of Early Times, drinking to the miracles of Easter morning in the Square, where the blind see, the crippled walk, and all Jesus can do is sit back and watch. God's will made no more sense to me here than Burke's voice did in my head, which was only right, I guess, since the voice could only be His will. I wasn't crazy, I was blessed.

I oughta tear this house down and jump on its bones.

"Are you listening to anything I'm saying, Frank? Can you hear?"

"I hear, Marcus. I hear Dispatcher Love. She's calling us."

He pulled the radio out from behind the seat. "Twelve Young, answer the radio. Twelve Young, I've got one for you." The warden's voice in an all-girls prison film.

Marcus turned up the volume and rested the radio religiously on his lap. "She's not calling us; she's calling me. Remember that. Even when she's talking to other units, she's talking to me. She told me that once. I used to call her on the phone when she went on break. She's a lot different when she's on the phone and not giving out calls. She said to me, Marcus, I love the way you talk on the radio."

"I can't wait all night, Young. I'm holding priority calls. I'm going to knock you out of service if you don't answer me now, and you know I'm not kidding."

Marcus keyed the radio. "Don't you worry, hon. Young is here and he's gonna help you out. Just remember you owe Marcus one when this is all over."

"I'm holding the bottle right now, Young. I'll cash it in whenever you're ready. You're going to 508 Ninth Avenue, cross of Thirty-eighth Street, for the eighteen-year-old female cardiac arrest on the fifth floor, no further information."

"Ten-four, Love."

Marcus carefully pulled the bus out into the empty lanes of Seventh Avenue and I held myself tight, rocking back and forth. "Every call is a cardiac arrest," I yelled. "What ever happened to chest pain, trouble breathing, a fractured leg?"

Marcus turned on the lights and sirens and slowed down. "It's the nine one one operators. They're afraid they'll get fired if they call it a fractured leg and the guy winds up in cardiac arrest, so they just make everything a cardiac arrest. It's simpler that way."

"But why is it always an eighteen-year-old female in a yellow raincoat who's died a dozen times already? What the hell is that?"

"That shit runs in cycles. You can't do anything about it," he said, and stopped at a red light. He hit the horn three times and started forward, stopping when he saw a car approaching from halfway down the block.

We pulled up in front of 508, a building that could have been condemned the day they laid the first brick. Half the windows were boarded shut, the others lightless, broken, empty, except for one yellow bulb hung from a wire in the top right apartment, always at the top. "I hate this block," Marcus said. "It's all junkies. I ain't goin in there without the cops."

"Well, I'm going. It's easier than waiting. Better to get it over with. It's what we do."

"Then you do it alone."

Though I knew it wouldn't make any difference, I strapped on all the equipment, thirty pounds over each shoulder. The front door was half open and I kicked it the rest of the way, steel ringing against stone. "EMS, ambulance," I shouted, to give those inside plenty of time to load their guns, sharpen knives. Into the black hall I stumbled forward, feeling for the stairs with my feet. Under the weight of the useless equipment and the impenetrable darkness, I searched for matches, one empty pocket after another, until, giving up and steeling myself to go blindly up, I heard a scratching above me, then the scrape of a match on the wall, a candle being lit, a tan face turning toward me. "It's my wife," the man said. He didn't look more than fifteen. "Please hurry."

I followed him up the stairs, and near the top of the first flight he lowered the candle to show me the two missing steps. Then he grabbed my hand and helped me over. On the second-floor landing, plastic vials crunched under my boots, their painted red skulls twisting in the candle's light. "Wait right there, Frank," came a voice below. The man shone the candle on Marcus, slowly making his way up. I pointed to the gap in his way. "You leave me down there, and then you want me to kill myself on these stairs," he said. "Is that the way a partner acts, just forgets the oldest rule, number five, partners before patients? Help me." I grabbed one arm, the boy took the other, we pulled, shadows convulsing on the walls, a scratching biting bloody struggle to get him over and up. "This is how medics get killed and lose their pension," he said.

"Please hurry," the boy said, already on the next flight.

"What's wrong?"

"It's my wife. She's dying."

"I didn't know she was married," I said, still sure it was Rose waiting for me at the top. I followed the candle to the third floor, Marcus telling us to slow down, the ache in me made worse by the waiting. Three steps missing on the fourth flight, two jagged window-size holes in the ceiling. I climbed over the gaps, thinking Rose must be having it tough, living in a dump like this. Her life was hard enough now, dead and dying over and over – what a rough time the dead have of it. Then, while helping Marcus, I thought of how I had to control my thinking. The guy probably told the operator his wife was Rose, and they naturally made it a cardiac arrest. I walked toward the dim light at the end of the hall, thinking this was our third call and our last. All I had to do was get through it, and then Marcus and I could get an early start on the drinking.

On a mattress on the floor in the middle of a room whose only other furniture was a box of dirty coats and a crucifix, there lay a giant of a girl covered in stained sheets, a great heap of hyperventilating linen. Only her hands showing, big and white, holding her middle as she cried out in Spanish. I moved in closer and grabbed her wrist with one hand and pulled the sheets away from her face with the other and lowered my head, because no matter how desperate and demented I became on the subject, there was no way I could ever think this was Rose. She was just too big.

"Look at that," Marcus said. "A fat junkie. That's a first."

"What's wrong?" I said to the girl, who looked younger than her husband, and more afraid than hurt.

"No English," the candle holder said. "She has a terrible pain in her belly. She says it's very swollen, big." He looked like an altar boy at a stock car race.

I placed my hand on the girl's stomach, and she screamed and pushed it away. "She's pregnant," I said.

"No, no. That's impossible." The boy shook his candle.

"Are you pregnant?" I asked the girl. "Está embarazada?" She turned her head away, embarrassed, and I had to say it twice more before she finally looked at me and shook her head as if I'd asked her if she'd kissed the devil recently or was running a brothel. She pulled the sheet back over her face.

"A fat blushing junkie," Marcus said. "I don't believe it." He moved over to her other arm and took her blood pressure. The husband grabbed my shoulder. "No, man, we don't do drugs, and no sex, no alcohol, no cigarettes, no TV or radio, no underwear. We are very devout."

"Well, the vitals are good," Marcus said. "She ain't bleeding out. Lungs are clear, ain't no fluid overload. Appendix? Kidney stones? Myself, I think she's got gas."

"She's pregnant."

"You tell her."

There were no chairs, no table or dresser, one window, no curtain, and the one corner where I thought I might sit for a while and think the case over – think, actually, about Mary Burke – looked like a roach park. To carry the girl down the stairs was unthinkable, and, I was sure, inevitable. The only adornment to the room was on the ceiling, a water stain that resembled a prison barge. "Can you walk?" I asked. "Puede caminar?"

The girl cried out and swung for my face with her open hand. "She says she's in great pain," the husband said.

"Thanks for the translation." I held her hands to keep her

from hitting me, and without hesitating, I pulled the sheets off one by one. "I have to see," I said. "You've got to let me." Beneath everything was a white dress. I pulled it up to reveal the belly, swollen taut.

"She's pregnant," I said. "Full term from the looks of it." The woman screamed again and grabbed her stomach. "We have to look," I said, and Marcus and I each grabbed a knee and slowly pulled her legs apart. She howled as if she were being sawed in half, and then she raised herself up to look between her legs and we all looked then and under the meager light of the yellow bulb a tiny white foot appeared, followed by a knee, a baby thigh.

"Oh Jesus, we better go."

"I'll go," said Marcus from the hallway. "I'll get the longboard and call for a backup. I'll get the fire department and the army. Don't worry."

The girl was beating on her husband now, hitting him pretty good to the face and arms, some low blows. I took a sterile sheet out of the bag and wrapped it under her and the baby's foot, which was bent down at the ankle like it was checking the air with its toe to see if it was okay to come out. I kept expecting it to be pulled back, never to be seen again, but rather than go back in, another leg joined it, the two now suspended over the world. "All right, then, let's do it," I yelled. "Come on, push. Push it out." She pushed and screamed and pushed and swung at us and screamed and tried to reach down to pull the two legs out herself. "Hold her," I said to the boy. "I think it's coming." The two of us pinned her shoulders to the floor as Marcus walked in, dropped the board, and fell down exhausted behind us. She let out a scream that will be with me always, and together we all stared at the place where there once were two legs and now were three. That's when she started to get upset.

"What's that, Frank?"

"Three legs now."

"That's too many."

"What about the backup?"

"Love said she wanted to help me, that the first unit to come available . . ."

We laid a sheet on the board and carefully rolled the girl on it and strapped her down properly. She lay there half dazed like she'd just delivered a litter of babies, though she was no skinnier for her work and no lighter, and Marcus and I almost lost her twice on the first flight. We put her down in the darkness of the fourth floor, her husband holding the candle over her face, asking me, "Is she dying?"

"She's going to have a baby."

"That's impossible."

"You can trust me on this one."

She started screaming again on the third flight, more holes than stairs, and halfway down she was able to free one arm and swing it wildly against Marcus, who was screaming also. "We have to put her down, down, now." The girl used her free arm to pitch herself forward and grab the tiny protruding legs, and as we reached the second floor the strap broke and all of us went down. My head lay somewhere beside her knee, and when the husband raised his candle, I noticed that a fourth leg had come out to be with the other three, and that the girl had decided that four was too much. She grabbed two legs with each hand and worked them back and forth, down and up, like she was forcing water from a pump. Marcus and I tried to break her grip, but she pulled so willfully, cried so powerfully, that the two of us gave up and bowed beside her as if in prayer. She screamed once more, her most impressive howl yet, which echoed across the island and returned to blow out the candle.

In the blackness I heard voices behind; a door opened and closed, and at the end of the hall three dots of light appeared and floated toward us. I bowed down again and when I raised my head the lights were above me, three thin flames from cigarette lighters held by two skinny men and an old woman. One of the men bent down and poured water from a bottle into the girl's mouth. She spit a little out, then swallowed and groaned and asked for more. I crawled around to her mid-section and peered over the expanse of her thigh, and in the space where the four legs used to be there now lay two infants, a boy and a girl, ridiculously small.

I lifted the tiny girl as far as the umbilical cord could stretch. I shook her twice, and when nothing happened I rapped on her feet and cheek. Oh God, I said, and with my shirttail wiped the goo from the baby's mouth and bent over and covered the mouth and nose with my mouth and began to blow, light quick puffs, mouse puffs. I looked across the girl to Marcus, who was doing the same to the other baby. For half a minute I breathed like that, until I felt myself start to pass out and had to stop. The tiny girl was breathing now, but so shallow and slowly you could hardly know it. Then Marcus laughed, and I looked up at the little boy wriggling in his arms, swinging at him; he let out a ferocious little scream that should have made his mother proud.

"How's yours doing?" Marcus asked.

"She's breathing," I said, "but not by much."

"Let's cut the cords and go. You better use your shoe-laces." I wiped my laces with alcohol pads and tied the cords. I did my best to sterilize my medic shears before cutting. Marcus gave the boy to his mother, who wrapped her thick arms around it. Her husband put down his candle and spread his arms around the two. "It's a miracle," he kept saying.

"You two known each other a long time?" Marcus asked.

"Two years," the father said. "Ever since we left the island together."

"This is a personal question, but I have to ask it. In all that time, you never had sex?"

"Never."

"Maybe you had a couple a beers one night last summer. You know it happens."

"Never. No drugs, no cigarettes, no beers."

"No underwear."

"We are virgins."

"Okay."

The baby's mother, who was little more than a baby herself, held the boy tight to her neck and face, smiling and making soft humming sounds. I tried to show her the baby girl, brought the infant close to the mother's face, but she did not look up, and when I pulled away I saw my little baby girl had stopped breathing again. "We'd better go now, Marcus; can't wait here for any more to come."

Without speaking, the two men who had been standing over us with their lighters reached low and with one hand each lifted up the longboard and carried the now smaller but still quite sizable mother down the broken stairs. The last of the flame carriers, the skinny old woman who, I realized, was probably my age, held her light over me as I made my way, step by step, little puffs of air into the baby's mouth, to the street, to the bus, my laceless shoes flapping noisily. I placed her on the bench seat, my ear down next to her soft blue nose to listen to the little bubbles of air rising from the bottom of a stream. I left her there and grabbed the longboard from one of the junkies and lifted it onto the stretcher in the back. The mother was calling for her baby now, and Marcus placed the newborn boy on her stomach and helped the husband up to the seat near her head. "It's a miracle," the boy kept saying as we made the turn onto Thirty-seventh.

The mother held her son so tight I was afraid she'd suffocate him, but the baby cried as if all the air in the bus was his and his alone. The mother cried too, softly now, the two of them shivering. I wrapped them both in blankets and when I turned back to wrap my baby girl I noticed she had stopped breathing. Again I breathed for her, and after half a minute she was holding her own, better than before, so much better that, for a moment, I thought she might let out a cry like her brother. I slid a sheet around her, carefully tucking it in under her legs, not too tight around the arms. I lifted her up next to the mother, wanting her to see how the girl was breathing better now, but she turned away to face her son, almost as if to protect him, like it was a storm cloud I held. I put the infant back on the bench seat and closely watched her straining chest, the gray inching back across her

face. This is not their baby, I thought. This is Rose's baby, or
Rose as a baby – the reason I was called.

Before Marcus had finished backing in, I was through the
ER doors, the baby cradled in my elbow like a football. I
gave her two breaths while running across the waiting room,
one more waiting for Griss the guard to open one eye and
shake his head before punching the buzzer. "She stopped
breathing," I said to Nurse Constance, who came over and
pried the baby from my arms to lay her on the white-sheeted
stretcher. She felt the arm, then the neck. "She had a pulse,"
I said. Nurse Constance rushed the stretcher into the
treatment room, crying, "*Code*, Code Blue," nearly running
over Nurse Crupp, who managed to push the overdose out
of slot one just in time.

"Oh Jesus," Hazmat said. "Let's put her on the monitor.
Where the hell is the pediatric code cart?" he yelled, though
Odette the orderly had already pushed the cart into his back
and was pulling out the baby-size laryngoscope, a breathing
tube no wider than antenna wire. "Look out, Odette. Give
me that tube. All right, flatline – let's do some CPR here.
Frank, how many months?"

"Can't tell," I said. "The mother didn't know she was
pregnant until about fifteen minutes ago. It was a breech,
twins. The other one seems okay though. Marcus is taking
him and the mother to Maternity." I was walking backward
as I spoke. More hospital workers filled the space I left:
Mishra the pediatrician, Stark the surgeon. I watched
Hazmat get the tube in, then push epinephrine through

it. Dr. Mishra took an osteocatheter out of the cart and forced it into the baby's shin, pushing hard to break through the bone and into the marrow. When she was able to draw blood back with a syringe, she hooked up the IV tubing, more epinephrine. Nurse Constance used two fingers on the chest, up and down; half an inch was all you needed. She stopped for a second and felt the baby's neck. "I think there's a pulse," she said, but the flat green line over her head said something else. It never pretended to be anything it couldn't. She placed two fingers on the chest, up and down.

Hell is here. Hell is right now.

I walked over to Burke's slot and pulled back the curtain. There he was, the voice that wouldn't die, the patient who never left. Quiet now, no movement, no shaking hands. The long night of getting better had worn him out, left him back where he started. Up on the monitor, the green lines seemed to be at war with each other, a series of normal beats marching against wild-looking rebel rhythms, the heart working hard and not getting much done, the face returning to the night-sidewalk blue of when we first met. Only the voice in my head showed no sign of failing. *Go to the bank, boy, and take out everything you can.* I stared at the EKG, at Burke's heart losing the battle, the green line a series of low bumps followed by bursts of loud spikes. I felt the wrist for a pulse; nothing. I turned up the amplitude of the EKG, the lines above more a measure of the voice in my head than of the blood in his face. The sound swelling and ebbing on the screen, pulsing. *I'm going. I've had enough.* The heart had lost and shook with its surrender, a thin quaking line. The alarms started, EKG hollering first, followed quickly by the bells of the oxygen saturation monitor, then the low drone of the ventilator.

The curtain opened behind me. Milagros stepped in. She looked at the monitors and shut off the alarms and felt for a pulse at Burke's wrist and turned the hand over to study the palm. She shook her head and lifted the defibrillator paddles from their pockets next to the EKG. She raised them up, to hand them to me.

"Ah, no." I stepped back. "You do it."

"I can't reach. Can't get good pressure. You're taller."

Don't do it, Burke said, and I should have walked out then, walked straight to Captain Ed and told him I was leaving. "I thought he was getting better."

"It's okay," Milagros said. "He is better. He was trying to talk before. Shock him. He'll come back. He always comes back."

I grabbed the paddles and placed them on his chest with all the weight I could bear and yelled, "Clear," like you're supposed to, even though Milagros was standing well away. What I forgot to do was look down to make sure nothing was touching the person I was buzzing, because if I had looked, I would have seen Burke's hand against my side, and when I shocked him at full power, the world wouldn't have gone black and thrown me back three feet off the rail. It felt like someone hit me in the chest with a baseball bat. *Ow,* I cried out with Burke's voice in my head. *You son of a bitch.* The beats on the monitor returned to formation. Milagros matched them with the beats at Burke's wrist. With her other hand she reached up to one of the five IV lines leading into that arm. "Should I increase the lidocaine?" she asked, but I was stepping backward, my head down, hands rubbing vainly at the pain in my chest, the curtain that separated the units rising up my back and over my head, falling in front of me. Suddenly Burke's voice was gone, replaced with another familiar sound, not in my head but behind me. "Excuse me, sir, excuse me, I would please trouble you for one cup of water. The smallest thing in the world to ask for, water. A man is dying, and that is me."

His hands tied and rattling against the rails, eyes racing left and right and back again, nose swollen from Walls' punches, dried blood on the lips now chapped and split, as if he actually were lying in the desert and not in a stretcher next to Patrick Burke's. "For days I've eaten nothing but sand. O Lord, I have waited for you so long." Then Noël, dry as he was, began to howl.

"Jesus," came Hazmat's voice from the other side of the room. "Who the hell woke him up?"

I was once called to the Plaza Hotel for an ambassador from a very small oil-rich country. He complained of crushing chest pain. I told him we'd take him to Our Lady of Mercy. Is it a good hospital? he asked, a question I preferred not to answer. I gave him some nitroglycerin and morphine, which eased the pain some, and we took him in and slid him into slot one in the treatment room and hooked him up to Misery's machines. I noticed then that the curtain between slot one and slot two was open and that on the stretcher in slot two was a cardiac arrest I had brought in hours before, who had been pronounced dead and was waiting to be bagged and taken down to the morgue. I noticed, too, that the dead man bore a striking resemblance to the ambassador. The ambassador observed this also. "Is it me?" he cried. "Is it me?" That question, as well, I preferred not to answer.

12

"Don't give me that look," I said.

"What look?" Marcus pulled to a stop under a green light, morning traffic flying past us. Patiently I waited for the thud from one of the newspaper trucks striking us from behind, ten tons of newsprint, then darkness.

"You know what I'm talking about," I said. "It's all over your face. The I-just-saved-the-little-baby-boy look. I don't want to hear about it. Okay? That's three jobs for the night; it's over."

"That's right, Frank, but let me tell you something. When you hold a dying child like that in your arms and you breathe life back into him, your life into his – "

"I don't care about that. Three jobs and it's time for a drink. Six o'clock. The cocktail hour. Pass the bottle, Marcus; I know you're holding." I reached behind his seat and pulled out the brown-and-green gym bag he must have bought in '76.

"Here, here." He grabbed the bag. "I'll do this." He removed a pint bottle of vodka, a jar of orange juice, and two brown-and-green coffee cups, which came with the bag and could not be thrown away, as they were ceremonial. "The bar is now open."

"I don't need anything except this." I grabbed the bottle

and unscrewed the top and poured in as much as I could stand. "I hate vodka."

"Take it easy, Frank. The cocktail hour. A little decorum, if you will."

Time has already happened. Time is over. I took another drink, the vodka doing its work. Burke's shouting had moved from the back of my head to somewhere in my left cheek, no more annoying than the taxis' horns on Ninth Avenue, the new day belching over midtown. Marcus grabbed the bottle and poured into the ravaged cups. I put up my hands to block the growing light.

"What I'm saying, Frank, is that I'm holding that little baby, I'm breathing my life into his, and then I watch as that child comes alive because of me, in my arms. I feel like I'm twenty-one again, like when I was holding my son for the first time. That's right, you didn't know that, but I got a kid, must be fifteen by now. Looks just like me, so I've heard." He raised his cup. "Here's to the greatest job in the world."

I lived for something and died for nothing.

Burke's voice was barely a whisper, and Marcus's eyes had stopped twitching, and the sun was definitely up, bumping its way across town. This day wouldn't kill me, no more than any other. "To the greatest job in the world." I finished in two gulps. "I'm ready for another."

Marcus poured, left to right, vodka and juice, his brown hands steadier by the minute. "A call like this makes me think maybe I'll take a trip out west, see my son again. Maybe even go back to working three nights a week instead of two. Start running again, cut down on the drinking."

"I'll drink to that." We smudged our cups together over

our heads and poured the juice into our mouths. Marcus said something that sounded like Hebrew and fell back into the seat, instantly losing ten years from his face. Though his features couldn't have been more different from mine, the look in his eyes was my own, born under the same blue song. "You're just like me, Marcus. I'm going to be just like you."

"Well don't look so down when you say it, man. You should be happy. We make a hell of a team, Frank. Here, let's have another." I held out my cup, he held up the empty bottle, then dropped it on the floor. "You hear that?" He was smiling. "It's Love, man. She's calling me." He put the radio on the dash and turned up the volume like it was playing his favorite tune.

"Twelve Young, I have priorities holding, sick people all over the city. I'm putting you out on your ear if you don't pick up that radio. I swear I'll never call you again."

"Don't do it, Marcus. That's three jobs. We're through. Tell her the bus died, our radio's not working, our backs are out. Tell her we're too drunk to do any more calls."

"No, Frank. She wouldn't call if she didn't need me. You don't know her." Marcus sat up in the seat and set his chin. He keyed the radio. "It's Marcus, Love. Only for you."

"Twelve Young, you're going to Forty-eight and Eleventh Avenue for the forty-eight-year-old male with difficulty breathing. Okay, units, let's update those signals."

"It's him. It's him," Marcus said. I put on my seat belt. There was no hope. There was only hope. Marcus placed both hands on the wheel to keep them from shaking. The effect was to double the twitching in his neck, his eyes blinking hysterically; they might as well have been closed.

He struck the first car on Ninth, a double-parked van. He backed up and started off again, gas pedal pressed to the floor, weaving wildly, losing both mirrors in the tight quarters of Forty-ninth Street. I went through a list of best possible crash positions, head down or head up, hands on the dash or on my head. Marcus was screaming, "I'm coming, I'm coming." When he took his third red light without looking, I decided the proper thing to do was cover my eyes and scream.

Now you're gonna get it.

I've been in my share of ambulance wrecks, and they're all basically the same: the scream just before impact (when you see it coming), the grunt of air rushing out, the neck twisting in a way it's never twisted before, head striking dash, mirror, glass, followed by the rest of the body, jealously imitating the head, each part striking out on its own, hitting whatever it can before retreating home. The moment after is painless and infinite, and within it there is an almost mystical clarity, the kind of world-sealing feeling many spend their lives searching for. If you could plan for this, you would make your most important decisions there – career, marriage, children. I've come out of every such moment with the same overriding thought: I quit; that's it.

"We're here," Marcus said. Only my left eye would open and only slightly. It provided a detailed view of what, after some thought, I called the street, one square inch of pavement one inch away. The other eye was held closed by a very heavy soft object, which also pinned my arms and legs, everything except for three toes of my right foot. It spoke to me. "Where is he, Frank? Do you see him?"

"Get off me, Marcus."

He was laughing, his whole body shaking with it, or crying – I couldn't tell – but he moved enough to free my right arm and leg, and I reached for the center rearview mirror, whose only function in an ambulance is to pull yourself up when it's flipped on its side. I climbed, stepping over Marcus's head and the steering wheel, raising myself through the driver's-side window like a tank commander. The bus rested quietly in the center of Eleventh Avenue at Forty-eighth, a block of empty sidewalks, shuttered car dealerships, the long-deserted Eagle Piano Company. Commuters from the tunnel slowed as they passed, studying the ambulance undercarriage as if it reminded them of something they forgot at home and considered returning for, just a moment, before hurrying on. "I don't see anybody," I said, and sat on the door. Marcus's head appeared at my elbow. "He's here, Frank. He's here."

"I know," I said. "That's why I quit. I'm through." I jumped to the street, sirens coming from the west.

"You can't leave me now," he said, but I was already walking east, flapping my elbows like wings in the warm sun.

Soon after Mona started working in the theater, and before the worst of my patients had caught up with me, Mona and I were married for the second time, by a Second Avenue bartender who claimed to have studied for the priesthood. For four straight weeks our lovemaking opened and closed each day. Nighttimes the bed was hers and by day it was mine, and every morning I left work to climb into her warmth and in the late evenings she left her job to climb atop mine. We kept so strict a schedule, I began to believe that the city couldn't work without us, as important as the power lines and water mains. If we missed one of our appointments, some calamity would strike. Then one morning I was too tired and bloody to do it and nothing terrible happened and that was the greatest calamity of all.

13

My mother had trouble adjusting to my father's leaving. The first three months she wore the same sad yellow robe and spent her days on the frayed recliner watching game shows and soap operas, getting up during commercials to walk around the house, moving furniture into the center of rooms, sometimes forgetting to move it back.

She slept in the den, where she stayed up late reading medical texts, searching for the name of the illness that had become her life. That first summer she convinced herself she was going blind. She wore sunglasses even at night. Dr. Bruce, her optometrist, assured her everything was normal. She insisted on more tests, made appointments once a week. "My eyes are killing me today," she'd say. "I better go see Bruce." He owned a royal-blue Century, and afternoons they'd drive to Mount Gary and park behind the charred pilings that used to be LaMonica's. I heard about it from our dentist, a friend of my father's, during a break from drilling. LaMoaningcars, he called it.

Bruce came for dinner, and pretty soon we were sharing breakfast. The thick glasses he wore made his eyes seem twice their size, and I could not look at them. Every morning over cereal he would tell me about Jesus. His sentences usually began with, Before I found Jesus, or, After I was saved. I was blind, he liked to say, now I can see. They were married in the church on State Street and spent their honeymoon with an encounter group in Pennsylvania. He bought her a new Buick, its bumper covered with news of Christ's resurrection.

On Tuesday nights Bruce directed AA meetings in the church basement, and on weekends he volunteered to rake the cemetery or paint a classroom. My mother practiced for the choir while tending herbs in the church garden. She'd be out weeding even in the worst storm, crouched in the mint, singing. The priest came to our house once a week for dinner, said a short prayer for each vegetable. He baked bread in our oven. "Francis," he said to me, "come in and look at the dough rise. The whole world is in this oven." I didn't trust him. I missed the way my mother broke plates in the sink, the way my father did nothing but grunt for days at a stretch.

We moved into Bruce's house, and I spent most of my adolescence among the five couches scattered over three floors. My favorite was the patio love seat, dark green with premium foam-rubber cushions. I lay there for hours after school, reliving those days with Jimmy Corcoran when we played in the rubble-filled lots off Eleventh Avenue. Evenings I spent in the den, dinner and television in the soft comfort of a burgundy leather sofa. At night I retired to the basement convertible, darker than the deepest cave. I traveled the world down there, ancient Egypt, the Amazon, the Gobi and the Sahara. I slept and slept, waking only for the simple pleasure of drifting off to another place, the road back to morning always taking me through Manhattan, a place of unlimited adventure, villainous traps, last-minute heroics, saving the city at ten to six, just before the automatic lawn sprinklers burst on, water spraying the black-papered windows.

My mother became a model for the community, all the more pity for her only son. School psychologists wrote to her often and at length on my array of disorders. I was taken to doctors and counselors, dieticians. A nun from Philadelphia hypnotized me twice, but no one could convince me the world was worth waking for. I was content in my dreamed life. Days differed little from nights. My parents' lives, the lives of that town, were little more believable than those walking through my sleep.

I slept through high school and two months of college, left there to sleep through six jobs in two years: factory worker, grocery clerk, messenger, security guard. There were several close calls: I nearly drove a forklift into a group of retirees, almost sliced the deli owner's hand into a ham sandwich. Once, my co-worker in the security field fired at me when I wandered into his post. He grazed his foot and was promoted. I was terminated. Officer failed to adhere to fundamental security policies, my supervisor wrote, officer failed to answer warnings, failed to take cover under fire. Officer walks with unusual looping strides, refuses to wear collar pins or badge. Officer is detrimental to unit morale and a danger to all mall employees.

But I never considered myself in danger. Those guards were more likely to shoot themselves than me. Walking the world half asleep, I felt protected. Chaos reigned all around. It was the woman next to me in the factory, the buttonholer, who had the heart attack, the driver ahead of me who slammed into the church van, my best friend, Ronald Bailey, who was knocked unconscious by a falling branch as we sat together smoking pot by the brook. I began to think of myself as both an accident attractor and deflector, and felt in some strange way responsible for the misfortunes of those nearby.

My last job in those years was my favorite: limo driver. All night I drove from the small towns to the airports and back. I stayed out on the roads even when there were no calls. Driving was like dreaming, the V-8 humming through sleeping Main Streets out to the lightless back roads, the rushing shadows of trees and hills, an unshakable silence. I looked forward to each night's work, no matter who sat in the back or who shared the road.

One night, alone on a back road two miles from Beacon, I saw a house on fire, every window in flames except where a woman stood waving to me, not frantically, as if calling me, but more like an aunt would, saying good-bye. She screamed as I carried her from the house. Another night, I passed a train just wrecked, boxcars piled up next to Route 7A. I helped the conductor out, and we watched his tanker bleed black water over the engine and into the river.

The other drivers said I could smell car wrecks miles away. I became accustomed to rounding dark corners into a wash of ambulance light, was disappointed if morning came without my passing a car flipped against the divider or torn in two by a tree. I got to know the local cops by name. Stopped to chat on the crash scene, or in the diner, listening to their stories.

After dropping off a salesman in Poughkeepsie one night, I got on 9W and opened up. That section of road overlooking the river winds like a grand prix course, and I used all the lanes, the car sometimes skimming the stone wall that marks the cliff's edge. Incredibly, while I was squealing around the hairpin, a Mustang passed me on the inside. The driver, a woman, weaved in front of me, drunk or crazy, out of control. I tried to keep up, knew she would crash and wanted to be there. She went through the wall and down about twenty feet, into a tree.

I crawled around the back of the car, taillights tilted up to the road, an oak planted in the engine block. Smells of earth and gasoline, sounds of crickets and steam. Bits of hair and blood stuck to the crack in the windshield. She was still breathing. I pulled open the passenger door and sat next to her. Broken glass everywhere, my hands already bleeding.

I knew not to move her, tapped her shoulder twice. Grabbed her hand and pressed it to my face to feel its coldness. Her breathing was getting worse, her head bent over the wheel at such an awful angle I thought it might be choking her, so I took a chance and carefully pulled her back. Her body sagged against the seat; her breathing stopped. Then she took a long breath and opened her eyes. "Everything will be okay," I said. "Don't move. I'll get some help."

I fell climbing the hill. My head against a rock, blood running over my eye. Three cars passed before a truck stopped, an old man hauling rusted pipes. He was running late, he said, but would call the cops in Highland Falls if he had time. When I returned she was holding her side. "I'm cold," she said, her skin the color of an old razor. I smelled whiskey and looked through the gum wrappers and cigarette boxes until I found the bottle, wedged under the brake. She swung her arm for it, missed, again, grabbed it, unscrewed the top.

"Maybe you shouldn't."

"Stuff it," she said. "You're too late." She gulped twice.

"I'm always on time. That's the strange thing."

"Jesus, how old are you?"

"Nineteen."

"I had two kids by the time I was your age." She took another drink and pushed the bottle into my chest. I drank, a moment's warmth, followed by a loud pressure over my right eye, like the hangover getting an early start.

"I'm an orphan," I said, the words falling out.

"Here, let me see your head – you're bleeding, you know." She covered my eyes for a moment, and I saw my blood on her hands when she pulled them away. Using her foot, she searched through the junk on the floor, and then she looked up at me, and holding her side from the pain of bending over, she slowly pulled off her panty hose and carefully wound the soft fabric around my skull.

"It's a concussion," I said proudly, remembering symptoms from the hospital dramas – dizziness, nausea, your hands feeling tied to your hips. I prayed she would never stop wrapping.

"My son once split his head like this; blood was spraying out. I just kept screaming the whole time. He had to drag me to the hospital. Some mom, huh?"

"Was his name Frank?"

She started laughing. "I don't remember." She took more whiskey and groaned, grabbing her side. "You look like Lucy of Arabia. Say, do you know anything about internal injuries?"

"You're not supposed to drink anything." I put my jacket over her. "You have to stay warm."

We took turns passing out, and once when I awoke she was an old woman and the next time an angel, her eyes staring blankly at me, her face fuzzy white and grainy, like in a silent movie. I was crying and rubbing her hand to warm it when the medics arrived. "Mom," I kept saying.

The medic sat behind me and put her hands around my face, to hold it steady. "What happened?"

"It's my mother."

Another medic coolly pulled the drunk woman's cold hand out of mine and inserted his own. "Squeeze my hand," he said, "wiggle your toes. Are you hurt anywhere else?"

I tried shaking my head, but the medic behind me wouldn't allow it. They fixed a cylinder to my neck and cut off my clothes and fitted me for a straitjacket. Then they bound me to a longboard and carried me up the hill. Two stars were all I could see.

In the back of the bus they gave me oxygen and took my blood pressure. With impassioned conviction they poked me and listened to my insides, each action moving to the next like a second hand. "What day is it? Do you remember what happened?"

I was afraid they would stop if I answered. I didn't want the ride to end. "Mother," was all I said.

"Your mother is dead. I'm sorry."

I stared at the ceiling as they started IVs and rebandaged my head. The rest of the trip I spent listening to the sirens and thinking over the power of those words: Your mother is dead. He knew all along. To hold such knowledge, I thought, you would have to be a god.

In the hospital, the nurses fluttered too much, the doctor pulled at his toupee. I answered all their questions and they grew to despise me when I explained that it wasn't my mother who died in the car, that my mother was singing in the church garden. Quickly they downshifted me to the backwaters of emergency, and rather than lie next to the infections, I waited for my discharge outside, watching the medics smoking and joking. I walked up to the woman who had brought me in and asked, "How do you become a medic?"

At Fiftieth Street, I looked back at Marcus, still sitting on the side of the ambulance, the last wreck in my life of wrecks. "I quit, Marcus," I said, and raised my head to the morning. "I quit, Rose. Find someone else to follow. I quit, Patrick Burke, you and your crazy family." I turned east into the sun and stretched out my hands, resting them on the April air, feeling winter's end for the first time. "It's spring," I shouted, as if years had passed since the last one, as though an evil king had just been thrown out of power. Four young lovers strolled past me, arm in arm, two boys and two girls or three boys and a girl, or four boys or perhaps four girls. They kept switching hats, kissing or biting each other in turn.

I stopped in front of 440 West Fiftieth and climbed the stairs and rang the bell for 3F. I pushed the hair out of my eyes and tucked in my shirt. I hadn't seen Mona since the morning she left. She'd been back to our apartment, but only late at night, while I was at work. Those days I came home to find something else gone: books, a mirror, two chairs, her dresser. I had called the theater and all her friends until one of them finally told me, "She doesn't want to see you."

I checked my watch and rang the bell again, waiting for that picture of her gliding down in her white gown. So many times in the last month I'd stood in front of that building, thinking of that picture, then walked away without ringing. I'd met her neighbors and their dogs. I was even called there once for an old man who had died in the bathroom on the top floor, the newspaper lying next to him, open to the obituaries. I wondered if he saw his name there. On the way out I put my ear to the door of 3F, trying to hear her breathing.

Mona's roommate always left for work at seven; it was ten after. I rang three more times and waited five minutes, and then, checking to see that there was no one on the street, I climbed up on the stone railing and jumped, grabbing hold of the bottom rung of the metal ladder, pulling myself onto the fire escape. The window on the third floor was open, a steel gate locked behind it. I looked in on an empty bedroom and moved over to the other window, also open and gated, and there was Mona, sleeping on the couch in the living room. "Mona." I opened the window all the way and banged on the gate. "Mona." I banged harder and screamed her name loud enough for all the Monas in the city. She opened her eyes and stared at me. "Who is it?"

"It's Frank."

"Oh," her eyes closing.

"Mona, I only came because I just wanted you to know that I quit. I'm starting over." Her eyes opened again, brown leaves floating in a well. I banged the gate. "Mona, did you hear that? I quit." I watched her sit up and stand and move slowly toward me, her dress bunched up below her hip, her eyes half closed, her lips a foot away. "Frank."

"I'm thinking of going back to school, finally getting that degree we were talking about. I'll find some job part time to get me through. Hell, I don't care, I'll deliver pizzas, open a restaurant, I'll run for mayor. I'm thinking maybe we could try us one more time. There's a bartender I met downtown who was once a justice of the peace in North Dakota. What do you think?"

"That's nice."

"No rush, though. Things are going to be very different and you just take your time and when you're ready . . ." I stopped and stepped back, her face so still, breathing. "You're sleeping, aren't you?"

"Uh huh."

I pressed my face against the gate. "I love you, Mona, always will. Don't you love me?"

"Uh huh."

"Then kiss me." I pushed my mouth through the gate and waited as Mona silently leaned forward and pressed her beautiful lips to the cold metal above my nose. Then she turned around and, back on the couch, she closed her eyes. "Good night, Mona." How I wanted to sleep like that.

I took the steps down three at a time, shouting as I dropped from the ladder. So what if she was sleeping. It was a start. On the sidewalk, I joined the ranks of the gainfully unemployed – can returners, dog walkers, street peddlers, and the rest of the jobless, off to church sales, cheese giveaways, computer lessons. I bought a hot dog from the stand on the corner. "What did the Buddhist say to the hot dog seller?" I asked.

"What?"

"Make me one with everything."

"That's very funny." He wasn't laughing.

"I can do this," I said to the man. "Do you make any money?"

"No."

"Yeah, but you never go hungry."

"You get sick of hot dogs pretty quick," he said. "In fact, I'd rather die than eat another. And the stink, it's like a second skin you can never get off."

"I could do it."

I bought a beer on Fifty-first and drank it as I walked north, practicing my resignation speech to Captain Ed. "I quit, that's it. I quit, that's it." The beer finding its way up to my head. A familiar swagger in my drunken gait.

I smoked a cigarette in the hospital parking lot, taking my last look at the rusting engines, the line of broken ambulances, the filthy gray hospital bricks. Someone walked out of the waiting room, and through the open doors I saw Mary

Burke and her brother sitting together and surrounded by ulcers, shingles, tuberculosis. Good-bye, Mary.

I walked through the crew room, past Luther sleeping on the couch, Marcus at the busted table, writing up the accident report. In the office, Captain Ed slept with his eyes open and his feet twitching on the desk. I leaned over and shouted. "I quit, Captain, that's it."

"Pierce, you're finally here. I've got some forms for you to fill out on this accident."

"I'm not filling out any forms. I quit."

"What are you saying, Pierce?"

"That's it."

"I can't talk you out of it?"

"Not a chance, Captain."

"Well, I'm sorry to hear that. You've been with us a long time. When were you due to come in?"

"Twelve."

"So when are you coming in? One?"

"I'm not coming in."

"Tell me, Pierce, how many times have you quit this month? Three? How many times last month?"

"All that was just practice for today, a long time coming. You have no idea how serious I am right now. This is it, the one. I'm looking at my watch, and in ten seconds I am going to disappear from here, never to be seen again."

"I'll put you in for one. I'm leaving the paperwork here. You can give it to Captain Barney when you come in." Captain Ed wrote a note on his desk and then covered it with his feet.

"Do whatever you want. I'm through."

I was working with Suzette on one of her rare midnight shifts, and we were called to an overdose on a tenement rooftop. At the top of the stairs we opened the door and found a man lying on the roof, not breathing. Sitting next to him were two of the biggest, ugliest dogs I'd ever seen, their teeth turning toward us. We closed the door and called the Emergency Service Unit, who arrived in five minutes with a tranquilizer gun. "You're not going to shoot the dogs, are you?" Suzette said. "It's not their fault – it's the guy who's the asshole." "We're shooting the dogs," the cop said, and pulled out two prefilled plastic darts. "Here, give me one of those," Suzette said, and took the dart, and using a syringe from the drug box, she withdrew the serum from the dart and replaced it with Narcan. "Don't shoot the dogs," she said. "Shoot the asshole." The officer opened the door, quickly shot the man in the right rear cheek, and then closed the door. A minute later the overdose appeared, and without a word he led his two dogs down the stairs.

14

In the lot again, I took my first gasps of freedom, a new life beginning. I smoked another cigarette. I would stay up all day, go to sleep by midnight, get up early, coffee and eggs and the help wanteds. New clothes and a haircut. Mona.

I looked at my watch. The Dark Bar opened at eight; one beer to think more about this, a pen and paper to write down ideas. I took a step and heard the emergency room doors open, Noël running past me down the lane, looking both ways on Fifty-sixth, then hopping on one foot toward Ninth. "So long, Noël." The doors opened again, and Mary Burke nearly knocked me down, running into the street like she couldn't see, a taxi skidding. "Good-bye Mary," I said. Griss walked up behind me. "What's going on, Griss?"

"Your friend there just untied the water beggar. Griss was coming out here to thank her. Probably just saved Griss a murder charge." We watched her turn right on the other side of the street, bent over like she was crying. She ran through a group of homicidal-looking high schoolers, who yelled to her and turned for a second as if to chase her before they continued on their way. "Having a tough time of it," Griss said. I started running. I didn't want to talk to her; I'd quit. I just wanted to make sure she didn't get more hurt. So I followed, keeping a block behind, my head down every time she looked back.

Five blocks of running and hiding and, near the end, so low on air, praying she would stop. I turned into Forty-eighth, almost bumping into her. She was holding a rusty fence railing with one hand and crouching down, breathing fast, and I stepped back around the corner and sort of fell against the wall, bats flapping in my lungs, their droppings clogging the bases. She was halfway up the street when I looked again.

From the corner it seemed like a decent block – two restored brownstones, a few trees, an old church – but looking further in I saw that the center had been cleared away as if with a giant spatula, and out of that concrete pan two towers rose, old before their time, one hundred feet apart. Black balconies on the top floors made the buildings appear to tilt in a little, as if they wished to lean on each other. The concrete plaza between them was a surreal landscape of miniature Aztec pyramids and barn animals molded in cement.

When Mary Burke stopped in front of the church and gazed up at the grease-stained glass, I assumed that was her destination. She'd be okay there. I would not. I pointed myself toward the Dark Bar, but when she turned her back to the church and walked across the street, I stayed low, following the line of parked cars until I was just across from the cement animals. I crouched behind a forsaken Ford, watching her as taxis zipped by, pushing brown air over me.

She stood in the center of the plaza, so that the animals formed a circle around her, looking to her as if for guidance. She stared up at the buildings for a long time, and I was drifting off, thinking of the calls in that building: an old man who died standing, his elbows on the sink; a teenage boy who swallowed rat poison; another who tried to get rid of his crabs by spraying roach killer on himself. It burns, he said, hopping on one foot. *I quit. That's it.*

Mary Burke tapped me on the shoulder.

"Excuse me," I said. I untied my shoe and tied it, and then I stood clumsily, looking for something else to do. "You seemed like you were in trouble."

"I'm all right. It's just that I can't stand to see people tied up. I'm in the waiting room for hours, listening to Noël screaming. I know Noël. The only reason he's screaming is cause he's tied up."

"That doesn't seem so bad to me. Can't go to work when you're tied up."

"Oh no. Don't say that. I wanted to cut my father loose too. They told me he almost died and then five minutes later they say he's better than ever and I go in and it's killing me to see him fighting like that, like he's in this terrible pain. One of the nurses pulled me away. And the doctor too. I don't think they know what they're doing in there." She stared up at the building as if waiting for it to fall on her. "Look, since you're here, maybe you could do me a favor. I need you to wait for me outside this building, okay? Only take a few minutes. I have to visit a friend who's sick."

"Okay."

She took ten steps and turned around. "I'm only asking because it's a dangerous building. There's been some robberies, you know, a woman was raped not long ago. And this person I'm seeing, she'll want to talk to me all day, but if I can point to you out the window and tell her you're waiting for me, then I can be out quick. I just have to pick something up, and if anything happens, I'll be in apartment Sixteen M."

"Right. M, like in Mary. Maybe I should come with you."

"No, I'm just going up for a few minutes. In fact, if I'm not back in fifteen, just hit the buzzer, and that way she'll let me go."

"Sixteen M," I said. "Fifteen minutes. Nothing's going to happen. I'll come with you."

"No, I'll be fine. I'm just visiting a sick friend."

I followed her inside, the front steel doors half open, their locks ripped out. In the gray-tiled foyer, a man slept on a desk where a security guard once sat, years ago. The man was breathing only a few times a minute, but each breath was probably worth five of mine, a breeze blowing in through the door when he inhaled, snoring like his tongue was rusted and his throat full of holes. As Mary waited for the elevator, I shook the man, and when he didn't move I lifted up an eyelid. The flea-size pupil: heroin. I remembered then all the overdoses on that block, cooling in the doorways and stairways. I put my knuckle to his ribs and gave him the rub, and he groaned and pushed my hand away. This dose wouldn't kill him.

"What are you doing?" she asked.

"I'm just visiting a sick friend."

"Don't wake him. He might get mad."

The elevator arrived, the doors opened and closed and opened. She stepped in and I waved good-bye. The doors closed and opened. I stepped in and they closed. The elevator jumped up three feet or so and stopped. Then it began to rise, so slowly I couldn't feel it, knew we were moving only because of the metal friction as we crossed each floor. I remembered the call for a woman shot on one of the top floors, in the hallway, a massive woman who had been shot in the head, and all the time I was taking care of her – she said only the word "frip" a few times in rapid succession and nothing after – I kept wondering what kind of fate had led this woman to be shot in the head, which was so small compared to the rest of her, a little larger than her knee. The hole over her left ear was no bigger than her smallest toe. I knew this for a fact, because Hector and I had cut off her clothes and rolled her onto a backboard and, with strength neither of us knew we had, wedged the board into that little elevator so that she stretched diagonally between us, her head at one corner and her feet at the opposite, Hector and I unable to move or to feel the elevator's drop, it was so slow. Thinking we would be there forever, until all of us were no bigger than the little hole, and the sound of the blood dripping onto the floor.

"I shouldn't have asked you to come." Her hands shaking.

"You asked me not to come."

"Promise me you won't go inside."

"Fifteen minutes."

"Everyone in that hospital is crazy. I'm going crazy too. You understand. I just have to relax a little, not feel so guilty the whole time."

"I'm the one who's guilty," I said. "If you ever have any doubts, it's my fault."

"I can't take care of everyone there. I can't even take care of myself. I'm full of water, all bloated up. I feel like someone left a sponge in here, soaked with all their problems."

"That was me." I guessed about twelve floors, the elevator exhausted but fighting upward. Mary Burke had worked herself into a wet corner. Pale and breathing fast, she had her arms wrapped tightly around herself. "We can still go back," I said. "I'll walk you home. You sleep for a couple of hours, watch some TV, take a bath. Then go check on your father. You seem to be the only one in your family who hasn't lost it. Maybe there is someone else you could call, an uncle or something."

"Dead, dead, dead and gone. You really look like a cop, you know that? A strung-out junkie priest who's really a cop. You're the one needs the rest."

It was hard to argue with that, and I was silent for the last minute, the last floor. We stopped, lurched up, and then settled in. The door opened, dry cool air circling us. She moved into the hall and turned to me. "I'll be all right. I was just upset before. Don't pay any attention to it." She had improved greatly in the hall's white lights, cool, confident, like a cigarette ad.

"You go on home, okay? I'm fine really. I don't need you. Thanks. Good-bye." I stood and watched her walk to the end of the hall. She knocked three times. A woman opened the door, wearing a paisley robe, a leaden glow behind.

"Well, what do you know: Mary," she said, then, yelling to someone behind her, "Hey, Cy, guess who's here. What's it been, two years? Mary – Mary Burke." Another voice: "Maaary." The woman grabbing her arm, pulling her in.

It was the first elevator I knew that descended faster than

it rose. The floor was greasy and black, like the church's glass, and still I thought I could see, rings of fire rushing at me. In the entranceway, I checked to make sure the man at the desk was still breathing. I went out to the concrete lambs for a smoke, checking my watch every couple of minutes. *I quit. That's it.*

When it was time, I walked back in. I held my breath in the elevator but was gasping by the fourth floor. Sixteen Mmmmm. The girl in the robe opened. "Can I help you?"

"Mary Burke, please. I'm a friend."

"She's not here." Orange and blue lights in the hallway behind, dreamland.

I stood waiting, silent, until her eyelids drooped and she leaned against the doorframe, enough space for me to get through. She woke up to grab my arm, and I pulled her behind me. "Wait a minute. You can't go in."

"It's okay, Kanita." A man stood from a chair at the end of the hall. "Come on in."

"But I don't like him," Kanita said. "He looks like a cop."

"He's not a cop; he's a medic.... I'm Cy Coates." He stepped into the hall, the universal sort: medium-built but strong, a light-skinned black or dark-skinned white who appeared twenty-five though he was probably forty-five. He looked a little like me, I thought, same height, same eyebrows, though I was whiter, whiter than peppermint Life Savers, and I appeared forty-five though I was twenty-five. He rarely blinked. I blinked all the time.

"Frank Pierce." I shook his hand. The room was tan and smoky and cluttered with weather-beaten love seats. The only light came from a dusty floor lamp and a couple of fish tanks glowing blue-green in the corner. Several faded and slightly torn travel posters had been taped over the windows: tropical places, lagoons and white beaches. On the sofa, a man and a woman stared at the only framed picture in the room, a three-foot-wide volcano from which occasional puffs of real steam rose. The couple looked like glue-sniffing Mormons, blond and stoned. Next to them, a dark man in a light suit slept in a brown chair in the corner, his face pressed against one of the tanks, tiny bright-blue sharks swimming over his cheek.

"Mary said you might be coming."

"Where is she?"

"Sleeping in the back." He pointed down the hall.

"She asked me to come by to pick her up. We're going out for a movie and a malted, and then I'll bring her right home."

"I know, but she told me to tell you she says she wants to crash here a few hours. She said she's going back to the hospital after she rests up. Terrible about her father, isn't it?"

"She said a lot."

"That's Mary for you." His eyes never left me, as I waited for another puff of smoke from the painting. "I better just go in and see her," I said, but was still standing there when Kanita brushed past me and sat on the sleeping man's lap. He opened his eyes briefly and closed them. She rubbed his head.

"I call this the oasis," Cy said. "Refuge from there. Did you know that two people were shot in this building last week? And just two days ago a gang of ten-year-olds held up the priest across the street. Then there's all these middle-aged women with their little dogs. I don't have to tell you. You've seen plenty. Everyone's got some wound to talk about – truth is, you can't walk down the street without something threatening your life, be it the poisons in the air or the taxis running you down or the shit they call food over at the Chinese fry palace on the corner." His eyes opened wider and wider, and just as I thought they might pop out, he blinked. I started down the hall, Cy right behind.

"I mean that food will kill you almost as fast as a bullet. At least you can feel the bullet when it hits. What about the microwaves from the sky, electrical waves from the ground, Freud waves from the past? All around us, the signs of a civilization tearing itself apart."

I opened the first of four doors. Inside was a desk, a couple of plastic chairs, a fat man sitting at the desk punching the keys to a computer that gave the room its only light. On a chair in the far corner I could barely make out another, much thinner man, sleeping or unconscious. A straight line of dried blood at the side of his mouth.

"Careful," Cy said. "That's the tiger, my office; the lady's down the hall. Be with you in a bit, Sam." He closed the door. "Welcome, Frank, to Sunrise Enterprise, the stress-free factory."

Mary slept on a mattress on the floor in the room at the end, a yellowing sheet pulled up to her neck. "Mary," I whispered. Her head sort of rolled over toward me. "Mary, we have to get going."

"Oh no," she murmured.

"She's had a rough time of it, I'd say," Cy said.

"I think you better come with me. I'll take you home." I grabbed her hand, and she pushed it into my chest like she'd be happy to give it to me if she could keep the rest.

"She wanted something to help her sleep," Cy said. He reached for the door to close it.

I pushed in again, grabbed both her hands, and pulled her up into a sitting position. "Mary, we really have to *go*," shaking her until she started to cry. She freed one hand and swung it in a high arc over my nose.

Cy's hand on my shoulder. "Frank, she's suffered enough. She's okay, I promise. Probably be asleep in two minutes."

I felt a sudden urge to act responsibly, though I couldn't say exactly what I was responsible for. When this feeling comes upon me, I usually try to imagine what a regular person would do, someone more in tune with the supplies and demands of human nature, and once I realize a regular person would never find himself in this position, I try to think like a hero in the movies: the script was clear, the part fast approaching where I pick up the girl and fight my way out. I was about to do just that, and then I thought how peaceful she looked, what a fight she would give if I lifted her, the comical appearance blood gives you after it's trickled down your mouth and dried.

The hand tighter on my shoulder. "Come on, Frank." I let him guide me out the door and watched him close it. At the end of the hall, the couple stared at the volcano. Puff.

"Here, sit down," Cy said, and sat across from me, on the edge of a coffee table decorated with cigarette burns and empty ashtrays. "I am always interested in people in stressful occupations, and being a paramedic is about as stressful as I can imagine. What's it like? Tell me some war stories, like what's the worst thing you've ever seen?"

"Lima beans on a pizza," I said.

"That's very funny. Conversion reaction. If you weren't laughing you'd be crying. You don't have to talk about it if you don't want. What you need is one of these." From his shirt pocket he removed a pin-size joint, bent in three places, which he slipped into his mouth and pulled out straight between his lips.

"No, thanks. Do you have any beer?"

"That shit is poison, Frank. We don't drink alcohol here." He pulled out a lighter and put the flame to the joint and breathed in deep and held.

I looked around the room. "Did you give Mary the Red Death?"

"Red Death?" Cy coughed and handed the joint to Kanita. "Tell me something, Frank – does killing your clients make good business sense to you? The kids selling that shit have no sense." As if he just remembered something, Cy walked over to the window and peeled back one of the posters and looked out. Then he jumped up and spun in the air, facing me. "What I mean is, they come into the neighborhood to make a quick dollar without any consideration for the people who have worked very hard to establish all the necessary connections for a strong long-term and productive business climate; but they'll be taken care of, don't worry about that. Stay still." He leaned forward and smacked his hands together just over my head. Brushed a dead fly from his palm. "I'm an important member of the community, Frank. I have friends in City

Hall, organized labor, the PBA. I own substantial percentages in Graceland Ballroom, the Venus Cinema, Joe Mars Carting."

"I should be going," I said. "I just quit." I looked over at the volcano and felt the exhaustion returning, on an entirely new level. "I have to get some sleep. Don't you people go to sleep?"

"Sleep is all stress reduction, Frank. Here." He pulled a white pill from his pants pocket. "You take one of these, sleep two hours, and that's all you need. Why do you think I'm telling you this, Frank – for my health? You ought to look at yourself, man, what it's doing to your face. Kanita, get me a glass of water."

I watched her get up and walk into the kitchen and return with a dusty glass and hand it to Cy and sit back down with the guy in the corner. Cy put the pill in my hand and I weighed it there, two hours of sleep. It felt so light. I thought of Mona sleeping on the couch, Mary Burke passed out in the back room, the first time I'd seen her smile. I felt the muscles breaking down, a roaring in my head, the dull thunder of dying cells. If I slept two hours I could stay up until midnight, sleep all night, and wake up with the rest of the world. "I just quit." I put my hands on the arms of the chair. "I better go."

"Oh no, Frank, drink up. I'm trying to help you."

I grabbed the chair once more, turned the key, nothing, engine dead, so I reached for the glass and threw in the pill and drank. Cy went over to one of the tanks and dropped in a few pellets from a box. The tank instantly clouded up, an occasional blue fin flashing by.

"Is this what you gave Mary?" Words unfolded over my teeth.

"That's the stuff. I call it the Red Lion. Very king-of-the-jungle. No language at all, you know, completely stripped away. Only power – total, brutal power. You can't believe how relaxing that is."

I placed the empty glass on the table and tried to stand. "I guess I'll be going."

"Just take it easy," Cy said. He walked down the hall and into the first room. Voices inside, followed by a groan. The door closed. Puff.

I waited a minute and nothing happened. Drugs never seemed to hit me the way they're supposed to: pot made me violent, caffeine kept me from exploding, whiskey sobered me. Somewhere in the last five years I had caused irreversible damage to vital connecting points.

I lit a cigarette, and when I exhaled, the smoke formed letters, then words, taken from what I was thinking – years, points, damage. I sucked in more smoke and more words came out, smaller print rushing by – lima beans, jungle, smoke. When I exhaled again the print was too fine to read, the words pouring out of me like coins I had been forced to swallow. I felt light in the seat, my head rising above the chair, so happy thinking I would never need any of those words again. I was bigger without them, my heart beating in big steps across my chest.

I looked through the smoke at Kanita, who was watching me. She stood and walked around the table, her hips rolling toward me. "Take my pulse." She held out her arm. I grabbed her wrist and tried to count, but the rate was too fast. Then I tried to compare it with my pulse, but I couldn't find my pulse. "It's good, isn't it?"

"Perfect," I said. I could have lifted her over my head.

"I knew it." She sat on my legs. Maybe I couldn't lift her. "I was wrong about you," she said. "You got more blood in you than I thought." She wrapped her arms behind me and started to gnaw sweetly on my neck, her fingers walking up my spine, dislodging the twisted metal, picking the damaged rivets. I gave up trying to pull her hands out of my pockets, let myself fall into her. I felt so good it scared me, as always the high tainted with this feeling something terrible was on the way, and sure enough, the moment I closed my eyes I saw Rose sitting on the sidewalk in her yellow raincoat, barely breathing. Rose always finds a way to find me, and this time I'd been caught with no room to run, nothing to do but sit through until the end. How do I quit, I thought, when I can never leave?

This is how it begins. The last time, the first time. Larry pulls the ambulance to a stop as we both see Rose fall to her knees on the sidewalk, then onto her back. From forty feet away I see her grab the railing to pull herself up, as if the air she needed was just a foot in front of her. I grab the tube kit and run to her. In those few seconds I know everything I need to know and everything I have to do. She is an asthmatic; the cyanosis, pursed lips, and retracting chest muscles tell me this, and I also know that I have only about one minute to put that tube into her lungs before they close up and her pulse stops and she goes flatline. Once asthmatics go flatline, they do not come back.

I'm not nervous as I slide to my knees near her head and pull open the intubation kit and prepare the tube and the lighted blade I'll use to lift up her tongue and see where to place the tube. I think only of what I must do. You want the best person here. Larry is a good intubator, but I am better. I have never missed when it counts, more than one hundred times like this, a last-second intubation, because you cannot miss. An eighteen-year-old girl not breathing. It is simply not allowed to miss, and though I'm so tired, hungover, though Mona and I are fighting all the time and I'm not the same medic I used to be, I am going to be the one here, and as I slip the blade between her lips I let myself think for just one second that this might be the save to turn the year's worth of bad luck around, to start a new start. She bites down, a reflex, and I have to pry her teeth apart with the blade, trying not to break them, her mouth open just enough to get the tube in, so little room to see. I pull up harder, not caring about the teeth anymore, and for a moment I think I see the bottom of the vocal cords and I wait for her to inhale and I shoot the tube toward the shadow of a hole. I hook up the ventilator and pump hard, Larry listening to the lung sounds in her chest and then her belly.

"You're in the stomach," he said.

"You sure?"

"You're in the stomach, man."

I pull out the tube and go in again. She's still biting down but weakly now, and though I open her mouth wider I can't see the cords. I point the tube under her tongue to where it's rising up, fighting to pull air in and not getting any.

"You're in the stomach," Larry says. "Let me try."

"One more time." I go in again, still unable to see but listening my way now, to the faintest scraping of air, and at its loudest point I know I'm close, and on her last breath I push it in.

"Stomach again."

"No way." I listen myself. Rose stops breathing. On the monitor, her pulse rate drops to thirty; it's going to stop. I never miss and her heart's going to stop and there's nothing I can do. Larry grabs the handle out of my hand and Rose's heart has stopped and he pushes me to her side to start CPR and then he intubates her easily. Air moving in and out of her lungs now, only now it doesn't matter.

I opened my eyes and found myself standing in the middle of the room, screaming, Kanita and company crowded into the corner between the fish tanks. Cy came up the hall, followed by big Sam.

"Frank, take it easy. What happened?"

"He just flipped the hell out," Kanita said.

I bent over, pain cutting all the way through. Things were broken inside. I didn't know what else to do, so I kept screaming.

"Frank, just be cool, man. You're having a paradoxical reaction. Affects less than one percent, but it can happen. Just be cool, cause Cy knows what to do. Now, I'm going into the kitchen for one minute. I want you to stay right there. I'm getting something to help you." He waved Kanita over and whispered to her: "Didn't I tell you this guy was stressed out?"

"Stressed? He's a goddamn psycho."

I turned toward the hall and with both hands on the wall made my way to the end, Mary sleeping soundly. "Frank, where are you going?"

I reached one arm under her back, the other under her legs. I threw her over my shoulder, firemanlike, and carried her down the hall. Cy stood in the center of the room, the others collected behind him. "You're making a mistake, Frank. Why don't you let us help you? Sit down and relax a minute."

I expected one of them to block the door, but my screaming fit had given me a clean path, and I walked out and waited at the elevator. Cy stood by the door. "She'll be back, Frank. You know that, don't you? And by the way, you owe me ten bucks." He slammed the door. In the elevator I felt Mary's eyes open and in the lobby she elbowed me in the ear and I leaned over and she stood. "I can walk," she said, and weaved out into the sun and collapsed on one of the cement animals. I sat next to her and lit a cigarette. I gave it to her and lit another. We smoked and watched three kids poking a dead bird with a stick and an old woman who looked like she didn't know what state she was in or what country and the men on the street drinking beer standing around an old car with the hood propped up and the other cars speeding past. When we finished, Mary pushed herself up and stumbled to the sidewalk and into the street. Taxi, I thought; taxis are good. I searched through my pockets, my wallet still there but everything else gone, money, keys, gum, remembering Kanita's loving fingers. I ran into the street and grabbed Mary under the arm and pulled her to the sidewalk, where she flung another elbow at my ear and screamed, "Let go of me."

The men standing around the broken car had stopped drinking and started walking toward us, but before they could raise their tire irons Mary ran up the block to Tenth. I caught up to her at the corner, where she was leaning on a mailbox. "You shouldn't have come up," she said. "I told you not to. I don't know what you were thinking, trying to get us both killed." She threw herself into rushing traffic, the tires screaming. I stumbled after her and caught up on the far side, checking myself for fractures, bleeding.

She looked up the avenue and down and back to me. "Did you have a nice talk with Cy? He tell you all about his Sunrise Enterprise, helping people? Well, I've seen him hurt people." She plunged southward, into baby strollers and postal workers, and then made a left on Forty-seventh, and where the crowds thinned out I caught up to her. "Why are you following me?"

"Because you can barely walk," I said, and grabbed her arm, more to support myself now. She broke free and when I reached her again in the middle of the block, she stopped. "You want to know about Cy? You want to know what he does to people that make him angry? He hurts them." She sat down on a pile of crooked steps, a building leaning crookedly over us. "You got another cigarette?" I pulled out the pack and handed it to her and searched my pockets again. No money, no keys. It was because of days like this that I kept an extra set of keys at work and sets at the Blarney Moon and the Dark Bar, but from where I stood, those places seemed at least a day's journey. Mona lived only three

blocks up Tenth, probably waking up about now. I considered climbing her ladder, passing out on her fire escape, a
great way to start our new life. So I sat down and rested my
head on the top steps and watched Mary Burke smoke,
talking herself straight. "I'll tell you about Cy. You remember Noël, right, from the other night, how Noël is now? He
wasn't always like that. He was a good guy, my brother's best
friend. They played baseball together and they set up a
league for the kids and fixed up this old building to be like
a drug-free community center. He was clean-cut, good-
looking, had a great way of talking with kids, and he'd hang
out at the basketball courts or the schools or the arcades,
talking about drugs, usually pointing out Cy, who was the
biggest dealer around, and finally one day either Cy or Sam
or one of the other goons put a bullet in Noël's head. He was
in a coma for three months. Crazy ever since." She finished
and stood and walked up the stairs and opened the front
door. "Wait," I said, and grabbed the cracked stair railing
and pulled myself up.

"What is it? You want to help me, is that it? You feel sorry
for me. Keep it for yourself."

"I just need to sit down a minute."

"Or maybe you want to fuck me, huh? God knows
everyone else has."

I reached the stairs first and started up – I just assumed
that everyone lived at the top – Mary talking through the
long climb. "Don't you see? It was Noël who got me to stop
going to Cy. And I did for a while, but when my brother
died I got really sick, overdosed, ended up in the hospital.
Noël stayed around the clock. Pretty soon we were going out

259

together. I was just a kid, you know, twenty-one, twenty-two. I stayed clean for a year. Then when Noël woke up from the coma, talking crazy, I wanted to help but I couldn't stand seeing him like that, and after only a few months . . . you want to know what I did?"

I waited at the top and she walked by me to her door. I didn't want to know. But I already knew; my head was starting to clear too. "I went back to Cy." She put the key in the lock and opened the door and looked back at me, eyes like rotting olives. "I knew he was responsible. I knew what I was doing. What do you think about that?"

She waited for an answer. I didn't have an answer. I followed her down the narrow hall, its walls covered with small drawings, and into the living room, with its walls of unframed oil paintings, ceiling to floor, many unfinished. I sat on the couch while she went into the kitchen. "I've been clean two years now. I got a job. I paint when I'm home. Don't bother anybody. Then all this shit happened."

I found a cushion near my head and fell toward it, my eyes closing, a dog licking my face. "Oh, no you don't, no you don't. You can't stay here." I felt her shaking me, and she sat on my legs, which by that point felt like they belonged to someone else. The sound of her crying was the last thing I heard.

I was working with Hector one night, and we were called to the police precinct for a hanging. When I got inside, the cops pointed to the patient, who was sitting in a chair, crying, his hand cuffed to a bar on the wall, his eyes swollen and red. One of the cops came up. "This asshole is so fucking lucky," the cop said. "He's busted on a bullshit burglary charge, right, and what does the asshole do? He tries to hang himself in the cell. If I didn't hear him doing it, he'd be dead right now, but I heard something, you know, something not right, and when I got in there he's hanging and he's thrashing around like all fuck, and I go to cut him down and he's kicking around and I can't get near him, and then the motherfucker kicks me right here, and so I Maced the fucker. Lucky I didn't shoot him." I took an IV bag out of the box and held the tubing over the patient's eyes, washing them. "Why," the man cried, holding his head up to the water, "why would you Mace a man who's hanging?"

15

I awoke to an ambulance siren. The driver was using the hi-lo tones, which sound like the sirens in French movies, chasing terrorists on the rainy streets of Paris. Only one ambulance in the city made that noise – Franco, the bus that wouldn't die. Three months ago, Tom Walls had promised to destroy Franco once and for all, and while chasing a suspected purse snatcher he mutilated a series of sidewalk fixtures before flattening Franco's nose on a subway entrance. Tom's partner was so traumatized he immediately left the city to attend law school, and the damage to Franco appeared so irreparable a dozen medics showed up to cheer the tow truck that lifted him away to the ambulance graveyard in Astoria.

Franco's inevitable return was a bad sign, but his siren was the only one that didn't whine and bleed inside me. There was something hopeful in his warning, an allusion to an afterlife – the other sirens were all atheists – and so I awoke smiling, and the smell of clean sheets, the feel of a soft blanket under my arms, cheered me enough that I tried sitting up. I searched my memory until I could place myself on Mary Burke's couch. "Hello," I said. A dog licked my cheek. It was nighttime, the only light from an alley window. I could just see the dog's teeth, the black outline of his fur.

"I'm Mary's friend," I said, "a very close friend who loves animals." I pulled the sheet away and stood. The paintings on the wall looked like cave drawings. I wanted to build a fire. "Hello," I said to the kitchen.

I explored the two small rooms in the dark, the dog with his nose in my sock. Everywhere I stepped were hard-angled objects of the same painful height. I kicked over a tray bursting with various-size metallic noises. In the bathroom, a glowing Mickey Mouse switch turned on a thousand blinking Christmas lights, and in her green-and-red sink I washed my face with three kinds of soap, each smelling like a different season. I filled the tub with hot water and mixed in shampoos, conditioners, and toothpaste. It felt good to be in a woman's room again, especially a woman who wasn't comatose or severely disabled. I wallowed in blessed stupor until the small sequined arm of her Elvis clock pointed to eleven.

On the street, I walked without my usual tripping or stumbling. I counted three separate piles of dog mines that on any other day I would have set off. The Jeep parked near the bank machine was playing Hendrix as if just for me, and the broken glass in the street glittered like a fable. Against my feet, the sidewalk felt soft, as if I'd had sex recently. I tried to remember just before or after passing out, searching for clues to the possibility of sex. I finally had to dismiss the idea for lack of evidence – I awoke with my clothes on, no stickiness – but I couldn't help thinking we would sometime soon, and the thought made me walk down the center of Ninth Avenue bent over a little and holding my hands up, remembering how I carried her out of that building, the feel of her pressed against my back, my arms wrapped around her thigh. I saw her picture on the side of a bus, the cover of a magazine. When I sat in the diner on Forty-fifth, her face was on the menu, next to the souvlaki.

"What do you want?" said the green-skinned waiter.

I pointed to the menu. "I want her and a cup of coffee." She was the best hamburger I ever had. I wandered out of the diner with my head raised up to the night, the strange peace in being neither hungover nor drunk, taking corners randomly, one street to another, thinking my life had turned a corner, like I'd saved someone, though I wasn't sure who. Who cared? I was on the mend, mending others, the only thing I knew how to do. So what if we were chronically doomed. It was the fighting back that counted, Mary and I.

I turned south on Ninth and walked into a crowd gathered at the entrance to Forty-third, Patrick Burke's corner, last place I wanted to be. Two cops were standing before a police car, and behind them fire trucks, firefighters, residents, and derelicts had gathered at the front of Burke's building. Fire hoses fed up the stairs and into the door, and since no flames were visible on the top floors, it appeared as if the hoses were pumping in the smoke that rose in bushels from the roof and upper windows. I saw the firemen walking around on the top floor as if looking for something, the source of the flames.

The Reverend Scythe was on the scene too; fires were Scythe's specialty. He'd chosen the top of Burke's stoop for his pulpit, hopping over the hoses even as the firemen were carting them back to their trucks. "Look up, people, remember the smoke that came before the fire, for when the flames of Judgment Day arrive, there'll be no room for smoke." Scythe waved his arms as if to fan the missing fire, the smoke that was quickly tapering off. "As Brother John foretold, fire will be the sky, the sun, the moon, the earth, fire the ocean and the fields, everlasting fire the air you will breathe everlastingly. Take heed, see now those words written in the smoke, because tomorrow is already too late."

I caught one of the firemen as he finished packing up the truck. "What's going on up there?"

"Just a smoke condition. Couldn't find the fire."

"Doesn't there have to be a fire if there's smoke?"

"Generally, except around here. It's weird."

"Anyone up there?"

"Nope. Super let us in. Second time we been called here tonight." He jumped on the truck as it pulled away, the Reverend Scythe shouting after it: "How many times have you been here today? What good has it done? How many times will you come back? When will you realize your trucks and your hoses are not going to work here? Already the fires have started, but your eyes can't see them. The dead are rising, but you can't tell their faces from their smoke. When are you going to wake up and prepare?"

The firemen waved at Scythe as they passed. Though he denounced them as hell-bringers, the men of Ladder Company 4 treated the Reverend as an unofficial mascot. No firemen had ever been seriously hurt in a fire at which Scythe preached. They had given him a black turnout coat and the oversize helmet that swung back and forth over his skull like a church bell. Scythe figured that firemen, by their name alone, worked hand in hand with the devil, but he wore the helmet with pride, and when all the trucks had left he turned to the dwindling crowd. "Go on home, sinners, ignore the last call. Go back to your opium pipes and whiskey bottles, back to your child pornography and gay marriages. Back to your slot machines, ribbed condoms, Mexican divorces, your sex clubs and martinis. Back to your hot-oil wrestling, Washington lobbying, organ donation. The list is long, but it's all written down – your state-subsidized brothels, liposuction, Oriental cooking. Add it up, you know what it spells: f-i-r-e."

I looked up at the dark smokeless rooms on the top floor and felt the sickness coming back, an old man hammering on a steam pipe in my skull. It seemed like every day I had to wake up two or three times just to remember the day before. I thought of Mary and me going to visit her folks, bringing gas masks and a defibrillator, calling the fire department, shopping together for our own volcano painting. *I quit. That's it.* I started toward Tenth, the Reverend's voice disappearing behind me, though his list, of course, went on forever. "And the Lord said if you can find one that's not a sinner, just one, I will spare the city. People, believe me, I have tried. I looked everywhere, and everywhere I looked, Satan and his firemen stared me back. Your Frederick's of Hollywood hormone supplements, Texas guitars, aromatherapy, elevator shoes . . ."

I wasn't afraid of the Apocalypse. In some ways I was looking forward to it. Just had to make sure I wasn't at work when it happened. The airport crash of '92 was bad enough: dead bodies, fire, silence. I won the medal of honor that night but don't remember how and had to take a week sick after. That's when I should have quit.

I headed north on Tenth, gripping my forehead with one hand and holding the other open and wavering in front of me. Whenever someone bumped into me I said excuse me and made a left turn. Fighting back was no longer an option. You can't fight what's not real. You don't attack madness, you rest from it, take lots of medicine. Retreat, the best defense. Only then did I remember the events of that morning: telling Captain Ed I was leaving; Mona climbing from her couch to say she loved me. How could I have forgotten? As if each day darkened everything before, making the morning feel like just another case of Mona speaking in my dreams, though this time it was I speaking in hers, the only real thing in my life.

I ran up Tenth to Fiftieth, where I had to stop and catch my breath, smoke a cigarette. Mona usually left the theater at eleven-thirty, home by twelve. I remembered two months before, when I caught her waiting at the end of the block, waiting for me to leave for work so she could go in without seeing me, similar to the way I took the long way home in order not to see her, the miles we walked to avoid each other, too many streets, too few destinations. We need to get away from this place, she said before she left; we're choking here. She had accepted the job as manager of the theater's summer-stock session, and in July we were to rent a barn on a field near the woods under a hill by a stream. Eight weeks in the Green Mountains of Vermont, Mona's recipe for resurrection. The family there leaves for the summer, she said, and we have to take care of their chickens and a goat you milk and there's a farmer who rents the field and comes to cut it with a tractor and we can use their pickup truck and I hear the stars are so clear at night you want to sleep outside in the newly cut grass and it'll be the best sleep you ever had.

At the time, it sounded to me like another rose-colored lie, the truth made more painful by it, like our last trip to the lake, but as I finished my cigarette on the corner of Tenth Avenue and Fiftieth Street and looked toward Mona's front stairs, it didn't seem like such a long walk to our room in the woods, the unfenced backyard where we'd hang our wet clothes in the sun. It was important we leave as soon as possible; the biggest mistake would be to wait for the ghosts to leave us: Rose and the Burkes had extraordinary staying power. All we needed was each other and a few hundred miles, sufficient distance to handle the forgetting. And as I imagined myself walking to that red barn, chickens and a goat, I saw Mona turn the corner, and I walked toward her not knowing what I would say. Then I saw that the man walking behind her was actually walking with her, and he seemed to know exactly what he was saying. I crossed the street and sat on the stairs opposite hers and watched them climb to her front door together. They said a few words and then what looked like good-bye, and Mona put her key in the door and opened it. Good for you, Mona, I thought, and then she let the door close without going in and he put his arm on hers and they kissed for a long time. They said good-bye again and he jumped to the sidewalk and turned and waved to her like Errol Flynn in *Robin Hood*. A goddamn actor. She watched him walk away, and I watched her shadow climb the stairs.

I followed the man toward Ninth, trying to imitate his walk, like Brando in *On the Waterfront*. What else could I give her? More heartache. My role had played itself out. I imagined drinking whiskey under the stars with the goat and Burke's ghost, breaking empty bottles in the barn. Rose lying in the driveway near the mailbox, not breathing. I caught up with the man at the light. He had that look, as Marcus would say. I stepped in front of him and turned. "*You* take care of the fucking chickens," I said, and headed up Ninth.

"You're late, Pierce, I know, but I can't fire you. I've got nobody else to work Sixteen XRay." Captain Barney held out keys and a radio. "You're in bus number eighty-six. I'll fire you tomorrow, Pierce, though I'll make no promises."

"What if there is no tomorrow?"

"Go on get out of here, Pierce, before I give you a big hug. I love this guy," he said to Miss Williams, who did not look up.

Bus number eighty-six sat in the far corner, leaning some-what, as if a great hand had crumpled it and tossed it there, a monument to too many red lights run, too many broadsides and head-ons, too many cracked-up drivers. The sides and front were chewed with dents, and a municipal-brown rust spread like a rash from the hood to the pitted lower panels. The rear bumper lay in a pile of broken parts nearby. Franco, the bus that would not die. In the dark he looked like an abandoned furnace.

Tom Walls stepped out of the driver's seat and met me at the passenger door. "Father Frank, what do you know?" punching my back and arms. "It's you and me tonight, the Rough Riders, tearing up the streets again, just like old times. Hey, call the morgue truck – you look DOA. We need some coffee, stat. Zip-a-dee-doo-dah." He kicked the front tire. "This old bus is a warrior, Frank, like us. I have tried to kill him, and he will not die. I've a great deal of respect for that." He jumped into the driver's seat and revved the engine. I opened up the back doors and climbed in.

"What you doing back there, Frank?"

"I'm sick, Tom. I need a cure."

I opened the drug box and set it on the stretcher and pulled out an IV setup and a tourniquet which I wrapped around my left biceps and held tight with my arm against my chest. I wiped the vein and grabbed a slim intravenous catheter and plunged the needle in. I hooked up a liter of saline, and while that ran through I mixed up and shot a vitamin B cocktail and followed it with an amp of glucose, a drop of adrenaline. Not as good as a beer, but it was all I had. The drugs were cold, like steel worms crawling over my elbow. I looked through the glass vials lined up in neat rows in the box – epinephrine, Isuprel, lidocaine – lifesaving medications that could kill me in a minute, end it all. "Come on, Frank," Tom cried from the front. "There's blood spilling in the streets." End it, that is, until Tom found me and brought me back, or halfway back. I'm sorry, Pierce, but you're out of sick time. I opened up the main oxygen tanks and ran the tubing through to the front cab. I carried my IV around to the passenger seat, and as Tom pulled the ambulance into the treeless lanes of Ninth Avenue I held the oxygen mask close to my cheeks and concentrated on long, deep breaths.

Tom drove with his seat forward, his face near the windshield, arms pressing down on the wheel like a jackhammer. "Father Frank, looks like you been doing overtime on the holy wine."

I pulled off the mask. "These are hard times, Tom."

"Yeah. It's great, isn't it."

"Great to be drunk," I said. "It's sobriety that's killing me."

"Look up, Frank, it's a full moon. The blood's gonna run tonight. I can feel it." He slapped the dash. "Our mission: to save lives."

"Our mission is coffee, Tom, a shot of the bull, Puerto Rican espresso."

"Ten-four, El Toro de Oro. Blast off."

Through five minutes of delirious turning I breathed in the oxygen. Tom finally slowed down for the hooker traffic near Forty-fifth, and there I saw Mr. Burke crossing the street in front of me, looking fine in a black overcoat and the suit I'd seen hanging in his closet, the suit I figured he'd wear to his funeral. It's a miracle, I thought, then thought again. I held the mask close and sucked in the oxygen and watched Burke make a left up Tenth and disappear in the huddle of pimps on the corner. The light turned green, and then they were all like ghost figures in the distance.

"Tom, I'm sick. The cure's not working. Maybe we should go back to the hospital."

"We were all sick in Nam – malaria, dysentery, you name it. But we did what we had to do. Don't worry, kid. Tom'll take care of you. Put your head out the window, get some of that spring air. Listen to the music. El Toro de Oro. Andale. Pronto."

Tom turned up the volume of the radio he always kept tuned to the year 1968. All I heard was the dispatcher's voice. Only right, I thought, that it would be Dispatcher 801, from whom no one can hide.

"Okay, units, it's suicide hour. Fourteen Boy, I show you in the hospital for sixty minutes, but I know you're in the diner on Fifty-second. Put down the burger. I've got a call for you, around the corner, Fifty-one and Ten, for the man with a noose around his neck and nothing to hang it on. Thirteen Zebra, you can forget about watching the shift change at Go Go World. Ten blocks down, at 220 West Thirty-second, in apartment four Charlie, there's a forty-year-old female who can't stop swallowing aspirin. Sixteen Xray, don't even think about getting a coffee, I have a call for you too."

Tom scooped up the radio. "Sixteen Xterminator here. We like our coffee bloody. Make it good – my partner's dying to help someone."

"You're in luck, X: your patient awaits you with bleeding wrists outside the bus terminal, Forty-two and Eight."

Tom drove as if he could hear his mother screaming for help from twenty blocks away. I pulled off the oxygen mask and pulled out the IV; grabbed a tissue out of the air and held it over the hole in my arm. I searched through the menus in the glove compartment for a dressing. "Tom, where are the Band-Aids? This is an ambulance, isn't it?"

"Look out," he answered. Franco's nose dropped, struck something hard below the street, and leaped up. The Band-Aid lay atop a pile of menus in my lap. It only slowed the bleeding.

The usual collection of lost souls milled around in front of the bus terminal: fifty drunk men staring at the sidewalks as if somewhere in the cracks they'd lost their tickets to a better life. Tom and I stood together near the ambulance, trying to guess which patient could be ours, and then from the center of the crowd a trio of hysterical derelicts pushed before them another, sobbing, like they were taking him to be sacrificed. He collapsed when shoved into the ambulance door.

"What the hell is going on?" Tom commanded.

"You've got to take him to the hospital," one of the intoxicated Samaritans said. "He tried to kill himself. He's cut bad. Show him your wrist. Show it." The crumpled form he referred to straightened himself against the ambulance and began shaking like a trout on a dock. "See what I mean? He ain't right. I'm telling you." The friend started to open the door and the others joined in, toppling the patient to the ground.

"Hold it right there." Tom slammed the door. "I will not take anyone anywhere against his will. This is America. People have rights." Tom looked over and I nodded patriotically.

"But he's going to die if you leave him here." The unofficial spokesman pulled the man's arm, turning the wrist over. "See?" All I could see was dirt and what was either a rash or a crude tattoo. "He was bleeding before," he said, and the others joined in. "He kept spilling his beer," one said. "I gave him mouth-to-mouth," said another, smiling shyly.

"You're lucky you didn't kill him." Tom pulled the patient to his knees. "We're going to hear it straight from the loony's mouth. Are you crazy? Did you try to bump yourself off?" The man's blubbering could be heard in three states. Tom shook him again, and the man seized briefly and from the corners of his mouth let out a long salivatory "Yessss."

"Why didn't you say so?" We dragged him into the bus, and the three brothers stumbled back toward the crowd. Tom pulled out one of the plastic electrode patches from the EKG monitor. "Sir, I am going to give you a medicine that is still very experimental. It's from NASA, and though the astronauts have been using it for years, we are the first service to try it. I will put this patch on your forehead like this, and in about a minute you will have to relax. You will forget all your suicidal feelings. It's very important that you wear this for at least twenty-four hours and keep checking in the mirror. If the patch turns green, you have to see the doctor immediately; the side effects could be fatal."

The man nodded and Tom moved up front to drive. A little time passed, and I told the man he should be feeling calmer now, and he stopped sobbing and sat quietly. It never failed. I sat next to him and looked at his wrists.

"You don't want to kill yourself like this, do you?" I said. He shook his head. "I mean, this is the worst suicide attempt I've ever seen. You feel the pulse? Here. That's where you cut, and it's not across, it's down, like so." I took out my knife. "Here, take it."

I had my finger on the artery, the blade shaking in my other hand. "I can't," he said, as surprised at my anger as I was.

"With all the poor people of this city who wanted only to live in peace and were viciously murdered, you have the nerve to sit here wanting to die and not going through with it. You make me sick. Take it."

He looked at the blade and me and his arm, all at the same time, and then his whole body struck the back door latch and he fell out, rolled over in the street, and stumbled onto his feet like a long jumper. Tom stopped the bus and came around to the back and we watched the man turn the corner, still holding the patch to his head.

"We cured him, Father. When we work together there's nothing we can't fix."

El Toro de Oro was white plastic and chrome, strings of red lights draped over heart-shaped mirrors. At the center table four old men played a hybrid pinochle rummy they seemed to reinvent with every deal. They drank from deep cans of beer and bet with fist-shaking threats, laughing or nodding after each performance. Behind the counter, the man who made the coffee stood where he always stood, wiping off the Formica beaches with a damp cloth and staring out the window into the blue charging seas. A young man shouted into a phone in the corner. "Don't lie to me I know where you been I called you your brother says you been out all day don't lie to me I'll kill you bitch." He slammed the wall, kicked the phone, and threw himself into a chair next to two friends, laughing.

I stood at the phone, not knowing who to call. I opened my wallet and pulled out a handful of identification, along with bits of torn loose-leaf, illegible scratchings, newspaper clippings, a coupon for a free hamburger. I thought of Mona at the door, my father in his chair, my mother praying in the garden. All the scattered pieces of my self. Only Tom Walls had stayed. Only right that my first partner should be the last. Ashes to ashes, Tom to Tom. I threw everything in the trash can and walked out. Franco's front seat wheezed when I filled it.

"Where's the coffee?" Tom asked.

"I don't know."

Tom hit me in the eyes with the ray from the two-foot lead-filled flashlight he had named Bronson. "Hello. Hello," Tom called. "Father Frank, where are you? Time to come home." He placed his stethoscope on my chest, tapped a few reflexes, pulled down my eyelids, and pronounced me dead. "Vomitus biscuitus. Spirito stinko. Flatulus glorious. Amen." He crossed himself rapidly three times, sighed respectfully, and walked into the coffee shop.

The diner was parked in the middle of a dead-end street between West End Avenue and the elevated highway that ran along the river. Amidst the steel pillars below the road, the homeless had built a village of scrap shacks, and I watched the shadows of men picking through the debris, like migrant workers harvesting rubble. I stepped out of the ambulance. Only walk to the end of that street and I would disappear.

A young woman, a teenager really, emerged from the darkness and walked toward me. She wore a yellow raincoat in the dry air and tried to move like a model despite the high heels that caught every crack in the sidewalk. Swinging her hips awkwardly, pushing out her small chest, she unbuttoned the top of her coat and pulled back the hood and smiled at me from halfway down the block. My Rose.

She looked surprisingly well, I thought, but I knew that at any moment the trouble breathing would start. She spread the raincoat around her bare shoulders, and as she passed she looked at me and smiled again, and with those same eyes that stared at me so blankly a month before, she winked and tossed back her hair with a turn of the head, showing a black mole behind her ear.

The three boys in the diner, seeing her walk past, came rushing out whistling and howling, pulling at their crotches. "Venga, puta."

Behind them came Tom, a coffee in each hand. "That's not very nice," he said. "You boys are going to have to apologize for that."

The boys looked to each other and laughed. Tom stopped. "Now, you apologize to this young lady," he said. Rose came back to stand behind him, a rare opportunity to have one's honor defended. I kept staring at her, looking for any signs of the asthma.

"You crazy, man. Look, she's a whore."

"That's enough of that. You're just getting yourself into more trouble. I think you better say something like 'I'm sorry' to this woman."

"You gonna make me, old man?"

Tom dropped the coffees, and the tallest of the three took a step forward, while the other two circled. Tom and the boy pushed each other twice and grabbed hold and rolled to the ground and then the boy was lying alone, Tom standing over him.

I watched these events roll out like a twister across the plains, fascinating until you're whipped into its center and the air explodes. I reached into the bus and turned on the lights and sirens, and then I jumped on the closest one, swinging my arms against his head. Thrown off and almost falling, I jumped on the other. Tom Walls holding Bronson over his head, bringing it down on shoulders, heads, and necks. Fists in my side without pain, the whisper of a knife pass near my neck, and then the fight was over, Tom swinging at the air behind them as they stumbled off.

I turned around to see Rose standing a foot away. "Thank you," she said, and looked as if she was going to hug me. I stepped back, but the thought of touching her gave me an awkward thrill. "You guys are my heroes."

"It's our job, miss," Tom explained. "That's what we do. Save lives. You go on home now. These streets aren't safe."

"I will."

I searched myself for holes, feeling so good, like I'd died in the fight and been born again, younger, stronger. I jumped into the driver's seat, the sirens still blaring. "Cmon, Tom," I yelled. "It's a full moon. The city's burning without us."

He stood laughing, tucking in his shirt. Not a mark on him. "I feel it, Father, but I don't ever remember you fighting like that."

"Are you ready, Tom?"

"When you are, Father."

"I've never felt better in my life." I drove with the sirens flashing, lights wailing, skidding around corners, running red lights without blinking, the power that had been gone for years. Tom cheering by my side.

About once a week during those years we worked together, Tom and I would go shopping for groceries for a family Tom looked after in East Harlem, the wife's daughter's children of Tom's friend who had died in Vietnam. Something like that. After dropping off the packages, we stayed a few minutes while Tom awkwardly bounced one of the kids on his knee. The daughter always made us coffee and asked Tom to tell stories of her father, but the mother, the woman I guessed was the dead soldier's wife, never said a word, never acknowledged our presence. I would sit with her on the busted sofa, watching Spanish shows on the TV Tom had brought.

16

The lights on Ninth Avenue glowed green as far as I could see, and I took the center lane, my gas foot anchored to the floor. Passing Forty-second, I put my left foot hard to the brake, locking it, sliding into the turn, left foot off, right still down, the gas grabbing the wheels a foot away from hitting the taxi. I was rising, lighter and lighter, with every turn another piece falling away. Soaked with suffering for so long I could hardly move, tons of it, my compassion so doused with woe it was useless, a dead thing inside. When I let it go I was free, careening up Eighth, skidding around Fifty-seventh, just missing a couple wearing green shoes. Entering Broadway on two wheels, I stood on a level field, nothing behind or ahead, above or below.

There's no better cure for the blues than driving an ambulance extremely fast and without direction, red lights beating against storefronts, sirens screaming for you, gas brake turn, gas brake turn, circling a block four times and then straight down the avenue. Guaranteed to cure you if it doesn't kill you. Drive as fast as you can and then go faster. Turn only at the last possible moment and without reason. If you have to hit a car, make sure it's one that's double parked.

"Where are you going?" Tom yelled. "Did you hear something?"

The ambulance and police radios at full volume, I turned up the FM, a song by the Doors, and with the yelping overhead, the dispatcher's pleading, it all formed a hysterical symphony, perfect for this kind of steering.

"I am driving out of myself," I cried.

"There's no brakes."

"I've taken that into consideration."

Tom believed the copilot's role was as important as the driver's. The eyes around the corner. He leaned forward, his face near the glass. "You're clear, you're clear, garbage truck, baby carriage, taxi, taxi, taxi." The copilot needed to be calm at all times, fearless, and over the years we worked together, it became the driver's job to scare the hell out of the copilot.

Most other medics would be screaming by now. Larry would stand on the seat, his back against the roof, crying. Tom was tougher. I considered it a victory if, when crash seemed imminent, I heard a slight gasp of air through his teeth, followed by a choked-off grunt. I had almost given up, but when I clipped a mirror off a double-parked delivery van on Fifty-second, I saw his knuckles whiten on the dash and I knew I was close. I charged the red light at full speed, screaming with Jim Morrison, immaculate.

"Garbage truck," Tom said, then again, louder, "Garbage truck," and he let out this hard low whistle like a tire going flat and I spun the wheel right, the truck cutting left, and just when I thought we'd roll, the bus straightened out and skidded to a stop in front of the Armenian deli.

Tom walked calmly around the front. I locked the door. "Get out," he said. "Get out of the bus."

"I got you good." I imitated the whistle.

"Yeah you got me. You're a psycho. Now come on. One minute I think you're going for suicide, the next it's partnercide. Unfit to command this vehicle."

"But, Tom, I'm cured. The fight fixed me. Let's do some jobs."

"You look like someone who just stepped out of a three-day firefight. You ought to look in the mirror, Father Frank."

"Don't call me Father Frank. I've changed. Call me Frank Evil. Heartless Frank."

"You're a bleeding heart, Frank. You can't help it. That's what you are."

"I'm bled out, Tom; can't bleed without blood. And then the heart stops."

"All right, Frank Evil. It's your turn to get the coffee."

Tom was behind the driver's seat when I returned and we started moving as soon as I got in, left side of the street, three miles an hour. He would drive all night like that, on patrol. "You listen to the ambulance radio and I'll listen to the police," he said. Trauma calls were usually dispatched first to police, and Tom enjoyed beating them to the scene. He said the job wasn't worth doing if you couldn't smell the gun smoke in the air.

I watched the street, the police radio to one ear and the ambulance dispatch to the other, waiting, knowing that nothing would happen without me. I wanted an explosion, a multi-casualty incident, bodies on four corners, shooting victims in every room, buildings collapsed, trains derailed. I could not control the living or the dying – their fates were determined long before my arrival – but I believed my presence was necessary for the event to occur, as action requires a scene. I was the scene. The city and I were one. Those ten years I was away, when my father took us out of the city, left me behind and out of sync with Manhattan, its cycles of death and renewal. Five years of relentless chasing and falling to catch up. Now it was hard to tell if I had made it or gone insane trying. I wondered if it was all the same thing.

We drove up Eighth, the avenue clustered with people moving absently and boneless from the neon chicken shacks to the slave shows at the Circus Cinema. Crowds watching and listening as if waiting for the one particular moment that would begin the night. Tom pulled over to watch a fight on the corner of Fortieth, two men rolling in the gutter, and, in front of the bus terminal, two more men fighting. One had his arm in a sling and the other had suffered some kind of stroke that paralyzed his right side and the two of them swung their good arms at each other until the bottle they fought for was empty.

While stopped at a light, we heard a scream from one of the buildings across the street. An old man ran out dressed only in tattered, deeply stained undershorts. Another scream, a woman chasing him. Short and dark and wearing a red bodysuit with a long red cape, she held a butcher's knife over her head. In the doorway they'd come from stood the figure of Mr. Burke, his coat and jacket gone, white shirt stained with blood, white arms raised to the sky.

"Go ahead and do what you want," I yelled to him. "I don't care anymore."

"You tell em," Tom said, and made a left on Fifty-first, a

left again on Ninth, and when we finished our coffees he pulled Franco onto the curb in front of the Puerto Rican bakery. His foot still on the gas, he yelled over the engine. "There's a woman in here, uses the old cheesecloth and the black bean. It should be against the law, this coffee. Are you ready, Frank?"

"Double them, Tom."

He stepped out and pulled from behind his seat a ten-pound weightlifting ring and balanced it on the gas pedal until the rods were thumping against the hood. "My high idle," he said. "He stalls without the weight. Can't let him stall. It's like dropping the flag."

From the corner ahead I saw an old woman approaching, searching left and right. When she was closer, I recognized Mrs. Burke, looking years older. I lowered my head in the seat. She knocked on the window. "Have you seen my husband?"

"No." I shook my head, looking away.

"I can't find him. I've been looking everywhere. He's sick, you know. He shouldn't be out."

She continued on down the street, and Tom brought the coffees. The moment he sat down the bus was in drive, the speed of a brisk walk up Eighth. "We're supposed to be covering the Upper West Side and Harlem," he said. "That's where the trauma is, but they keep calling us for midtown."

"I can't escape this place."

"Sixteen Xray, Xray." The dispatcher on cue.

I keyed the radio. "X."

"First of all, I want you to know how sorry I am about this. I've always liked you two. Sixteen Xray is a legend in

our lunchtime. A unit above none, and so it hurts me deeply
to have to do this, but I have no choice. You must go to
Forty-six and Ten. In front of the liquor store there you'll
find a forty-year-old male, unconscious, lying next to his
wheelchair. Do I have to say any more?"

"You've said too much," I said.

Tom stared at the radio. "Mr. Oh."

"It's early for him."

"That's all right," Tom said. "We're not meant to do Oh
tonight. Something else is going to happen. I can feel it." He
continued at the same speed toward Ninth and south and
then west on Forty-fifth, and I began to get the same feeling
and I watched the sidewalks and storefronts, at any moment
expecting a man to come running out to the street, blood
pouring from his throat.

"Bingo," Tom yelled. He turned up the volume on the
police radio. "EMS to Central," he said. "What was that
call?"

"Pedestrian struck, Fifty-fourth Street and Tenth Avenue."

"Ten-four, one minute out."

Tom let off the brake, pressing me against the seat, the
siren in my throat, shutting off everything that had happened before.

"I love that police dispatcher," Tom cried. "Her voice is
like caramel flan. Her breasts are huge."

"She loves me," I said, and forced myself forward, my
head near the windshield, scanning the streets ahead. "She
whispers to me at night, in French. Taxi, you're clear, taxi,
you're clear."

"Her name is Yvonne, Hungarian. She cooks for me, topless. The bread she cooks is a part of heaven."

The police lights three blocks up, the crowd around a garbage truck. "She swore herself to me when she was fourteen," I said. "I've painted nudes of her in oil, crayon, on black velvet. She still cries when she sees them. The garbage truck up ahead."

I was out of the bus before it stopped. A cop standing in front of the crowd, near the garbage truck's rear wheels. Another cop suddenly next to me.

"This one's definitely different," he said. "The body's alive, but no head. I'm having a lot of trouble accepting it."

I grabbed the airway bag and started moving through the crowd, mostly garbage workers and homeless men who had worked in sanitation or who wished to someday. At the front of the truck, three more trucks were parked, all part of the notorious Mars carting fleet.

"Move it. Medics coming through." The garbage wrestlers parting in front of me. All singing the same song: You see that shit? un-fucking-believable.

The cop stood in front of them like an auctioneer at a cattle show. "If I didn't see it," he said, "I would have never fucking believed it." He moved aside to let me next to the body.

It lay on its back, new white sneakers pointing straight up, a purple sweatsuit zipped over the great middle but open at the white-haired chest to show the three gold chains that wrapped around the wide neck that disappeared into the slim space between the mammoth rear wheels. I could see nothing of the head, only neck and then tire.

The cop's voice above me. "Apparently, the driver here was backing up when he struck the man here knocking him to the ground and running over his head with the most rear of these two wheels. Someone on the sidewalk saw the whole thing and told the driver to stop, fortunately, or unfortunately, depending on how you look at it."

I watched the chest rise and fall, equal and full. Listened to the lungs, clear except for some stridorous sounds near the top. I checked the pulse, slow and strong, and then the hand moved. Carefully it turned over mine, grabbed my wrist and with amazing strength twisted it – numbing pain up to my shoulder. I punched the hand, the stomach. I stood enough to kick him in the ribs before he let go.

"Did the same to me," the cop said. "Almost ripped my leg off. I thought I'd have to shoot him. A tough guy."

"You better believe he's a tough guy," one of the wrestlers said. "That's Joe Mars. You can't fucking kill this guy."

"Is there a tow truck coming?"

"We ordered the biggest one; ten-minute ETA."

Tom Walls arrived with the stretcher piled up six feet with equipment: traction splints, suction machines, life preservers, bedpans. "Prepared for anything," he said, and pulled out a body bag.

"He's not dead yet."

"Must have a small head."

"Well he didn't before, but he does now. It's Joe Mars."

"That's a fitting way to go. Run over by his own truck. Who hit him?"

The cop didn't have to point out the driver, who looked like he was standing naked in a meat locker, arms wrapped around himself, feet tapping, cigarette shaking in his hand.

"Be getting a call for him next," I said. "The sons of Mars ain't gonna like this."

"He snuck behind me," the driver said. "I didn't even touch the gas. My foot was on the brake the whole time." He looked over to the man standing next to him, short, with silver teeth. "You were with me. You saw it. Tell em."

"All I knows," the man said, "is he's racing around all night asking me where's Joe hanging out, where's Joe. Why you care so much about Joe? I keeps saying to him."

"Some partner," said the cop, writing in his book.

"Hey, Tom," I said. "Let's lift it."

"Lift what?"

"We got thirty meatheads here. I mean, it's garbage, right? These guys know how to lift garbage."

"Never happen," said the cop, but Tom was already arranging the men around the rear of the truck. "Never say happen," Tom said, and took up his position next to Joe Mars. "Let's go, men. On the count of three."

A memorable groan and little else. A quart of rainbow-colored soup spilled over the wheels that had displaced Joe's head.

"I don't believe it," Tom cried. "You call yourselves garbage men. You are girly men, veal boys. If only we had thirty medics here we'd know how to move this thing. All women please step away from the truck. If there's no men left then I'll do it myself."

"I don't need this shit," said a woman in a green Mars uniform the size of a steer skin. She raised her hands from the truck and moved away.

"Get back in there," Tom yelled. "You're a garbage man and don't forget it. We're all garbage men. The world is our garbage. Now lift, lift."

Kneeling next to Joe Mars, I watched the tires expand against the ground, one inch, two. Not enough to see the face.

"Hold it, hold it," I yelled. Men snorting like mating bulls. I opened my knife, stuck it into the tire, and twisted. Then the other. I grabbed the cop's arm. "Pull up on the tire, near the head." He did, and still not enough space, and the oxygen in the air getting thin, muscles breaking down, men whimpering now like whipped dogs. I had taken a chance cutting the tires. If they dropped it now . . . "I need another inch," I said. "One more." Dying groans.

I closed my eyes and breathed in and held it, feeling the truck rise, and I pulled Joe's white sneakers as hard as I could, the head sliding free like taking off a wet shoe. The truck fell. A cheer went up from the crowd, which now numbered near a hundred, and then another sound, like a bad smell, and silence as all saw for the first time the remains of Joe Mars.

The face was flattened significantly, so that nose, cheeks, and chin all settled in the same plane. The skin was peeled back from a line down the center and bunched up where the plane ended and the sides of the face began; no butcher could have cleaved cleaner. Add to this the flattening in the back and Joe's natural and well-known flattop. The result, a near-perfect square, the human blockhead, mouth, nose, and eyes huddled together in the cube's oozing center. With his every gurgling exhalation, blood and spittle showered the table of his face.

"The skull must be fractured in a dozen places," I said. "He won't live an hour."

So I taped a mask to Joe's head, more to control the bloody spray of his breath than for any good oxygen might do. He improved immediately, at least he appeared to, for the mask gave the impression of a more human-shaped face beneath. By the time we reached Misery, his breathing had become very shallow, pulse down to thirty. Not much time left. I took down the IV and jumped out. Tom pointed to Mars. From the gaps in Joe's face a lumpy gray foam billowed. It filled the bloody plain that made up the top of his head, and then it seeped evenly over the sides.

"Look, Tom, that's gray matter. He's puking up his brains."

"A tough guy," Tom said, and we pulled the stretcher out and wheeled it through the packed waiting room, the inevitable wait for Griss to open the door.

"Griss, open up," Tom said. "We got a celebrity here. The famous gangster Joe Mars has been run over by one of his trucks."

"Griss says all the more reason to slow down and appreciate the ironies of street justice."

Hazmat waited at the end of Skid Row. "What kind of nightmare are you handing off to me now?"

"Garbage truck over the head," I said. "Must be a huge basilar skull fracture with brain tissue leaking into the esophagus because he just vomited a load of gray matter in the back of the ambulance."

"His mind doesn't agree with him," Tom said.

"I don't believe it," Hazmat said, and as if to help

persuade him, Joe Mars opened another well of gray. The doctor made a thorough examination of the product, and then he looked up. "He can't be alive."

"He's not," I said, my hand on the wrist. "He's dead."

I went into the bathroom half blind and came out clear-eyed. Dr. Hazmat stood outside slot three, his arms crossed. "Nurse Crupp, we're gonna need some more Valium over here. He's awake again. Five milligrams, stat."

Behind the stale blue curtain, Patrick Burke continued his battle with the cloth tied to his wrists, the plastic lodged in his throat. Unable to scream, he gnawed viciously at the tube, as if trying to close it off, choke himself. The ventilator alarm rang out and I watched Burke's face turn the color of the curtain, his teeth clamped tightly over the tube. "Give me a hand, Frank. I've got to get something between those teeth." Trying not to look into the eyes, I helped Hazmat pry open the jaw enough to force in a bite stick. "Nurse Crupp, where's that Valium?" he shouted, though she was standing next to him and jabbing a syringe into one of Burke's many IVs. Seconds later, Burke's arms rested quietly on the rails. The alarm quit its crying, and the ventilator started up again as if nothing had happened, pumping air in, pulling it out.

"You can't believe how much he's improved," Hazmat said.

"He looks great," I said. "How many times have you shocked him tonight?"

"Fourteen. We finally got him a room upstairs. Should be up there in a couple of hours. He might even walk out of here someday."

"What do you do, just have someone follow him around with a defibrillator?"

Hazmat laughed. "That's good, Frank. No, but they might surgically implant one, about the size of my thumb. It goes up near the shoulder here, with two electrodes connected to the heart. It sends a shock down the line whenever it senses a drop in blood flow. Amazing, isn't it?"

"A medical miracle," I said.

Mary Burke stood in the rear of the waiting room, talking to a group of about ten people. I walked over and stared at the back of her head. Gone were the lost daughter, the scared junkie. Tonight she had dressed for strength, her suit of armor – leather jacket, blue jeans, heavy black shoes. She turned toward me and then to the group. "Everyone, this is the medic who brought my father in. Frank, these are some of my father's friends. They've been coming in all night."

One of the women stepped forward and shook my hand. "As soon as we heard, we came right over," she said. "We live out on the Island now, but we used to live right down the block from Pat. He was like a saint to us. When Ron got sick and lost his job, Patrick helped me get cashier work down at Food City, and then when Ron got better, Patrick talked his boss into giving him back his job."

Everyone in the group had a story to tell attesting to Burke's charity. I watched Mary listening with her eyes closed. For the first time I noticed freckles on her face, three per cheek, each placed perfectly, clear sign of a higher hand.

"I'm going for a smoke," I said to her.

We stood in the parking lot. A wild breeze turned a corner and blew out my match, and then the air was as quiet and still as a country well. I saw Tom sitting behind the wheel of Franco, his hands moving back and forth, the motions of driving. More calls, more calls.

Mary coughed for half a minute. "I heard that was Joe Mars you just brought in. He looked pretty bad."

"He was. He's dead."

"Good. He was Cy's partner, a real son of a bitch. You know, Cy called me up today. I don't know how he got my number, but he asks me do I want to come over and see him, and then, when I tell him I'd rather go to a leper colony, he says there's a new gang wants to kill him, take over the business, like I'm supposed to feel sorry for him. I told him I hope this time he's right. That they kill him. That's what I told him."

"You're not going back."

"Look, last night I was weak. It won't happen again. And all that shit I said – it was just cause I was stoned, talking out of my head, you know. Forget it."

"Sure. No problem. Thanks for letting me crash. It was the best sleep I had in months. I used some of your soap."

"Forget it." She ground out her cigarette and looked back through the emergency room doors. "I wish these people would leave already. I can't listen to another story. It's like we're at a wake or something, like they're here to bury him. He's not going to die. Did you see him?"

"I'm not sure."

"He's responding to me when I talk to him. He can blink for yes, twice for no. The doctor says the brain has come around but they're waiting for the heart to stabilize. He says they still have to keep him tied up. It's like pulling teeth getting any information out of that guy."

"Have you seen your mother?"

"No. Why? I been here all night."

"I don't know." I stared at the constellation of freckles on her cheek, smelled again the hothouse fragrance of her bathroom. "Can I bring you back something to eat – a falafel, some pizza?"

"No, thanks. We just ate. Nino's sent over three pies this evening. Someone must have told them. I forgot how much my father meant to these people. All I saw was how tough he was with us. But now I know he had to be like that, to make us tough. This city'll eat you up if you aren't strong enough."

"No," I said. "The city doesn't discriminate. It gets everybody." Franco's lights lit up the parking lot. "I have to go. Another call." I stepped closer, blood pressure soaring, my heart racing to a finish. Tom hit the air horn, running out of time. "We're all dying, Mary Burke."

She stared up at me, six inches away, five. "This is not a good time."

"There is no time," I said, and placed my hand on her back and kissed her once, solidly, lips mashed for a second, then I was running to the ambulance.

On Broadway, Tom took his foot completely off the brake, and the overdrive kicked in like a mail truck hitting us from behind. Franco was the last of the light-framed 450s, the fastest in the city, and Tom was pushing him to the limit, breaking open the smallest holes, cutting, sprinting, dodging tackles. I forgot how good a driver he could be, always in control, even at terrific speeds. I put my boots on the dash and tilted my head back, eyes half closed, the windows like walls of light, blurry, banging, flashing, like sitting in a pinball. The kiss echoed inside me, spreading out into the lights rushing past, everything rushing behind. Movement was all that mattered. "Where are we going?"

"A shooting," Tom said. "Confirmed. Forty-fifth Street, Nine to Ten."

In the middle of the main hooker block, two cop cars were stopping the traffic, and the corner of Forty-fifth and Nine had become a crazy stampede of johns frantically reversing away from the crime scene. Tom turned in from Ninth and climbed the sidewalk, skidding just short of the cops and whores standing in a half circle around the stoop. We grabbed the trauma and airway bags, oxygen and backboard. Cops pushing people back, the man's body lying on the bottom steps.

"Where's he shot?" I asked the cop.

"He ain't shot. Just dead," the cop said.

"Stone cold dead," said his partner.

A futile search for a pulse. The hand cold. At least an hour gone.

"It's the Outlaw," one of the hookers said.

"How do you know?"

"He's dressed in black, isn't he?"

Black boots, black pants, black long-sleeved shirt, and a wide-brimmed black hat covering his face. I pulled it back to see the hooked crooked nose, the tiny cross tattoo like a tear under his right eye. The Outlaw was well known in the Kitchen, a one-man terrorist organization. There were celebrations every time he went to jail and public warnings every time he got out. So the only surprise in finding the Outlaw dead on this stoop was not finding any bullet holes. His body lay in a strange position, as if he'd been attacked in some way, though I couldn't see a trace of trauma. The head rested up against the fourth step, the back ran flat along the third, and his legs trailed down the last two so that his feet reached the sidewalk. The arms were bent at the elbows, hands near his face, palms open and up, as if a cathedral was trying to sit there. His face had that look too, of someone fighting off a fatal weight.

I checked the head and torso again. "Maybe he OD'd."

"No way," one of the hookers said. "The only drugs the Outlaw used was sex and violence, usually together."

"Well, how did he die?"

"Musta got killed. Everyone knows the Outlaw's working for Cy, and everyone knows that Cy's running out of time."

The other whores stepped up for a better view. They seemed to think the Outlaw's death very funny. "Looks to me like he died from pure ugliness," one said. Another, leaning almost off her heels, "I think Dorothea parked her big fat trailer on his face." "Suck this," said Dorothea.

"Any of you ladies see what happened?" Tom asked, and one of the women stepped up.

"I did the man a couple of hours ago. I'd never forget that nose, and I can tell you he was fine then." The one next to her looked hard at her face. "Damn, girl, your pussy killed that man." Everyone laughing, like fat men in a barbershop.

The patient and I were sitting together in the back of the ambulance. "My brother was killed in a fight in a bar and he went to hell," the patient said. "But he can still talk to me. You can't believe how bad it is down there. He's been telling me that he can get out if I kill someone, that's the only way." The man was staring through me and I had to avoid his eyes. I looked up through the little window, at Larry in the driver's seat, eating a cold hamburger. "It's one for one. I kill somebody, and he gets out. He says it doesn't matter who. I don't want to kill anybody, but I can't stand it, it's so bad for him down there. I don't know what to do." The man stopped talking and then he turned to the back window, staring out intently, as if someone there was speaking to him. "No, I can't," he screamed, and covered his ears with his hands. "No, you can't," I said, moving to the front of the stretcher. He pulled his hands down and turned back to the window, listening again, and then he nodded his head and mouthed the words "Yes, I know."

17

Tom was driving to coffee, lights off, keeping to the left side, idling low, obeying all traffic laws so as not to tip off the dispatcher. Number 801 had returned, and though he worked in the basement of a warehouse in Queens, his eyes were everywhere. "Ten Henry, go to the bus terminal for the man shot three years ago in the hip and says his arm hurts. Thirteen Boy, at the bus terminal also, Ninth Avenue entrance, you'll find a woman at the ticket booth who can't remember where she's going. Fourteen Adam, in front of the bus terminal is a Norwegian who says he's never been to an American hospital before and would like to see one. No further information. Units, I know you're out there. Fifteen Zebra, Fourteen Young, Sixteen Xray – update, update."

"Stay away from the bus terminal," I said. "The bastard's trying to clean it out."

"He'll never do it. Take every unit in the city if he tries that."

"Not so loud," I whispered. Dispatcher 801 was hated and feared by all who heard him.

"We'll hold the signal on the Outlaw; wait for a real call to come over and grab it." Tom turned off the lights and parked in a dark hole in the middle of the block. "Get ready, Frank, cause there's gonna be a lot of trauma around here.

New vacancies for top mobster, top renegade. Some people willing to go to extreme lengths to get those positions."

"As long as we keep moving," I said. "I don't like standing still." We were sitting on one of the few tree-lined blocks in the area, a reminder of what the neighborhood never was: brick houses all occupied and cared for, sidewalks uncracked and junkie free. I turned up the police radio but couldn't shut out the quiet. On the FM, the music about cars and girls only worsened the effect. I closed my eyes. Pictures in my head. The faceless Joe Mars. I looked down the row of brick, remembering the call on the third floor, building on my right, the man lying in bed, shotgun on his chest, empty above his neck. Up ahead, two young women turned the corner, walking toward us. One wearing a yellow raincoat. It had to be. Rose, catching up.

"Come on, Tom, let's give up the signal, pick up a job."

"You want some bum from the bus terminal? We'll wait for a real call."

"Let's get in a fight, then."

"Who with?"

"That's your job." Rose leaned over an alley fence, a little short of breath. Her friend helped her sit down. "Let's just keep driving, Tom, keep moving. No stopping. We're sharks. If we stop too long, we die." Tom put the bus in gear. He always liked it when I called us sharks. I kept my face down, bowing to the floor.

East on Forty-eighth, passing two cops kicking a bum and two whores kicking a bum and two bums kicking some cans around. On Ninth, the corners were heating up, dealers runners and buyers, gods prophets and slaves, the defeated ment, bomb something."

"What do you want to break?"

"I don't know – let's break some windows."

"Why?"

"Destruction, distraction, I just feel the need."

"You need a reason, Frank. You don't just go around breaking people's windows. That's anarchy."

"What's a reason? Give me a reason, Tom."

"Let me think," he said, and when we reached Tenth he made a right and took his foot completely off the brake, passing buses, taxis, diplomats, until he pulled up alongside a wildly weaving gypsy cab. At the wheel, a white-turbaned man scanned the sidewalks with the intensity of a soldier on a battlefield. "All right, you take this towelhead here. I bet he's been in this country a year and still doesn't speak more than ten words of English, could be longer and less English. Only one thing we can be sure about – that is, he drives like a maniac. No concern whatsoever with the most basic rules of the road. Probably has forty moving violations, ten accidents, pedestrian-strucks, three at least, and I think I'm being kind here. Look, look, a classic cabbie move."

305

The driver stopped for the red light about a quarter into the intersection, completely obstructing the crosswalk so that pedestrians had to move around through the passing traffic.

Tom pulled up alongside and yelled out to the driver, "Hey, swammy, that's called a crosswalk. You stop before it, not on it." The driver directed the top of his turban in our direction, a gesture I guessed might have gotten someone killed in Kashmir. Tom turned to me. "Do you think it was freedom that brought him here, the love of America? I don't think he gives a damn about America. He wants money, and what he doesn't spend on hats or halal he sends out of the country. I say the man is a detriment to our people and our society, he never should have been let into the country, and now that he's here he needs to be dealt with."

The light turned green, the cabbie already halfway across the street, making his move left into our lane to avoid the construction in his. Tom gunned the engine to steel-mill level, took his foot off the brake, and we were beside the cab, Tom's two hands on the wheel making the slightest move to the right, into the taxi without touching, the cabbie skidding through sawhorses and under a bulldozer and Tom talking all the while. "We need to be vigilant, Frank. The keepers of the flame, of the ideas that started this country, the free expression of opposition. Fight back, Frank."

"Who, Tom? I don't care about the motives. Just tell me who." And right then I wanted to hit someone more than ever in my life, more than Wade Dombrowski, who stole my girl in eighth grade, more than my father, more than Dispatcher 801. I was tired of cleaning up the blood of all the people who suffered at the hands of all the people. I wanted to spill a little, get my own licks in on someone I could hold even marginally responsible for the troubles I'd seen. Time was running short.

Tom made a right on Fifty-second and stopped, two doors down from the building I grew up in. "I know who to go after," he said, his finger stretched out toward a point near the middle of the block. "Him."

Noël stood next to a white Mustang, a baseball bat resting on his shoulder. He wore the same bloodstained suit, and along with the tires tied to his shoulders and elbows, he had wrapped his chest and belly with steel wire, at least a mile of it, and around his bare brown arms and neck he had tied blue and black rags, rags also around his black boots and rags woven between the thick clumps of black dreadlocks also tied wildly with colored string and more wire and thin curly strands of white paper that dangled from each ear. He wore two watches on each wrist, and now he checked the time on all of them, and sighing like Nurse Constance coming off her coffee break, he grabbed the bat with two hands, lifted it up, and swung it through the Mustang's window. Then he put the bat down and used it like a cane as he walked up to the next car.

Tom punched the speedometer. "This guy has been terrorizing the neighborhood for weeks, ever since he got out of jail, scaring half the population, wreaking general havoc, contributing heartily to the bad name of the place. The term 'menace to society' was made especially for him."

"He's crazy," I said. "He can't help it."

"Well, why don't they put him away? Prisons don't want

him. I took him in to the hospital yesterday, and here he is again."

"He took a bad beating when he was younger."

"Not bad enough."

Noël reached the next car, a Bronco, and carefully he hefted the bat and smashed it through the windshield.

"Look at that," Tom said, "and tell me this is just a crazy person. Each move is calculated. See, he knows exactly what he's doing. If you're going to hit someone, this is the one. I've been after him for weeks. He's quick, though, shifty, and he runs like a rat, tough for one person, but with two people and a good plan, maybe . . ."

There was no doubt that violence and mayhem followed everything Noël did, but how could I hold him responsible? He had a bullet in his head. We were all responsible. "Okay," I said. "What do I do?"

"If he sees me he'll run, so I'll get out here. You start talking to him about baseball or something to divert his attention for a minute, while I sneak around behind him and get down on my hands and knees and you push him. When he falls we'll both get him."

"That's ridiculous."

"Believe me, it always works. The simpler the better."

"They teach you this in Nam?"

"No, in Flatbush."

Tom got out and crouched down and moved behind the ambulance. I climbed over the console and behind the wheel, tripping the siren with my foot. Noël never noticed. He was sending his bat through the hatch of a Pinto when I pulled up.

"That's a hell of a swing you got there, Noël." Standing about fifteen feet away. "I'm thinking Mattingly in his prime."

He stared for a while like he wasn't sure who I was, but then he smiled, walking over to the Pinto's passenger window, talking. "Ah, man, Mattingly had so many swings, always changing every week, toes up, toes down, elbows over the head, elbows on the hip, but the best year chasing the Boggs, it was the elbows up in the back, hips off the plate like so and let it go." He put out the side window and cheered. It looked like fun. He moved over to the windshield. "Me, I swing like all Reggie, Mr. October." He lined himself up. "Look at the big step, man," and sent the bat through, shouting, "See ya, number three, game six, World Series, 1977." He dropped the stick and ran once around the car with his fist in the air. He picked up the bat and held it out. "Here – you try."

"No, no, I better not."

"Sure, sure, give go."

"Yeah?"

I forgot all about the plan, to hit Noël. More than anything, I wanted to break something. "All right. What the hell." I grabbed the bat. Put it down. Spit into my hands. Picked it up. Looked out to right field. "The next year," I said, "tiebreaker for the division, in Boston, Yankees down, two to nothing. Bucky Dent steps to the plate."

"Oh man, Bucky."

"The pitch in from Torres, his trademark, the high heater. Bucky knows what's coming. He steps in and smash, over the green monster. The crowd silenced by that rocket. The

309

Yankees are going to the playoffs." I trotted around the car, taking my time, enjoying every second. Pieces of glass in my hair, my face and shirt, glittering in the night lights.

"Frank, what the hell are you doing?" Tom was standing in the half shadows of the building. Noël picked up the bat and sprinted for the next building and before Tom could cut him off he was down the stairs into the alley.

Tom turned to me. "You go down those stairs over there. Meet me back here if you can't find him in ten minutes. Call out if you see him, and get with the program, Frank." He disappeared down the steps.

I stared into the alley entrance I remembered so well from my childhood, the dark home of the bogeyman, where my mother told me never to go, and though at the time it was my policy to go everywhere I wasn't supposed to, I never went down there, not even when I was dared. The only place in the city I could say I was scared. But that was seventeen years ago; I was older now, on speaking terms with the bogeyman. So headfirst I dove into the darkness, toppling the garbage, kicking the rolled-up carpets, the groaning mounds of blankets and tiles. I walked into a pipe right above my left eye, the pipe gonging, my head ringing. I held it tight, thinking how much smarter and wiser my eight-year-old self was.

I pulled out my mini-flashlight and shone it on the wet ruined walls, pipes corroded and bent. On the ground the garbage I had been kicking was actually about a dozen people sleeping, their possessions piled above them for warmth. Two sets of eyes stared up from under the blankets, little brown faces. It appeared to me their shoulders were connected. That feeling coming back, about how strange and hopeless every single thing was.

I walked the length of the wall to the alley's end, and under the stone steps leading up to a red door I found a passageway, just wide enough, cornering left, right, and left, into a warm corridor which felt half a block long and the more I walked the hotter it became. I passed a series of metal doors nearly glowing with heat, what sounded like the rush of flames behind. It already felt like summer, like the hottest night in July. I heard the noises of the street getting louder with each step, until I could make out the quivering hum of the air conditioners, babies crying as if in a room next door, garbage trucks passing just over me, their summer's reek lingering.

A door slammed ahead of me, something metal hit the wall to my right, a drunken groan, followed by a woman's voice: "Get out before I call the cops." I turned around and started back. My mother was right. The alley was a bad place, worse than the street, like the worst of the street all the time. I reached an alley intersection and was trying to decide the nearest way out when I heard a woman crying down the passage to my left. I should have needed no further directions, to turn quickly, fearlessly to my right, but I had been walking into disasters for too long, the only route I knew. I pointed my flashlight toward the sound, down the corridor and around a corner, where I found her standing against the back of a dead end, wearing her yellow raincoat and nothing else, one arm holding it closed over her chest, the other rising up her leg. "Why did you kill me, Frank?"

"I didn't mean to."

"You should have helped me."

"I tried to help. I wanted to."

She reached out her arms. "Don't you love me, Frank?"

"You know I do," and I started walking toward her, with my hands ahead of me and reaching for Rose, who shrank into the wall until she was just three thin lines of yellow light coming through an old door of warped wooden boards, where I rested my head. The door opened, pulling my ear with it, and in the blinding new brightness Noël's hair appeared and then vanished into the light.

The tiny room could have been home to any number of vagrant lunatics: the bare bulb in the peeling ceiling, the floor full of old newspapers and coffee cups and filthy clothes and bed linen, a soured mattress, a despair-ridden chair. It looked like my room, actually, everything except the home-made coffin in the corner, made of cardboard and duct tape, and the bones inside. Noël was kneeling on the floor next to it, trying to find room for the wooden bat among the junk that was piled so high it was coming over the sides: baseball equipment, trophies, photos, rocks, crutches, and bones, mostly cattle bones, I guessed, too big to be human, but there was no doubt about the skull, all *Homo sapiens*, sitting on the pile like a white crown, with a quarter-inch hole over the right eye socket and a wig made out of strips of black paper and tape, a remarkable likeness to Noël's jumbled pate. I'd seen enough. "Noël, how do I get out of here?"

"Almost finished, almost finished."

"I don't need you to come. Just give me some directions." I looked back at the door, at any moment expecting Tom Walls to jump in. Having to explain why I hadn't called, why I was such a lousy vigilante.

Noël picked up the skull and rapped its forehead with his own, a hundred-year head butt. "How many times you died?" he said to the skull. "How many times come back?" He shook the skull next to his ear. "Hey, that Noël, he never learns what's right isn't that right no that's wrong. It's who you are is who you'll be and who the hell do you think you are anyway, shoot that boy in the head, that'll teach him." Noël picked up the bat with his other hand and used it to threaten the skull. "Hey hey, can't you see that line, right there down the street, around the corner, huh, who let this crazy nigger in here, hit him in the leg, back of the neck, don't forget the face." He threw the skull back on the pile and pulled out a photograph and rubbed it over his cheek. "Oh, you care so much, Noël, you have such a big heart I want to just leave it in this chair one minute while I go powder my nose and oh no, did I sit on your heart, oh I squashed it I'm sorry."

I grabbed Noël's arm and pulled him up. "Come on, Noël, I can see you're busy and I don't want to take up any more of your time – if you would just show me an exit." I was dragging him to the door when Walls crashed in, like he'd run out of a massacre, one hand on his bleeding head, another victim of the pipes. "Hold him, Frank. I'm here."

"No kidding." I let go of Noël and watched Tom square himself in the doorway, his arms wide and waving in. "Come on, come on." Noël jumped up and down a few times and threw himself against the back wall, then into Tom Walls. The two rolled together on the floor, and somehow Noël made it to his feet and disappeared down the passage, Tom right behind.

I picked up the photo Noël had dropped. It was of Mary Burke, post-prom but still blond and smiling, still a heart-squasher. I placed it back on the pile and walked to the door, all of a sudden badly needing a drink. In the dark passages someone had turned the thermostat up, and with it the voices behind the walls. I turned randomly, feeling myself turning further in, almost looking forward to the surrender, lying down waiting for my bones to be found and loaded into some lunatic's box. I reached a section that seemed to take me under the street, horns overhead followed by explosions, cries of greeting and revulsion, getting louder as I came to another dead end. I stood before a steel door, and from behind it I could clearly make out the bellowing voice of Ralph Kramden from my father's favorite show, *The Honeymooners*. Then the snappy reply of his wife, Alice, followed by laughter, clearer, closer, a man in the room. "You tell him, Alice," the man said. Ten years since I heard that voice. "Frank." My father calling me. "Come here, Frank," the command that wanted something done now. I was so happy to hear it, the man I'd hated for so long, the one who'd know exactly how to help me out. I opened the door to tell him I understand and to pour another glass of gin and pull up the blue chair next to him, sip our drinks and laugh at the TV. Groaning when I found myself on the street, the ambulance half a block away. You run and run, and where do you go? Round and round, and where you stop you already know: Rose, my father, the circles always complete, each time around another bone in the box, waiting for it to fill up. What was I rushing for? The faster you run, the sooner you get back. No wonder Marcus drove so slow.

I found the super lying in the bottom of the shaft, two flights below where I stood, the elevator doors open and no elevator. "Get me out," he said. "Hurry up." I tied a rope to a beam in the shaft and climbed down, nearly stepping on the bone that was sticking out of his arm just below the shoulder. He spoke with a Russian accent. "It was a long time I didn't hear the elevator working and so I came to look and no elevator. Get me out." Except for the fractured arm, I couldn't find anything wrong. He wore a faded Hawaiian-style shirt, and when I began to cut away the sleeve to see the wound, he looked over at me. "What are you doing?" he said angrily. "Don't cut that. That's my lucky shirt." And that's when I heard a click from above, followed by a humming noise, gears turning. The man and I looked up and watched together as from the top floor the elevator began its descent.

18

I sat in the driver's seat and waited for Tom to finish killing Noël, and stoically I listened to the sirens ringing up and down the avenues. Farther away, much farther, a voice was crying on the radio, a desperate, static-filled begging that could only be Dispatcher Bailey. His first time at the controls after six months of psych leave, and Bailey's typical bad luck to be working on Hell Night – coming back right where he'd gone off. "I need units. I need units. We got fires in the hole, Forty-two and Broadway. Shots fired outside the Dynamite Club, Thirty-six and Ten. Fired workers shooting each other at the post office, Thirtieth and Nine. Where are my units?"

He sounded like a general gone mad in his bunker in the last hours of a war. I picked up the radio. "Dispatcher 801 sent them all to the bus terminal for cold sores."

"Sixteen Xray, is that you? I need you. Five Will, Seven Boy, answer the radio. We're getting slaughtered over here. They've raped her, oh Lord, they got her, 110 East Fifty-second. Somebody help her for Christ sake. He's going to jump, he's going to jump. Oh my God, he jumped. Is there any unit that can go to 530 West Forty-eighth Street, apartment sixteen M, and help that poor man?"

"La moutard est roulé dans la rue," I said, the few French

317

words I remembered from high school. French always put Bailey over the edge.

"Units, units, we're getting interference. Mother, you're not listening. Oh no, I hear them coming now. Foreign carriers in the perimeter. This is a level one alert. I want everyone to turn their radios off, and when I tell you to, turn them back on."

I turned the radio off, and Tom came out of an alley across the street from the one we had gone in. He sat in the passenger seat, holding his ribs to slow his wheezing. "I almost had him. The moment I get my hands on him he disappears into his hole, just like a rat. I'm gonna catch him, though, before we're through."

"You can't even catch your breath."

"Thanks for your help, partner."

I turned on the overhead flashers and headed for the jumper, 530 West Forty-eighth Street, 16M, Cy Coates's place. Who needed a dispatcher? I knew where I was headed. I rested my head on the back of the seat and let Franco idle forward. Left on Tenth, left again on Fifty-third, then charging down Eleventh at a walking pace. Every day is Judgment Day, I thought, the end is always here. I was starting to sound like Mr. Burke. *There is no tomorrow. Tomorrow is right now.* How many times have you died, Frank? How many times come back? I turned on the sirens and stopped under another red light.

"We have a call?" Tom asked.

"We're dispatching ourselves," I said. "Jumper, Forty-eighth Street, Ten to Eleven."

Tom, still breathing heavily, was waving his left arm

forward, as if that would make me go faster. "Come on. You driving to a jumper down or a garage sale?"

"A jumper sale. A garage down. There's always tomorrow, Tom. You can't go too slow."

"I think you're having a relapse, Father. Now I gotta go recount the bottles of rubbing alcohol."

I parked behind the police cars and fire trucks that filled Forty-eighth Street. In front of them, in the center of the stone animal park, was the massive Emergency Service rescue truck. From its side, SWAT teams pulled out air bags, scuba gear, shotguns, and riot shields. From its top, two men dressed like rabbis trained the great lights on the thirteenth floor, where Cy Coates appeared to be suspended from the balcony's railing, his body attached to it in some way that let his legs dangle below.

Tom and I stood in front of the ambulance, wondering what equipment to bring up. For a few seconds Cy didn't move, a sure DOA, then he rubbed his nose with his left hand and began crying out, "Get me the hell off of here."

"Better bring it all," Tom said. Not until we were underneath the balcony could we see the part of the broken railing that passed through Coates's back and came out his stomach and held him over us.

The foyer was crammed with cops and equipment. "The elevator in this building is broken," I said. "We'd never fit anyway." Tom held open the stairway door. "Come on, guys. A man's dying up there. Let's go."

"Forget it." Six voices at once. "That's thirteen flights."

"Look." Tom pointed out the door. "The news cameras just pulled up."

The cops stood at once. The sergeant, who looked like Will Rogers, called out, "The stairs, men, the stairs." A minute after they left, the elevator came, and Tom and I and the sergeant stepped in with our equipment. The long ride up.

"What's with the rabbis?" Tom asked.

"Like to follow us around. Deputized 'em. Put up a lot of money for the new truck."

"This guy a jumper?"

"We got a call for shots fired on the sixteenth floor. Then the jumper call right after."

The elevator opened and we knocked on three doors at the end of the hall, all locked. The only answer was from Cy, crying out, "Come on in." When the rest of the cops reached the top of the stairs, the sergeant pulled the first two men into the elevator with him. "I'm going up. Checking sixteen."

"I'll go with you," I said.

The door to 16M was open. The sergeant walked in, leading with his gun, his shoes sloshing through an inch of water. "She must have left the tub on," he said, and stepped over the woman lying in the hall, the woman from the morning before, Kanita, a perfectly round little hole above her eye, splinters of bone and blood down the side of her nose, her lips pulled back and dry. "Got another one over here," a cop said. The dead man was lying back in the chair, staring at a broken fish tank. Two new holes in his head. I looked up at the volcano on the wall. Puff.

The other cop returned from the hall. "That's it. No one else home."

"Don't look like a forced entry," said the first.

"What a shame." The sergeant crouched down and with the muzzle of his gun turned over one of the dead fish. "These babies go for five hundred bucks a pop." I took the stairs down.

The residents of 13M, the apartment Cy was hanging from, must have been out of town or out on the town. They'd have trouble recognizing the place now. In less than a minute, Tom and the handful of police had overturned every piece of furniture. The floor was covered with gas-powered metal cutters, acetylene torches, ropes, harnesses, and the large, important-looking boxes that were always brought to these scenes for reasons no one knew. The balcony-door windows were broken, and a trail of blood led down the hall, to where Tom appeared in a bedroom doorway.

"Get this, Frank – we got two patients. Number one, the scarecrow outside. Number two misses the railing but breaks both legs on the balcony. He then throws himself through this glass door, crawls down the hall and into the bedroom, where he proceeds to pull the covers over his head and is now sleeping like a baby."

"Well, he's the steakhead of the night, then."

"I don't think anyone can touch him on that, not even the pimiento out there."

"How's he doing?"

"I haven't had a chance to see him yet. I'm gonna take care of sleeping beauty."

Tom would never admit it, but he was deathly afraid of

heights, in the sense that he would rather shoot himself in the head than go out on a ledge. He could hardly conceal how happy he was to have found another patient, and when I stood next to Cy I could see why. Not only was he impaled on the spike, but the force of his fall had warped and twisted a few feet of fence, ripped it from the rest, and bent it at least two feet over the street.

While the cops strapped on the harnesses, I took Cy's vital signs. He'd lost some blood but not a dangerous amount. The danger was in taking him off the spike, which might be stanching the bleeding, so the spike had to stay in and the fence closest to it cut away. I looked around the wound. The metal had gone in just below the hip in the back and come out just above it in the front. Incredibly, the hip was intact. The spike appeared to have missed all mortal points along the way. I pressed his abdomen. Every time I said, Does this hurt? he screamed and said no.

I put an oxygen mask on him and prepared to start an IV. The only way to do it was to lean out over the edge, against the contorted metal not connected to the spike, and reach out and hit the vein. Looking up, I held the IV bag in my teeth, waiting on a cool breeze to hold me. I leaned over and farther out, the spotlights below like two moons in a concrete sky. Wondering what I would think on the way down. Hail Mary, fall in grace. My mother's laugh. Mona's navel. My last kiss, Mary Burke. The gaps stretching, the navel fading and returning, just a mole in the hole, everyone a ghost. I uncorked the needle, lined it up, and pushed it in. Slid the catheter over the needle and into the vein, the needle out, the tubing in, saline rushing through. Taped everything in place. During this time the cops were busy attaching their harnesses to pitons they had hammered in the brick wall. "You in?" one asked. "Yeah." "You in?" "Yeah." I wasn't asked.

The metal cutters were brought out, two of them; neither worked. The metal cutters back and the torches forward. A fountain of sparks arching over me. Good time to turn off the oxygen.

"Is that me?" Cy asked. "Is it Independence Day?"

"They're torching the fence. You're gonna feel the metal getting warm, maybe very warm."

"I can't hold up my head anymore. I have to lean back."

I passed the IV bag to one of the cops at the door, and Cy stretched back into my hands.

"So, Frank, am I going to live?"

"You're going to live."

"I knew it. You can't kill me – nobody can. I've been thinking about things. Meditating on my financial future. You guys gave me plenty of time to meditate on the future. What did you do, stop for Chinese food on the way over? I could have told you there's plenty of food at my house."

"I was tired," I said. "I needed a coffee."

"What about Kanita?"

"Dead."

"That's too bad. The way it is, though, price of having a vision, working hard to make it happen. Get some money, a nice-looking girl on your arm, and everyone wants to take a piece. Some kid I wouldn't even let wash my Mercedes is in my house, shooting at me. Try to give something back to the community, and this is the thank-you, Frank. Take note,

man, don't let it happen to you. Damn, I thought I could
make it onto the balcony, like Sam. He's fat, that's why, falls
faster. I'm tryin to watch my weight, and look what happens.
Hey, am I shot, Frank? Boy can't shoot for shit either." Cy
raised himself on his pole and flailed his arms, trying to turn
around. "Is there a phone inside? I got to make some calls.
Get some people over here to clean up this mess. Goddamn,
that's hot." The sparks flying over and on us, the spike near
Cy's hip turning red. He laid himself back in my hands.
"That's all right. I can take it. I took something already.
Besides, I got money, and money's the best drug there is.
Look at that." He held out his hand, resting atop the
northern skyline, a thousand sparks striking his palm and
raining upon the Upper West Side. "Isn't it beautiful. When
the fires start to fall, then the strongest rule it all. I love this
city. Look," he said, and then he was gone, over the side and
down. I grabbed his hand, and I was going over too. Okay,
was all I could say.

I had fallen, but I couldn't fall, held up by a belt on my waist
I didn't know I was wearing, bending me in half as I held
Cy's wrist in my fist, the rest of him swaying below. For the
first time, I saw some sign of concern in his eyes. "Look,
Frank, about that ten dollars you owe me: forget about it." I
looked down beyond Cy, people moving below us, a crowd
of at least fifty gathered around the stone animals. *Let him go,*
one shouted. Even from that height I recognized some of
them, mostly overdoses and shooting victims, a man with his
throat cut, a woman thrown from a roof, the boy shot from

his bicycle so long ago. "So, Frank, are you going to pull me up now?" *Let him go.* Many voices now, a chorus rising in the light. "Let *me* go," I shouted. "Now, Frank, why would I do that?" His wrist sliding through my hand. His hand in mine. *Let him go.* He was going. I pulled up and reached down with my other hand and grabbed him under the arm. Then I started to rise.

"Good thing we buckled you in, huh?" the cop said, pulling me over the side. Followed by Cy. "What about me? Who's supposed to buckle in Cy Coates?"

One of the cops turned to the other. "I thought you hooked him in."

"I thought *you* did," the other said, and they put Cy on a backboard and pulled the straps around him as tight as they could. Three inches of iron still stuck out from his belly, a half foot from his side. While carrying him out the door, a part of the pole struck the frame. Cy yelped.

"Be careful of that metal there, John," said the officer at Cy's feet.

"I'm so sorry, sir," said the officer at Cy's head.

"Look, man," Cy said. "Stop jerking my pole."

The man was sitting in his kitchen chair. He told me he was having palpitations; not pain exactly, just a strange, uncomfortable thumping in his chest. I placed the EKG monitor on the kitchen table and took out the cables and hooked him up. The screen showed a second-degree heart block with occasional premature ventricular contractions. I hit the Record button, and the machine traced the rhythm onto the EKG paper. As I was looking at the paper, measuring the QRS interval, I noticed the rhythm change. "Look at that," I said. "It's a third degree." "What's a third degree?" he asked, watching the screen with me. "A total block," I said, and pushed the Record button as the rhythm changed again, sinoventricular tachycardia. "That looks like a Wolff-Parkinson-White," I said, recording again. "Whoa, wait a minute, we're in a Wenckebach now. I haven't seen a Wenckebach in years." Every few seconds, the lines on the screen changed, running the full gamut of rhythms: runs of V-tach, PSVT, A-fib, the complexes narrow and tight together, then wide and far apart, and then there were no complexes, only a flat green line. "Look at that," I said. "Asystole." I hit the Record button and turned to the man, who was staring intently at the screen. That rhythm he knew. He fell from his chair to the floor and didn't move.

19

No backups available, and we had to take both patients. Sam was sleeping on a longboard strapped to the bench seat, and Cy was talking from his board strapped to the stretcher. His blood pressure had dropped a little, so I started an IV on his other arm while he told me the sanctified story of his life. The words seemed too far away to understand, like the sirens whose wails sounded blocks from me, though I knew they were just over my head. I checked Sam's vital signs, my actions calm and mechanical, and then I sat down in the chair at the stretcher's head. I couldn't decide if I was breathing. I felt the effort of taking a deep breath, but no air entering. I closed my hands into fists and punched my legs, and it wasn't clear if my fingers were numb or my legs or my whole body. Also, my eyes would not stay open, and I even tried propping them up with my fingers because there was a lot of paperwork to write and because I was convinced that I would die there if they closed. My arms casted in metal, I wrote the name Coates, Cy, and got no further. The hands fell to my sides and I closed my eyes, the gauze wrapping. We stopped moving. In the distance I heard Tom's voice telling me he was looking for a stretcher for Sam, and as hard as I tried I couldn't shut that voice out. No light coming in but still a small flame inside, a pilot in my chest. I tried my best to blow it out but hadn't enough air, so I closed my whole body around it and gritted my teeth and squeezed and snuffed it out, sinking to the bottom of my chair; finished, I thought, but the good feeling lasted only a moment. Tom was shaking me. Dead or not, I still had to help him take out the stretchers. "Gee, Frank," he said as we wheeled the two patients in. "You really look like shit."

In the waiting room there was Griss the guard and there was everyone else. He stood alone before the door to the triage desk, his arms crossed, pulling his chest out until he made himself the size of the door. He was surrounded by an entire shift of untreated patients, so furious at the nurse's neglect that they'd nearly forgotten the wounds and ailments that had brought them in. Within the semicircle around the guard they fought for space, pushing and pulling their way forward and back, but no one came within arm's length of Griss, as if a stone wall surrounded him, and when he stretched his arms from his sides, pushing out the wall and inflating himself further, the crowd moved back and split down the middle. Together with Tom striking people from behind, it gave us enough room to get the stretchers through.

"People, hear me out," Griss said. "The path to your salvation will not be paved over Griss's body. You can just forget about that, cause Griss gets off in forty-seven minutes, and then he's going home and he's taking a bath. You want to hold a revolution, you got to do it earlier, set it up with me before midnight, cause believe me, I'm not in the mood for this shit now. Everyone will wait until their name is called."

Inside, in the small triage room, Mary Burke helped Mr. Hand off the floor, while Nurse Constance concentrated on her magazine. "He's been waiting since the day before yesterday," Mary said, "and now he just collapsed outside." Mr. Hand grabbed Mary's hand like a monk holding an angel. Nurse Constance took out a thermometer and jammed it into Hand's mouth. "Honey, he's been collapsin since before you were born."

The nurses in the treatment area slept in their chairs, heads resting on X-ray orders and romance novels. The floor was littered with papers and unused bandages and cellophane wrappers, as if a parade had just passed through. All was quiet except for Sam's snores and the familiar rhythm of Burke's ventilator.

Dr. Hazmat appeared out of one of the curtains, and without a word he examined the two patients. I pointed to the iron spike's entrance and exit; Tom did the same to Sam's splinted shins. "All right, everybody," the doctor whispered, and the nurses quietly moved the stretchers into the surgery slot. I stood next to the doctor and pointed to Burke's slot. "How's he doing?"

Hazmat shook his head. "He just coded again. Took us half an hour to bring him back this time, and he hasn't made a move since. The blood gases were awful. God knows how much brain he's got left. Another code like that one and he's done. You know, when he was fighting before, I thought it was the survival instinct, fighting to live. Now I think maybe this whole time he's been fighting to die."

I threw the half-finished paperwork into the garbage, too

tired and dead to write. As I walked past the triage stall, Mary Burke came out and kicked the wall and shouted to the nurse, "God, what's wrong with you people? Why did you take this job in the first place if you're such a cold bitch?" She stood in the hall, not knowing how to get out. I pushed the button on the wall. "Thank you," she said, and walked coolly past the guard.

The waiting room was quiet again, Griss dozing at his desk, the night full of little storms that seemed to finish before they started. I followed Mary to the front row of seats, where her mother sat with her hands on her pocketbook. "One of our neighbors brought her in. They found her wandering the streets, having conversations with people who aren't there. Just now she was talking to my grandmother, who's been dead ten years. She speaks to me like I'm eight years old."

"Why don't you go play in your room, Mary?" Mrs. Burke said.

"Okay, Mom," Mary said, and turned back to me. "This is supposed to be a hospital. I mean, somebody in here should be able to help her. Give her a pill to put her to sleep, let her lie down, something, but that bitch in there says she can't do anything, there's no stretchers. You know, some of these people have been waiting days to see the doctor. Days. I just spoke to him. He says my father's getting worse. He says he doesn't think my father's going to make it. Well, no wonder. Every time I go in there, it's like a bunch of zombies walking around. Nobody doing anything."

I watched her talk. So tired I just wanted to hold my eyes

on her eyes. Not listening to anything except the air she took in. "God, you too," she said, and then she sat down and covered her face with her hands.

Tom threw the stretcher into the back of the ambulance. "We have a call," he said. "Cardiac arrest." The engine revving, two tries to reach my seat, then shooting through the brick arcades of Fifty-sixth Street. Night breaking into grays, dim hint of the future in the skies over the East River. I closed my eyes and felt the lights battering against the door.

"There's the son of a bitch," Tom said when we reached Forty-fifth, and then he was gone, the bus still rolling and nobody driving, my partner running toward the crowd on the corner. I climbed over the console to set the brake and saw the girl in the yellow raincoat lying on the sidewalk, a man on top of her, the bloody camouflage that could only be Noël's.

I pulled out the stretcher and equipment and pushed it to the sidewalk. Tom was already at work. The girl lay on the ground not moving, and next to her, Tom was beating Noël unconscious. He punched the face and then went to work on the ribs. I tried pulling him off and then had to kick him in the side. "Tom, help me. Put her on the monitor."

"I think that lunatic was trying to kill her," he said, already taking out the EKG wires and hooking them to her chest. I grabbed the airway bag and knelt above her head. Felt her neck for a pulse, watched for the rise of air in her lungs. Nothing. A flat line on the EKG. I put the mask over her mouth, connected the Ambu-bag, and squeezed. The same face Tom and I had fought for outside the coffee shop at the start of this shift. The same face I had seen die so many times. Rose. Her eyes opened, a brown so dark they were black, shining with terror.

"She's flatline," Tom said, and pulled open the raincoat, then yanked apart the buttons of her white blouse and began to push gently on the small space over her heart. I opened her mouth with the laryngoscope blade and carefully slipped the tube into her lungs. As easy as that. It's always easy after. She looked up at me as if waiting for the signal that this was a dream. "It's okay," I kept saying. "It's all right."

The crowd around us getting larger, her friend standing behind me. "What happened?" I asked, though I already knew. "What's her name?" I said, though I knew that too.

"Her name's Rose," the friend said. "She was fine and then she sat down here and said she couldn't breathe."

"You know how she is."

"I thought she was having like one of her panic attacks. She's been so down lately. You know her brother got shot three weeks ago."

"I know."

"And her parents are away most of the time, and when they're not out you wish they were, you know. She's been staying with me since her brother died. She's gonna be okay, right?"

"No," I said. "She's not." Tom had started the IV and given her a shot of epi and we both checked the monitor for changes but there were none of course and so we put her on the stretcher and wheeled her over to the bus. At the doors, I looked back at Rose's friend and others still staring at the spot where Rose went down. Next to them, Noël was just starting to get to his feet, Rose's friend pointing. "He's the one. It's him. She was fine until he came over, just having a panic attack, and then he got on top of her, like he was kissing her, choking her, or something. Somebody call the cops." The rest of those gathered were considering these facts. They circled around the still dazed Noël. I sat at Rose's head, squeezing the bag, and I watched Tom close the doors and run back over to Noël and push him down. "When I get back I'm gonna kill you. Do you hear that?" Noël with enough sense to get to his feet and start backing away. By the time we turned the corner he was running down the street like a blinded dog.

When Rose and I were finally alone, I said to her, "I'm so sorry, Rose. I'm so damn sorry I can't tell you." She was still looking up, but the light inside her was gone, and I pushed the lids over her eyes. On the monitor, the line was still flat, and so I put down the Ambu-bag and stroked her hair and bent over her and kissed the side of her mouth. I had intubated Rose dozens of times since missing that first one, and in the end they were all the same. Rose dies, that's what she does, there's nothing you can do and it's the hardest thing to take no matter how many times. If you can see that and understand, you will understand every terrible thing in the world, and you will be dead too, for to know it is to die. "I'm so sorry, Rose. I'm so damn sorry." I moved to her side and pushed her over a little and pressed myself next to her and I wrapped one arm around her shoulders and one under her neck, my hand on her head. I kissed her again.

I started CPR when we pulled up to Misery, and stayed in the treatment room crunching down on Rose's chest, the doctors and nurses working very hard to bring her back, though everyone knew it was without hope. One of them took my place, and I walked out of the room, past the nurses, the bums lined up in Skid Row, to the waiting room, Mary Burke curled up like a child in her mother's arms. I stood outside, next to the ambulance, the doors still open, the equipment in a pile on the tar lot. I threw it into the back and closed the doors and sat down next to Tom, who started driving. "I'm going to kill him," Tom kept saying. "I'm going to kill him."

I held tight to the door as we swerved down Ninth, the bus leaning over the shopkeepers pulling out fruit boxes and breakfast signs. We made a right on Fifty-first, the morning's long shadows crossing the street like arrows pointing the way west, right on Tenth and right again, and when we reached the line of broken windshields, site of Noël's home runs, Tom locked the brakes. On the sidewalk, Noël running toward the alley. "He ain't getting away this time."

Tom reached him on the steps, his flashlight Bronson over his head and down. Noël dodged and ducked and tried to go underneath, but Tom was ready, his arms wrapping around Noël's neck. Gotcha, he said, and they rolled to the floor, over and over each other, Tom like an alligator wrestling his prey, one arm around Noël's neck, the other pinning the arms to his chest. They rolled up against my legs and I grabbed and tugged at Tom's arm but he held tight, and though I kept pulling I could feel Noël dying. I punched Tom in the head and pulled back, punching and pulling, Noël swinging his arms wildly until he could swing no more, and when Tom finally let go and rose to his feet, Noël was on his back, not moving.

I knelt near the head. No pulse. I looked up at Tom, "Now you've done it. You killed him."

Tom took a long step back, staring at his work. "He's the killer, Frank. He got what he deserved."

"You killed him. You killed him." I threw all my weight up and into his chest and he fell backward to the sidewalk, his eyes never leaving the body. He made no move to get up, and I ran to the ambulance, pulling out the airway bag and monitor.

"Don't do it, Frank."

I knelt down and hooked up the EKG and pulled out the paddles, charged them to the maximum power, and placed them on the chest. A click, and the body jumped an inch, and when it came down it was Noël, eyes blinking crazily, crazy Noël. I checked for a pulse, bounding under my fingers.

"Get the stretcher, Tom."

"You're making a mistake," he said, but he walked over to the bus and pulled it out.

Noël still not breathing. I grabbed the intubation kit and moved over to the head. In one motion the kit open, the tongue up, tube in. I pumped it hard three times and saw the chest rising on its own, Noël's hands reaching to pull out the tube. Rose always dies, I thought, and Noël always comes back.

We strapped him in and rolled him into the bus. On the way to the hospital he freed one of his hands and it was all I could do to keep him from pulling out the tube. Tom taking the turns at one hundred miles an hour, shouting from the front: "You're never going to understand, are you, Father?"

"Never," I said. "I know." We hit a pothole and I fell to the floor, releasing Noël's arm. He yanked out the tube and screamed, tearing at the straps. By the time we pulled into Misery, he was standing on the stretcher, and when I opened the back doors he leaped to the ground, running down the drive, Tom running behind.

I stood in the waiting room. Griss was gone, and the day guard, whose name I didn't know, was busy checking the ID cards of workers filing in for the new shift. Cleaners, cooks, nurses, and orderlies stumbled past us and waited groggily on line, while Mary Burke and her mother sat in the front row, watching them walk through. Something remotely hopeful in the procession, visions of these workers sweeping through the hospital, raising the sick and dying, giving them back to the world. Followed by a morning mop-up, make the beds, coffee break.

I walked past the stretchers in Skid Row to the treatment room, where most of the staff were either coming or going, and in the small space where Mr. Burke's body lay I pulled the curtain closed behind me and stared at the machines that so diligently pumped air into his lungs and drugs into his arms, recording his heart's endless beating. One at a time I pulled each plug and waited in the new silence for the final rise of his chest. One minute I stood, the machines dead, the body fighting on, pulling at the restraints. I grabbed his wrist and felt the pulse slow, then stop; his arms sank into his sides. The clanging alarm of the EKG monitor filled the room and was soon joined by the bass honking of the respirator alarm and a complement of two tweetered IV-drip regulator alarms. I checked that the plugs were out. I hit the power switch and looked in the back for the final cutoff button. One of the morning nurses drew open the curtain and checked the blank screens and then behind them, and he plugged each one back in. He looked at me and put his hands at Burke's neck. "Code," he shouted.

Hazmat's replacement, Dr. Brunt, walked in and paused there like a commuter driving by an accident. "What's this?"

"He just coded," the nurse said, and crossed his arms.

Brunt looked at his watch. "Christ, what a way to start the day. Are we doing CPR now?" He put his hand over his eyes and squeezed and then pointed to me. "He's in V-fib. Shock him."

I took out the paddles and charged them and placed them on Burke's chest. "Clear," I yelled, and pushed down as hard as I could. I put my fingers over the buttons and made the motions of clicking. "Shock," I yelled.

"Nothing. Zap him again."

Again I went through the motions, jolting him with my hands to make it look like a shock. "Zap," I screamed.

"Nothing," Brunt said. "All right, start compressions, and let's get an epinephrine in."

I stood next to Burke's body and placed my hands on his chest. Two more nurses ran in, wheeling the code cart before

them. On the doctor's orders, I pretended to shock him
again. More epinephrine, lidocaine, nurses pulling out
syringes. I turned away from Burke's eyes and began chest
compressions, staring at the gray-and-white industrial-issue
curtain for what felt like ten minutes though it took less time
than a star falling. I saw Burke's face slide away and behind it
more faces, the shadows of faces, shadows of shadows,
moving from the center out. I recognized them all and all
the others I couldn't see yet knew were there, like an
astronomer gazing at the universe through a starless sky. I
felt myself expanding through all the pieces of people that
had passed through me, and as a medic, I was very proud of
this, a billion lives to every life. There was an infinite
completeness to the thing, a madness close to ecstasy.

"All right, that's enough," Dr. Brunt said. "He's dead, I'm
calling it. Let's get some coffee." Everyone filing out.

"The family's outside," I said. "They're likely to get pretty
upset."

"No tears before coffee." The doctor stood beside his
favorite chair, checking the morning's headlines. "Once they
start crying, I'm no good for anything. But they must be
prepared for this by now. He's been here for days. I mean,
I'm not going in there cold, am I?"

"No, but you know how they can be."

"Oh, I know, I know. I'm a mourning sheet."

In the waiting room, Burke's family stood in the front row
like statues about to be pulled down to make way for a new
family. Mary Burke was first. "How's he doing?"

"Why don't we go into this room inside?"

"You can tell me right here."

Dead dead dead. I shook my head. "His heart stopped. Let's go inside."

"Oh my," Mrs. Burke said, her face a strip mine, scattered rocks and construction equipment. Her daughter grabbed my arm. She should have hit me then but wasted all her strength on the words. "No, no. He was getting better before."

"It's all right, Mary." Mrs. Burke's hands were on her daughter. "Let's go in."

I was thankful the curtains were closed when we walked by the body. In the nurses' lounge, I pulled the chairs out, cleared the empty coffee cups from the table, and helped Mrs. Burke to a seat. "His heart never recovered," I said. "The body couldn't go on any longer."

"Bullshit. If he got the care he needed he'd be alive. It's a goddamn butcher shop. It is."

"Please, Mary," her mother said.

"It was his spirit," I said.

"What kind of hospital is this? Where's the doctor? Doctor," she yelled into the treatment room. "Doctor."

I felt the room's cold air warm, the floor soften, the vase of rotten orchids on the table shake and fall over. "Look," I said. "He's here right now." But she was too angry to know, as I knew, that her father had come into the room, that he was right then in the crook of her mother's arm where she rested her head, crying, in her own hair, even as she brushed her fingers through, almost pushing him out. "He's here," I shouted, and he was, everywhere I looked: in the teardrops on the table, the drunken lines in the carpeting, the pockets of oxygen that I tried to scoop together with my hands, to show her. I put the vase upright, "Look, look," but the vase didn't move. Dr. Brunt walked in and sat down.

"How can my father be dead?"

Brunt's hands moved over his face as he spoke. "He's not, but he is. He won't come back, though. He never really left. I'm so sorry I can't explain." The doctor went on to tell the story of his brother dying, a story none of us understood, and then he put his head down, his hands still moving over his face. I stared at the vase, hoping it would move again, but there was something else in the room now, much stronger.

"You killed him," Mary said to the doctor, and when he didn't look up, she turned to me. "You killed him." What was there to say? I could only marvel at the power of her hate. Enough to smash atoms if she wanted, turn me to dust with the smallest snap of it, yet all she did was leave. That was the miracle.

Nothing to do but go home and roll around in bed. Too tired to drink. In the lot out back, Tom Walls and Franco stood together, Walls in front, swinging his light at the grille, smashing chrome. He moved to the side and took out his biggest knife and shoved it deep into the tires. He saw me watching and held out the knife. "Help me, Father. Help."

I walked down the drive and into the street. Overhead I felt the ghosts of all the rooms I'd been to, and rather than haunt me, they seemed to be wishing me rest. "Sweet dreams, Frank," one of the windows said. I turned the corner of Forty-seventh and Eleventh and saw Rose sitting on my front steps, her yellow raincoat buttoned up in the sun. I stopped for a second, considered turning around, but there was no other place to go, no one else left. She stood when I reached the steps. I opened the door and held it for her.

I couldn't keep Rose breathing, but I'd kept her memory, stayed with her at the end a thousand times. Didn't that make me a better lifesaver, a true saver of lives? Hadn't I saved them all, each with their own room inside? I was so tired of running, of trying to forget. I would never forget, and for that, perhaps, I could be forgiven.

Going up the stairs, our hands almost touched. At the top I opened my door to the cat sitting in the bare living room. "Hi, you're home," he said. I headed straight for the bed, quickly took off my clothes and pulled the stale covers up to my nose. Quietly Rose took off her raincoat, shirt, and skirt, and crawled in behind me, her belly soft on my back, hands under my chest. She wasn't cold at all but hot, and her heat went everywhere through the bed. There was only a slight smell, but after five years on the job I was used to it, and this was nothing. I listened to her breathing and I felt myself sleeping before I was asleep. The sound of her breathing. I was going to sleep.

Acknowledgments

Special thanks to those who pushed: my partner Seth Greene; my teacher, Colin Harrison; my agent, Sloan Harris; and my editors, Jenny Minton and Sonny Mehta. And to my wife, Jenny, who was handed the too often thankless job of pulling – without you, these pages would still be in the woods.

In memory of Mary McKenna and Doris Jean Austin.

Warner Books now offers an exciting range of quality titles by both established and new authors. All of the books in this series are available from:

Little, Brown and Company (UK),
P.O. Box 11,
Falmouth,
Cornwall TR10 9EN.

Fax No: 01326 317444.
Telephone No: 01326 372400
E-mail: books@barni.avel.co.uk

Payments can be made as follows: cheque, postal order (payable to Little, Brown and Company) or by credit cards, Visa/Access. Do not send cash or currency. UK customers and B.F.P.O. please allow £1.00 for postage and packing for the first book, plus 50p for the second book, plus 30p for each additional book up to a maximum charge of £3.00 (7 books plus).

Overseas customers including Ireland, please allow £2.00 for the first book plus £1.00 for the second book, plus 50p for each additional book.

NAME (Block Letters) ....

....

ADDRESS ....

....

....

☐ I enclose my remittance for ....

☐ I wish to pay by Access/Visa Card

Number ☐☐☐☐☐☐☐☐☐☐☐☐☐☐☐☐☐☐

Card Expiry Date ☐☐☐☐